FLAME FOR REAL

They circled the cube slowly, gizmo-faced greaser and robed prophet, both probing and testing the object with penetration programs that caused sparks to fly off its burnished surface. Joey Jet was loading another macro when the cube suddenly twitched, and threw his icon into the air.

A beam of light shot out from the cube and smote Joey, smacked him, smoked him. He screamed, and Josh knew that wherever JJ's physical body sat at its term, he was shrieking in agony there, too. The cube began to rotate, its sides changing color and texture, mutating before his eyes. It grew a face—*JJ's face, horribly distorted*—then the cube squeezed itself tight around the face. Somewhere in the real world, the life was being crushed out of JJ. An unseen force pressed on his chest and his body exploded, and then the image was gone, the cube was gone, and before Joshua stood the grotesque peeled man.

"Was that real?" Josh asked, his heart a violent engine with a broken regulator.

"Is the Net real?"

□ □

ALSO BY STEPHEN BILLIAS

The Ravengers

Published by
WARNER BOOKS

HOLOMEN

STEPHEN BILLIAS

ASPECT®

WARNER BOOKS

A Time Warner Company

WARNER BOOKS EDITION

ISBN 978-0-446-60233-4   ISBN 0-446-60233-7

Aspect® is a registered trademark of Warner Books, Inc.

Cover design by Don Puckey
Cover illustration by Donato

Warner Books, Inc.
1271 Avenue of the Americas
New York, NY 10020

A Time Warner Company

Printed in the United States of America

First Printing: April, 1996

10 9 8 7 6 5 4 3 2 1

for David Shack

We are the hollow men
We are the stuffed men . . .
Our dried voices, when
We whisper together
Are quiet and meaningless . . .

                T. S. Eliot
                The Hollow Men

CHAPTER 1

MEET THE HOLO MEN

Joshua Victor could speak two hundred languages and dream in fifty. He could breakfast in Tokyo and dine in New York without jumping on a near orbiter. He could walk through walls. He could sing like a bird and look like one too if the fancy struck him. He was a Netrunner, one of the best, a high-flying, all fortunes good in these cookies, magical numbers coming up, certified crazy Edgerunner. He didn't pay for his Net time, he charged it to an obscure Corporate account that was never audited. Same with his term, he didn't buy it, he billed it to somebody else, and it was the latest, fastest, most interactive, holographic, top-of-the-line machine on the market. In the year 2020, he was nineteen years old, a twenty-first-century wonder boy.

Joshua had only one problem—he was starting to spend more time jacked in than flipped out. His landlord was get-

tin' ready to boot him out of his apartment, his parents
were worried about him, and his teenage lover, Sally
Thrower, was on the verge of splitting. Lately Josh'd noticed changes in his mental state, not attributable to lack of
sleep, sedentary lifestyle, or crappy diet. He was growing
new nodes in his brain, flickering strands of gray matter
that synaptically linked him to the Net in ways he didn't
quite understand. He no longer had to issue log-on commands, if he merely thought them his deck sprang to life.
There was more, but Sally'd freaked when he tried to tell
her about it. She'd wanted him to see a doctor, but how
was he going to pay for it, and anyway, he liked what was
happening to him, he was evolving, it was exciting. The
areas around the 'trode implants in his skull were swelling.
He was becoming one with the Net, he was losing touch,
disappearing from the real world into the elusive land of
the iconic. Sleeping on the Net. Dreaming on the Net.
That's what did it to him. Drifting in cyberspace, his alpha
waves modulating, his REM activity high, still jacked in,
his brain was vulnerable. Where was he? Was he asleep in
his room, or was he sleepwalking on the Net, his coordinates changing slowly as his icon moved, oblivious to en-
counters with others, not interacting but still visible,
protected by electronic shielding and deflection programs.

It was annoying to come up for air after three or four
days of Running and find Sally flitting over him like he
was the asphalt and she was a hovercar. The pizza boxes
and soda cans were pilin' up. Cardboard and aluminum
flotsam and jetsam floated everywhere in a sea of kulch.
The gasman'd shut off the heat but they still had electricity didn't they, the juice that drove the Net, that was all he
needed. Every time he left the Net he felt lethargic, irrita-
ble, fatigued, like he was used to walking on the moon and
was now draggin' his ass around on Earth at six times the

weight. The real world was too slow, bub, he was turbocharged, power-spiked, red-lined, undelimited, his calculator had an infinity function. Like now, he'd been jacked in for three days, poking into places he wasn't supposed to go, leaving little surprises for Corporate jerks he'd never met, dodging the ice and Runnin' hard, and he flipped out and there was Sally, lookin' pissed, combing her short red bangs, and thrummin' her fingers on the table next to his term.

"Nice of you to drop in on reality, asshole. I've been sitting here for two hours."

"Well, then, you're lucky, 'cause I've been jacked in for seventy-two."

"Don't ya think I know that, stupid? Who do ya think cleans up the mess you make when you don't even bother to look where you're going around here? You knocked over my dieffenbachia again." Sally was a perky redhead with green eyes, freckled skin, and an Irish temper. She liked Joshua, maybe even loved him, but she had a life too, dammit, she couldn't be expected to wait on him all the time. The blood surged up under her pale, translucent skin, giving her a flushed, excited aspect. She was bony and gawky, still shaking off the coltish awkwardness of adolescence, but she knew what she wanted, and being babysitter to Joshua wasn't it. She'd left her parents' home in a comfortable beaverville south of Night City to live down here in the techno-shanties with Joshua, a college dropout with uncertain prospects. At first it'd been exciting to be with a Runner, a guy who put his life literally on the line, an electronic on-line cowboy who was always coming back from his Net forays with a new angle, a piece of information to sell or a rippin' place they could go to party, but after a while it got old, having to tend to him while he sat there spacing into the machine. She'd tried jackin' in, but she was more connected to the day-to-day, maybe it was her job in the nursery, tending to plants—especially the endangered ones, hothouse bulbs from the shrinking jungles of Brazil and Southeast Asia, vivid, fragrant orchids and richly blooming, oversized rhododendrons—that made her feel like the real world still had more to offer than the virtual one. Even after Joshua color-printed fractal images of imaginary flowers created from mathematical constructs, they paled before the delicate and nearly extinct beauty of the rain-forest flora. It was her mission to save as many of the doomed specimens as she could before the last bulldozer effaced the natural wild for an orderly rubber plantation, or the last stand of teak fell before the cutters. If that meant leaving him, she would.

But Joshua didn't get it, he was desensitized to human interaction, he missed subtle clues of body language that would have alerted him to Sally's distress, because the Net had a shorthand for these gestures that was limited to a few hundred expressions. He too was just spouting from the rich loam of teenage mulch, a handsome boy with a cocky attitude and eyes that sometimes missed taking it all in because they were sending out such intense energy. He had straight black hair that was chopped unevenly in the back, 'cause of course he saw himself as his icon, a dashing fellow he'd designed himself in the image of his namesake as a tearin' down-the-walls, robe-and-sandal-wearin' bloodthirsty warrior from a Harry Grimes biblical holopic. He even had a trumpet that had very special physical modeling properties. He was too thin because he didn't give a shit about eating, it just slowed him down, diet soda and junk food was all he needed, until the blood sugar low hit, then he'd pop another chocolate power cube and zoom on. Sally used to have hot homemade soups waiting for him, but Joshua didn't understand or appreciate why she didn't

just open a can and 'wave the stuff, it could be ready in
thirty seconds, hell, he'd done it while he was piloting a
sim-cycle through cyberspace. Like right now, he'd been
flipped out for all of two minutes and already his fingers
were twitchin', he was itchin' to climb back into the box,
all he needed to do was relieve himself and maybe chomp
a kibble or two, but here she was in his face, wanting to
know when he was going to make some money toward the
rent, if only he could just climb right inside the machine it
would all be so easy. He'd heard about people who'd
turned themselves into AIs, like the famous Rache Bartmoss, his hero, the world's greatest Netrunner, now dead
but still transmitting from somewhere in the Net, his soul
a set of algorithms, but it cost millions and billions of e.b.
(eurobucks) and he was just a little shit with a programmer's facility for manipulating data, he hadn't done anything like the great Rache Bartmoss, no high adventure,
nothing but a little pranksterism—Jesus, he couldn't even
daydream in the real world without her chattering away—

"What, Sally?"

"I said good-bye." She was standing in front of him, and
funny, she was holding two big suitcases and she had her
hat on, the one she'd made herself, weaving dried flowers
into straw until it looked like she was wearing a bouquet,
and she was crying.

"Where're you going?"

"What do you care?" She was right, of course, he didn't
care, he was too far gone.

"Don't go," he said weakly, but he didn't get up, didn't
put his arms around her and give her the hug she longed
for, that would have made her drop the bags and stay, because what she wanted wasn't attention, not even sex but
just human, physical touch. You couldn't touch anyone on
the Net, that's what Sally hated about it, but for Joshua

there was safety in that, you were once removed, so to speak, if you didn't like somebody or how things were going, you snapped them off, you changed the pattern. Bland, that's what Sally called it, but to Joshua it was cleaner, easier. Life was so messy. His term started ringing, somebody was calling him on the Net, he was momentarily distracted as he checked the term screen for the incoming caller's ID to see whether or not he wanted to bother to answer it, but there was nothing being displayed, that was odd, he checked under the desk to see if he'd kicked the cord out, and when he looked up, Sally Thrower was gone. Just like that. Joshua had a sinking feeling, like when he dive-looped down out of the sky over the Pacifica grid, but this one wasn't because his senses were being tricked by a flight simulation program, this was real hurt. He loved Sally, why was she leaving him? He didn't have to put up with that shit on the Net, where he was trumpet-blowing Josh, Old Testament warrior-prophet-king. Joshua was torn between running after her and answering the still insistent pinging of his Net phone.

Finally he screamed into the mike—"What the hell do you want?!" but he was talking to the ether, there was no one there. Fractals were splitting on the holo display floating fifty millimeters in front of his eyes. As he watched they spun themselves into an old-fashioned confirmational message with an odd twist:

PROGRAM SUCCESSFULLY FAILED

Some goofball was playing with his head; it was probably one of his hacker buddies, maybe Joey Jet or Phreaky Phreddy, he'd call them later, but still it was a neat trick, incoming calls were always supposed to identify themselves, it was a strict Net requirement. Maybe if he dove in he could follow the data trail and hack back, jack! He forgot about Sally T and plunged into the Net, logging on with a blast of his trumpet macro that launched dozens of programs, and boom, the Net appeared all at once, humming with activity. Joshua entered at the beach, a safe spot not often patrolled by the Netwatch security ops, there was too much of it to cover and too few of them. From here one could stand and face the expanse of the virtual ocean, rendered in elaborate shifting patterns of green, blue, and white, sometimes calm, sometimes choppy, the tide running in and out, the beach sands and dunes changing shape and texture, the illusion distinguishable from the real shoreline only by the faint gridlines that delineated the sky above it, and the two spheres that hung there, one representing the sun and one the lunar disc, so that runners could tell the local time by glancing upward. Joshua had fine-tuned his deck to the point where the slightest shift in his focus changed the display. He rarely used the term keyboard and monitor that sat in his apartment before his listless, inert body. Instead he'd programmed everything to respond to voice commands or subtle eye movements, building on the work that had been done years before with quadriplegics to provide them with interfaces. More than once Sally'd said he'd be happier if he were a cripple, then he wouldn't have to make excuses. Out there he was a disappointment, to Sally, to his parents, who wondered why their child prodigy wasn't fast-tracking it to a Corporate power job, to everybody he owed money and favors, but down here in the Net he was a magician, a gymnast of the clandestine, a god. Out of nothing he would summon a sim-cycle to ride into the Night City of the collective imagination of thousands of Runners like himself.

He did so now. With a twitch of one eyebrow Josh made a low-slung speed machine appear on the sand, with wheels of Swiss cheese and a seat of nails, a machine festooned with lights, bells, and streamers like a Philippine jitney bus, and a cavalier touch, mounted on the handlebars, a horse's head that talked and turned to stare at strangers as it flew. The rounds of cheese gave off a waxy scent if you had a fragrance mod hooked to your term. It was altogether a flight of fantasy, this vehicle, yet it could propel Joshua to the farthest corners of the Net in a few minutes while lesser Runners walked or rode ordinary sim-devices in realtime.

"Gee up, Cyberslew!" he cried, evoking the name of a great racehorse from the recent past, one of those beasts of mythical proportions, forty hands high, that raced on the new tracks built to accommodate their immense bodies. The horsehead threw him a backward glance of boredom and showed its teeth. The cycle gently lifted off the sand, which blew around realistically as if from the backwash of a jet exhaust. He didn't need the icon, it was just a representation of the module that moved him, if he wanted to he could make it disappear and he could swim lazily through the sky. That's what he liked about the Net—no rules, at least for somebody like himself, who could make it up as he went along. The tourists, the gawkers, and the Corporate mojos who used the Net as their trading floor were confined to certain streets and locuses, conventions established over years of program linking, a mutually agreed upon reality. Sure, others toyed with their icons, made fanciful images of themselves as handsome creatures, mythical beasts, or known celebrities, but they trod the same paths as everyone else, the established city icons, the bars and bistros of Night City, for example, that they could visit in real life if they so desired. Runners like Joshua were more adventurous. Out there on the fringe, beyond the known coordinates, was Wilderspace, where anything might happen. The area was undefined and far removed from the LDLs (Long Distance Links) that were the electronic basis for the Net. If someone wanted to form their own city grid, or pirate some info, or cause any kind of trouble, they did it in Wilderspace. The place was unstable too, if you were Running in Wilderspace and it crashed, you crashed too, and sometimes it wasn't so easy to get out, you might be sucked into some data sinkhole and spun around for a while like a laundromat nightmare.

Joshua would venture into Wilderspace later, but first there was this weird message to check out, the one that had arrived on his term without caller ID. It could only have come from Night City. The flight from the beach took only a few seconds, now he was hovering over the grid, a crosshatching of icons representing the buildings and environs of that metropolis, which was set above the true horizon to give the pretty illusion of a city free-floating like the fabulous mountains of Buddhist creation myths.

"Program successfully failed"! Machine language, programmer humor, hacker glop Net sysops wouldn't allow, it had to have come from someone busting the mail relays. Joshua wondered if he was the only person who had received this message, and if so, why. He hadn't been running any programs at that moment, he'd been dealing with his hysterical girlfriend who was now his ex-girlfriend. Another pang of pain hit his stomach, but he pushed it aside and fluttered down until he was directly above the cluster of icons that represented the Night City LDL.

"Show me sender IDs of the last six hundred Net messages as points on a scatter-graph," he instructed the controller on the LDL, and instantly a corner of his display was filled by the peculiar spray-paint configuration of the chart. *"Heuristo!"* Josh said to himself, using the true Greek version of "Eureka!" Five hundred and ninety-nine

of the messages were aligned in a typical pattern as coming from other points on the Pacifica grid or through relays from the Olympia, Atlantis, or Tokyo-Chiba regions. Only one dot of the six hundred fell outside expected parameters. This point had no location attached to it, and had therefore been treated as exception processing and placed by the charting program in an irregular location at the crosshairs of the y and z axes. "Give me everything you've got on the anomaly" he commanded. The CPU churned momentarily then produced a blank screen. Joshua wondered if maybe he'd misspoke, there had to be something on this blip, unless—

"Run Shield Cutter!" he ordered, and his deck attacked the speck with a series of stripping and decorticating macros that would uncover any data hidden behind sheath cloaks. As he perched on the rim of the LDL's sat-dish icon, his macro bored away at the infra-coating like the proverbial Zen mosquito attacking the iron bowl. Within minutes the outer layers of the file were ground to dust and exposed a translucent pearllike nugget of pure information. It turned out to be written in a fifth-level machine language called Metatron III that Joshua guessed only a few hundred people on the planet could program in, but he was one of them. He ran a debugger on the jewel to make sure he wouldn't pick up anything nasty if he cracked it open, and when it ran clean, he read it.

"Data is the opium of the people. Next meeting in six hundred billion nanoseconds at the unusual place. Be there or B^2."

Curiouser and curiouser. The message had come to him, but not directly. Joshua had the distinct impression he was being tested. They could have simply invited him, whoever they were, but instead they'd laid out a data scavenger hunt. They were likely monitoring him right now, to see what he'd do next. Ye olde unexpected usually worked best on the Net. Josh's icon brought his trumpet to his lips and blew the stirring opening to *Bolero*, which was a macro to suck in the pearl of wisdom for further analysis, but apparently his gamesmen were prepared for such eventualities; as soon as the tiny sphere felt a tug on its coordinates it blossomed into a flower whose petals fell away on the breeze, vanishing into nothingness.

Six hundred billion nanoseconds was only ten minutes. If he hung around Night City for a little while he might be able to follow somebody out to Wilderspace where the meeting would undoubtedly be held on one of the pirate ships floating at the fringe of the visible ocean of the Pacifica grid between the defined coastline and Honolulu or the Gilbert Islands. Joshua wandered over to the strip of icons that represented downtown Night City. He had one or two favorite hangouts, like the Core Dump, a hacker's bar and freeware shop where the latest programs were traded, but today he decided to drop into the IF THEN ELSE Café. He popped open that icon like a can of kibble and took a table near a window that projected a simulated view of a Night City street. His icon was sharply pixeled and smooth in motion compared to the fuzzy edges and herky-jerky movements of the rental units that comprised most of the tourists in the café. It was a truism that all icons are equal, but some are more equal than others. If you had extra computing power or programming savvy, you could tell at a glance who was running with superior decks, who was hot and who was not. Most of the tourists were bumping around in standard iconic ware, done up in Hollywood celebrities or boring supyrhero (men) or supyrmodel (women) images. A few favored the man-beast look, wolf-men and lizard heads being the most popular, and aliens were in too, in a variety of styles from smooth-skulled bug-eyed waif to toothy reptilian, but Joshua found the Halloween-every-night motif uninteresting. If there was a member of the secret club in the café, he'd be something chill like Joshua's rendition as an Old Testament prophet. There at the bar was an oddity dressed in a ghoulish costume like skin turned inside out, or a peeled human, so that coursing arteries and veins pulsed atop the flesh rather than just beneath it, and the meaty body glistened with grease. The face was like that of a burn victim, eyes protruding from bony sockets, nose exposed, lips bared back. Others on the Net gave this freak a wide berth, but Joshua decided to run a little test himself. He slipped off to a private corner and pasted some text into a harmless little symbol sack that he then handed off to the waiter to deliver to Mr. Inside-out, and watched for the icon's reaction. Joshua's message: "Meeting in a few picoseconds," would be meaningless to anyone except his quarry. The man accepted the waiter's offering gingerly, and Joshua saw that he ran antipersonnel programs on it before his icon agreed to touch it. As soon as he read the message, he disappeared, and Joshua, with all his techiegear, was not quick enough to trace him. This proved nothing, of course. The man might simply have been bored or reluctant to engage a stranger in data exchange. This was typical of the antisocial nature of many hackers, who in real life were lonely programmers who lived with their mothers and didn't have the social skills of slop hogs. Joshua assumed his seat at the table. The waiter shrugged and cleared his place of the untouched sim-beverage. A pageant of peculiar personalities passed by, mostly browsers and touristos, but occasionally augmented by a true phenomenon that could only have been created by a code artist like Joshua. He quickly tired of the spectacle—this wasn't where he usually spent time on the Net, typically he was back in the guts of the machine, hacking away at some Corporate cube for fun and profit. A commotion caught his attention. Icons were bouncing off the café walls left and right as a small cyclone whirled into the IF THEN ELSE. Some jerk was wreaking havoc with the motion sensors. Joshua watched as a pair of Netwatch cops suddenly appeared in front of the spinning icon. These policemen were in full riot gear, and heavily armed. They let loose a pair of Bulldogs which attacked the intruder. The mini-tornado slowed down under the assault but managed to smash into a few more tables and wipe out a few more innocent bystanders before the effects of the heavy ammo caused it to implode. When the image collapsed, the Netwatch operators seized on its vestiges to trace it back to a source, but there wasn't enough left to make an ID.

Joshua was close enough to hear one say to the other, "Stupid prank!" to which the other responded, "Yeah, call in the sweepers," and the next thing that happened was a loudspeaker announcement that the IF THEN ELSE Café was being shut down for maintenance, would everyone please leave the coordinates for the next ten minutes.

In the instant before the icon collapsed and zoomed in, Josh saw one figure floating above the rest, spinning up in advance of the implosion that signaled icon contraction. It was like surfing, Josh'd done it many times himself, but it was dangerous, because if the wave closed down too fast you'd wipe out, just like at the beach. Josh jumped on the shimmering crest of the screen change to follow this character. When the icon suddenly shrank from a pictorial representation of the café to a static darkened symbol, the two of them were propelled into the silvery sky above the Night City grid and for a minute the sim-stars of the Night City sky lit up as they popped into near orbit altitude. What a rush! Of course, they weren't really flying—the two of

them were engaged in a consentual hallucination as they
traveled on the grid landlines. The two of them were like
miniature rockets, twin meteoric flashes of light. Netwatch
ops hated this sort of interactivity, it was expensive and
disruptive, but Josh and his fellow traveler didn't care,
they went streaming across the stratosphere, their momen-
tum carrying them far out over the ocean. Joshua lagged
slightly behind, hoping to discover where his unknown fellow traveler would land. The gridlines flew by like rows of
corn from the window of a passing car, when there used to
be corn, lashing and flashing parallel for an instant, then
strangely curved as they whipped by, only this was no
cornfield but the endless expanse of the simulated Pacific
Ocean. From this perceived height, the pirate ship icon was
a mere speck in the emptiness of the Pacifica grid as represented by the softly undulating plane of blue-green
water. Josh would have missed it if he hadn't been following the surfer and noted the dip and shallow angle of descent he made toward the floating renegade vessel.

He'd coasted through their defenses by tagging behind
in the shadow of the surfer. There weren't any posted coordinates for this icon, it was running a Shrouded Gate program that made it illegal but also invisible to ordinary
Runners, who rarely ventured into Wilderspace, and then
only at their peril. The icon didn't expand by zooming out
to offer him entry like an ordinary Net symbol, instead it
inserted him instantly into its interior, not a cozy ship's
compartment (why should it be, this was the Net, where
anything was possible), but a room like in a castle, with
walls and floors of stone, empty except for softly flickering torches mounted at angles in iron brackets set in rough-
hewn walls. The glowing flames illuminated the scene
with the sputtering variability of creosote-soaked rags. A
dozen or so shrouded figures stood in silence in a mystical

pattern with one of their number at the head of the arrangement. Joshua'd arrived at the meeting at the precise time
specified in the cryptic message he'd decoded. No doubt
he'd been led there by the icon surfer, even though Josh
had thought he'd followed undetected. He hugged the back
wall as roll call was taken. As the names were called off,
Joshua tried to identify who was speaking, but the room
echoed with the non-specific ringing hollowness of stone,
a wonderfully subtle audio-sim that Joshua appreciated
from a purely technical standpoint. The members of this
movement had taken the names and images of revolutionary figures from history as their icons.

"Trotsky?"

"*Da.*"

"Che?"

"*Sí.*"

"Mao?"

" 'A single grain of rice.' " The Chairman uttered one of
the famous sayings from his Little Red Book. And so it
went. Pancho Villa, Spartacus, and Ethan Allen checked in.
The taking of names concluded and then the assembly
began to chant in a mock-Gregorian style:

> *We are the holo men*
> *We are the stuffed men*
> *Our dried voices, when*
> *We whisper together*
> *Transform the Net forever.*

They all laughed together, synchronistically, like
Noroms, the feared random access (NO ROM equals
Moron backwards) vandals of the Net, but these were not
mindless surgically altered characters ganging up and busting through the interface, there was subtlety and pleasure

in the programmatic deviations of the Holo Men. They were artists, at least to a Runner like Joshua. Their programs were elegant crystal expressions grafted onto the fundamental structure of the Net like a plastic surgeon's handiwork, seamless and suture-free. If you didn't know exactly what to look for, you'd swear there was nothing here but the empty waving sands at the bottom of the illusory ocean. If they knew Joshua was here, they didn't acknowledge him. What was their purpose for meeting, what was their agenda? After the chant they milled around in a peculiar pattern, but Joshua couldn't grasp the essential meaning of their movements. He remained in the shadows at the back of the room, watching, until their shuffling, slow-motion pacing began to bore him. He materialized his trumpet and was about to give them an Old Testament wake-up call when one of the group broke from the pack and approached him. As he neared Joshua, the character shed his robe to reveal the tricornered hat, leather breeches, and silk shirt of colonial America.

"Who are you, comrade?"

"Abbie Hoffman," said Joshua, spontaneously evoking the name of the Yippie revolutionary prankster of the 1960s.

"Ah! Delightful. Ethan Allen here. Come, join us for the ceremony."

"I don't think so," said Joshua.

Ethan Allen quickly changed his icon into a crab and scuttled back into the shadows.

"You must not see my face," he warned.

"Whaddaya mean?" asked Joshua. "You can be anything you want on the Net."

"My data face. My encrypted signature. You have the ability, I know, to reveal it. We all do."

"We?" Josh asked. He was tightrope walking in a windstorm, bathing in the lava lake of an active volcano, carrying crystal in an earthquake.

"Aren't you holo?"

"Huh?" Josh didn't know if the crab character meant "hollow" or "holographic" and what difference did it make, the question was idiotic.

"Oh dear. My mistake. Good-bye." The crab mutated into a scary monster and tried to crush Josh's trumpet, but Josh could run his icon changes with the best of them, he blew a note and changed into a wisp of sound, wafting up from the mouth of the brass horn and trailing away into the ether beyond the grasp of the fantastic chimera. This game of iconic transformation could have gone on endlessly, but the thundering voice of the leader of the Holo Men interrupted their frolic.

"Joshua Victor, come forward!"

There was no refusing this summons. Ethan Allen resumed his robed form, and Joshua reverted to his own biblical depiction of himself. The other cowled figures parted to let him through, and he soon found himself in the center of the circle, surrounded by these quasi-monks. He stood before the leader, whose hood completely masked his face so that Joshua couldn't even see which historical figure he was supposed to represent.

"You have passed the first test. Well done. But why do you hesitate? Why do you not join in?"

"Join in to what?" Joshua asked.

"We represent the future. After the Revolution, there will be us, and us only. Don't you want to be a part of the new order?"

"If I knew what it was, I could tell you," Joshua said, because he didn't like playing games when he didn't know the rules, it was his programmer's mentality to seek clarity.

"Perhaps you are too young," said the voice from within the cowl.

"I've been hearing that mush since I was nine. That's what old people always say. Doesn't sound very revolutionary to me."

"Enough! The council will conduct further analysis of your qualifications. We will inform you of our decision." With these words, Joshua suddenly felt himself shrinking— oh, my God, the blackness, the blankness, the insensateness, it was horrible, the absolute nullity of it all. He was unplugged. No one could have prepared him for this, no one could have warned him, he would have laughed at the preposterous, outrageous notion that he was addicted to electricity, but it was draining out of him like oil out the crankcase of an antique int-com-bust engine. Suddenly he was alone in his scummy apartment. Booted off the Net. Shit, nobody'd ever been able to do that, not Netwatch, nor Corporate security geeks, not even his hacker friends in jest.

The apartment was cold and cheerless. What was different? Sally was gone, but there was something else missing, an element of life Josh couldn't identify at first, because he'd spent so little time there in the last few months. Finally he realized what it was—she must've come back while he was meeting the Holo Men, because all her plants were gone, the blooming flowers, misty ferns, trailing vines and creepers, all the greenery and splashes of color that had made their grungy flat tolerable. A track of dirt and shed leaves led to the door. Josh stood up, stretched, and gazed around despondently. His life was in tatters. Only in the invisible world of ordered electrons that constituted the Net did he feel happy.

"Frack it!" he said to the bare gray walls. He rebooted and dove back into the vibrant imaginary world that swam before his star-kissed eyes.

CHAPTER 2

CICADA BANANA

Sally stroked the leaves of the cypripedium, which responded by opening and waving its stamen suggestively. The hothouse thermostat was set at a hundred and five to mimic the sweltering jungle of Borneo. Rows of killer lady's slipper orchids, a fortune in fragility, lined the glass-enclosed room. Recent rips in the ozone layer required polarizing filters to be installed in the roof panes, tinting the light with a faint blue tinge. Like Josh in his Networld, Sally spent many hours here in the greenhouse, pruning, watering, prodding the delicate specimens to flower and pollinate. Japanese businessmen were willing to pay enormous sums for these rare plants. Her boss, Phil, was getting rich off the venture, but he realized he had a special talent in Sally, paid her well for her services, and he didn't object when she insisted that one in every twenty blossoms be returned to the jungle in an effort to reintroduce the species to a land decimated by clear-cutting and erosion.

With tweezers she carefully plucked a mite off the shiny leaves of the paphiopedium she was tending at that moment. She flipped down her magnifying eyepiece to examine the creature, then uttered a little shriek and jumped up. The bug was not a real insect, it was a metallic reproduction, mobile and articulated, but clearly a miniature machine.

"Phil!" she cried. "Come here!" Quickly she trapped the strange device in a specimen jar. It rattled ominously and buzzed angrily against the glass cage in which it found itself. The vigilant owner, ever mindful of the precarious nature of his business, had rushed over at Sally's call. His hands trembled as he took the vial from Sally.

"Are we infested?" he whispered in horror. A plague of mites would wipe him out for this season. The next shipment from the Far East wouldn't arrive for months.

"I don't know, Phil. It's not real. What does it mean?" She watched him turn over the jar in his shaky hands. Phil Talley, the owner of Phil O'Dendron's Nursery, was a diminutive man, smaller even than Sally, with a slight build and a passive face defined by rectangular wire-rimmed glasses. Sally had come to love him for his patient, tender way with the bulbs and shoots that responded to his touch and care. As far as she knew, Phil didn't have an enemy in the world. One of the big Corporations must have planted this bug in their nursery, they were the only ones with the money for such sophisticated devices. Orchids were highly coveted among certain Arasaka executives, but kidnapping for ransom and outright theft were the usual methods employed by flower robbers. Why would they deliberately set out to destroy his crop?

"Call the police," he told Sally, though he didn't really want to involve the authorities. They'd come trooping in here with pesticides and quarantine orders, slap a big orange CLOSED sticker on his store window, and confiscate the whole lot. He'd probably go under.

"No, wait, Phil, let's think about this." Sally knew as well as Phil what to expect as the result of a police visit. This nursery was her life—she wasn't going to let him throw it all away just because someone was trying to intimidate them. The poor man was smoking a cabbage leaf cigarette as he did when he was distraught. Flecks of ash clung to his clothes, another mark of his agitation, for he was habitually neat and even his gardener's khaki pants and work shirt were crisply pressed. "My boyfriend would know what to do about this, only—"

"What?"

"I left him, Phil. I'm kinda mad at him. He won't grow up. He spends all his time in the Net, which is why he'd know how to handle a micro-device like this bug. There's got to be some way to deactivate them all at once. I'll call him if you'd like," she said doubtfully, but Phil could see that she really didn't want to do it.

"That's okay, girl, you don't have to go back to him over this. You've given me an idea, though. I know what these machines hate that flowers like. Come on, we'll turn on the misters and drown the little doo-hickeys or rust 'em shut."

"It's worth a try." They sealed the orchid room and turned up the heat until it was just below the temperature that would kill the exquisitely delicate buds, then they doused the space with a fine spray of mist until the glass fogged over and every leaf was dripping with moisture, but when they reentered the room the tiny bugs were still crawling over everything, chomping their way up the shiny lower leaves on the stalk toward the vulnerable efflorescences.

"We're going at this all wrong," said Sally. Her red hair was limp from the effects of the heat and high humidity, and her pale skin was shiny. "We used the water and the heat like these were living things, but they're machines. What does in machines? You gotta cut their power. I've got another idea." She left the nursery area and ran to the office, where she grabbed the bulk eraser they used to wipe clean the holotapes they sent with each order that described how to tend the flowers, a special service of Phil O'Dendron's Nursery. She raced back to the nursery, plugged in the highly magnetized eraser, and ran it over the jar holding the one captive bug. It fell from the side of the glass onto its back on the bottom of the container and lay still.

"That's it," she cried, and she ran from plant to plant, disabling the bugs, which couldn't handle the disorienting effects of the highly potent magnetism.

"Way to go, girl!" Phil shouted. He was vastly relieved that his crop was saved. In a few minutes Sally had enfeebled all the encroaching machine-insects and swept them up into a hard plastic pail. There were several hundred of them, and though they couldn't reproduce like living creatures, in those numbers they would have been plentiful enough to consume the orchid crop entirely. Two questions remained: who had placed these voracious intruders in the hothouse, and why? The dreadful thought flitted across her mind that Joshua could have programmed these micropests, but she dismissed the idea immediately—he wasn't like that, and anyway he was too preoccupied with his own roamings in the Net to bother with an elaborate revenge scheme. No, it had to be somebody with something to gain from Phil's loss, a competitor, maybe. Later on she'd take these awful things to the landfill and see that they were buried beneath the thousand tons of garbage generated that day by the citizens of Night City.

CHAPTER 3

ICEBLINK

Iceblink: the yellowish glare in the sky above an ice field.
Webster's dictionary definition

There it was, looming in the sky, a signpost, a warning, the sickly yellow haze of reflected ice, like the gray pall that hangs over a battlefield, a carefully crafted illusion, of course, but enough to deter all but the most aggressive and reckless hackers. Josh was sniffing at a big block of the stuff in a quadrant he'd never noticed before, floating in the lee of San Morro Bay just south of Night City. Whatever was within this new data fortress must be valuable. He was touching it cautiously with a few special program openers when it shed its defenses all of a sudden and revealed a second nested icon within its outer bulk. In the few hours since his encounter with the Holo Men, Joshua had roved the Net restlessly, hoping to engage one of the

figures from the meeting, but he'd struck out. The only interesting phenomenon he'd discovered was this new cube,
but why had it dropped its electronic countermeasures so
easily? This required special caution. Joshua suspected this
was an Arasaka fort, they were active in this sector, they
practically owned Night City, didn't they, but why was it
out in the open like this, it was almost too easy, and there
seemed to be no apparent purpose for its existence, almost
like it was put there to attract hackers like Josh. So what?
He was up to a challenge. If they thought they could trick
him into a false move, they were wrong. He stepped back
and swung around the fort to the allegorical back door, the
tail where the program attached to the grid. This was where
hackers did most of their damage—if you could pry open
the link between the icon and the infrastructure of the grid,
you were in, no matter how fancy the rest of the defenses
were. Joshua tried a few flip keys, but nothing worked immediately. He was tapping and scraping electronically at
the data hinges of the connection when his sonar picked up
the trolling sound of a Netwatch clever dolphin program
cruising toward him. Ordinarily these automatic garbage
sweepers of the Net would pose no threat to a cool Runner
like Josh. One of every six dolphins was designed with
extra detectors to determine if intruders were Running
without proper link to the billing program, but Josh's icon
was so well masked that even a clever dolphin would think
he was either a part of the background or a legitimate Net
user. Today, though, Josh was slightly off balance, having
been struck from the Net once already, so he cautiously
withdrew from the area until the graceful mammal leapt
and spun its way past him and out to sea. Then he turned
again to contemplate the chunk of gleaming ice. He'd been
playing it too safe, he needed to take a gamble just to get
his confidence back. He wasn't going to repeat that un-

pleasant ultimate empty feeling of being dropped from the Net, but just in case, he decided to call up Joey Jet and see if he wanted to shatter some ice with him. Joey was weird, but he had a good set of tools for ice-breaking, and he and Josh had done some chill fort-busting in the past. Joshua sent out a covert signal on ultra-low frequency where he knew Joey would be monitoring the traffic, and sure enough, he responded within a few seconds.

"Hey, dude, what's the do?"

" 'S'up, Joey? I'm down here below NC in the San Morro quadrant, and there's something new. Come on down and check it out."

"Are you clean, kemosabe? I heard you got popped right off-line this A.M."

"Whoa. News travels fast. Where'd you hear that?"

"Oh, choomba, you're semifamous, in a bad way. Everybody's laughin' at ya. 'Hotshot programmer kicked in the butt.' "

"That's the grapevine line on me now? Maybe you can help me 'prove my image. Come see this hunk of stuff I found."

"Awright." Joey Jet signed off, and Joshua waited for him to materialize. You never knew in what guise Joey would show up, sometimes he was punked out, sometimes he took a Hollywood icon and customized it, so like he'd have a starlet's face on a weight lifter's steroid bloated body, weird shit like that. But nobody, not even Joshua, was better at cracking open the frozen security ice of data fortresses than Joey Jet. His specialty was Arasaka cubes, 'cause he'd worked for them as a line programmer until they discovered he was writing his own game software at night using their compilers. When they fired him he left them a big messy macro to debug that took three full-time Tokyo aces two weeks to unscramble before they could ac-

cess parts of the main database again, a little prank that
was said to have cost Arasaka several billion dollars. Joey
had to become a hide-and-seek cowboy, there was a permanent contract out on him, but that didn't stop him from
dipping into the Net anytime he wanted to, because like
Joshua, he could cover his tracks so cleverly it was almost
impossible to find him. Today he showed up as himself, or
the nearest approximation Josh'd ever seen of him, his
Joey Jet persona, a greaser hood in a leather jacket and peg
pants, Puerto Rican pointy-toed black shit-kicker boots,
and an impossibly high slicked-back pompadour haircut, a
look from history, the middle of the last century, with the
variation that his icon's face was a metallic cluster of
bionic implants and 'trodes on shiny aluminum skin.
Joshua and Joey were virtual friends—they'd never actually met in the real world. For all Josh knew, Joey could be
a fifty-year-old liquor store clerk or a waitress in a taque-
ria, but he doubted it, he guessed that Joey was a young
loner like himself, pushin' the envelope, lookin' for action
on the Net 'cause there wasn't any anywhere else.

His alloy visage was impassive, so Joey had to put all
his emotive technique into his speech, and here he'd managed quite a feat of programming, a voice like melted but-
ter that oozed out of miniature speakers into Josh's ear
with rhythmic cadence and mellifluous inflection, warm
and soothing. Girls went crazy over it, and even to Josh the
honeylike tones were pleasing. The tinny speakers of his
deck, though the finest of their class, weren't as sensitive
as the surround-sound amplifiers of a holopic palace, but
they conveyed Joey Jet's vocal strokes adequately. Like
right now, Joey was musing on Josh's discovery—

"Maxed out, man! Awesome hunk of chill! What's it
for?"

"I dunno. This is the inside, the shell fell away as soon

as I hit it with a testing utility." The two of them circled the cube slowly, an odd pair, the gizmo-faced greaser and the robed prophet, both probing and testing the object with penetration programs that occasionally caused sparks to fly off its burnished surface. Joey was loading another inquiry macro when the cube suddenly twitched and threw his icon into the air. He landed on his back and jumped up. JJ's eyes popped out of their metal sockets on springs, then snapped back with a satisfying click. Josh laughed, even though he'd seen the trick before.

"Hey! This is something else, Josh. It ain't what it seems."

"What are you talking about?"

"I just found out, it's not a data fort at all, it's—it's somebody's icon!"

Joshua stepped back from the monolith and withdrew the intrusive tentacles of his Feeler programs. "Get off it, JJ. There's Net limits on icon size, and this thing is about a hundred times too big."

"Don't take my word for it, pal. Ask him. Or her. Somewhere inside that thing is a hacker's brain just like yours or mine, only smarter, 'cause neither of us knows how to exceed the boundary of icon dimensions, and this character has blasted them wide open. Oh, and by the way, it's invisible."

"What do you mean? I'm looking right at it."

"Yeah, you are, and I am, but anybody else who cruises by won't see it, in fact they'd pass right through it even though we can't scratch its surface."

"Why us?"

"You tell me. Whattaya been into this morning, besides a lot of trouble?"

Joshua told JJ about his encounter with the Holo Men. He wondered if he should be sharing this even with his best Net friend, but it was too late, he'd blurted out his tale in a rush of excited words. The cube sat silently before them, but all of a sudden Joshua had the distinct sensation that it had ears and had been listening to him.

"Go ahead, ask it a question," he prodded Joey.

"What is this, the Wizard of Oz? Show me the little wimp behind the curtain." Those were the last words he ever heard from the honeyed voice of Joey Jet. A disembodied fist shot out from the cube, spewing blue fractal fire, and smote Joey, smacked him, smoked him. Hell Burner! He screamed, and Josh knew that wherever JJ's physical body sat at its term, he was shrieking in agony there too. Then he was gone, his icon dissolved in a dramatic puff of smoke. The cube began to rotate, shrinking as it turned, its six sides changing color and texture, the thing was mutating before his eyes, it grew a face, Joey's face, horribly distorted, for a second Josh thought it had all been a gruesome joke by his friend, but then the cube squeezed itself tight around the face and a pathetic cry emerged from the mouth of the tortured boy. Josh was seeing the actual countenance of his Net friend, somewhere in the real world, as the life was being crushed out of him. Josh's curiosity rose momentarily above his horror as he marveled at the technical mastery of the moment. He was startled to realize that he did know his Net friend, it was Myron Winklebottom, the geeky kid from his high school. Myron's real face was a pale, pimply plain, flesh-and-blood version of his Net facade, and his voice a mere teenage croak compared to that golden resonance on the Net. He rasped and moaned as an unseen force pressed on his chest and suffocated him. His body cavity exploded, splattering the viewing eye with pink lung tissue and dark blood, and then the image was gone, the cube was gone, and before Joshua stood the grotesque peeled human he'd seen in the coffee shop earlier that day.

"Was that real?" Josh asked, his heart a violent engine with a broken regulator, racing out of control.

"Is the Net real?" was the calm rejoinder.

"It is to me."

"Precisely."

"Are you Arasaka?" Josh asked, remembering that Joey was wanted by the Corporate giant for his expensive pranks.

"Far from it. You shouldn't have told your friend about our little meeting."

"You're one of the Holo Men?"

"Yes. But my identity mustn't be revealed to outsiders. Your loose tongue cost him his life—"

"No!" Josh screamed.

"Don't take it so personally. At 12:37 P.M. this afternoon an Arasaka assassination team was planning to eliminate your friend. I saved them the trouble."

"But why? Why? JJ—Myron was just like me, he would have played your game."

"He wasn't like you. He was a troublemaker—"

"So am I!"

"You're a visionary, like ourselves. Yes, you like to meddle, we know of your antics in Corporate accounts, but you're also experiencing physical changes, aren't you?"

"How did you know that?

"Because all of us are undergoing the same phenomenon. This is what separates us from your late friend."

"But did you have to kill him?" Josh wailed.

"Come, come. You never even met the boy. He's not worth this grief, believe me. I told you, he was doomed. Nothing could have saved him. I spared him a more unpleasant death than the one you witnessed." There was something shockingly cold in the gory icon's flat delivery, frigid yet fascinating, like the frosty sparkling allure of a diamond.

"Who are you?" Josh demanded.

"I am the first of the Holo Men, the architect, the Creator. I am God. My Net icon is Nietzsche." The flayed, bleeding image laughed harshly.

Joshua had no response to that grandiose statement made with the same unemotional assurance as his other utterances.

"If you're God, you can bring Joey—Myron back."

"There are limits even to the Omnipotent," the shucked human being chuckled cruelly. "Forget about him. Join us. Soon you'll be expanding at a rate unimaginable to you now, your memory increasing, your data cache growing, until you too are a god, one of the pantheon. Or, we can send you to the same fate as your friend. The choice is yours."

Joshua knew that he stood on the cusp, that he was being judged. His next words would determine his future. His brain was transforming itself, the Holo Men knew why, perhaps he really was one of them, always had been, maybe they were all the results of a genetic experiment gone awry or something. He had to know. He was sorry for Joey, but the bloody character before him had told him he was unique, nobody'd ever said that before, well, maybe Sally, and his parents, but they didn't understand why he was special. He was being swept up into a new way of thinking, one that matched his frenzied Net life. It felt good. "Sign me up," he said.

"Follow me!" his newfound mentor commanded, and off they went, out over the ocean into Wilderspace again, but this time their destination was not the invisible pirate ship. Once again they dove toward a tiny grain of an icon amid the ocean's vastness, and even this particle was protected by a Shrouded Gate so that only Joshua and his companion were able to see it. Again the icon sucked them in without the traditional zoom-out. Joshua found himself standing this time in a finely detailed reproduction of the office of the president of the dis-United States, a room familiar to all Americans from countless propaganda holo-broadcasts, with images of former presidents lining the walls, historical furniture of cherry-wood and maple laminated with the presidential seal, the desktop graced with a bust of Lincoln, a room now thoroughly meaningless in an era when the states no longer functioned as a union, but were divided instead into autonomous regions each vying for power, the president a mere figurehead with less authority than a hot-dog vendor. Joshua's guide had taken a seat behind the Jeffersonian-era desk. The monks still wore their concealing robes, which seemed out of place in the political setting, but Joshua barely had time to notice this anomaly before the proceedings started.

"You may think that this is a simulation, but we are actually sitting in the office you see before you," his escort told him with a matter-of-factness that belied the preposterous nature of the statement.

"What do you mean? I'm still in my apartment, and you're wherever you're Running from."

"Physically, yes. What I am trying to tell you is that your Net location is not the Pacific Ocean far in Wilderspace, but 1600 Pennsylvania Avenue, Washington, D.C. Verify that if you don't believe me."

Joshua flashed the coordinates of his icon in a corner of his view. Sure enough, he was in the District of Columbia. It was like they'd superimposed the Net sim over the actual place. That was a neat trick.

"Where's the prez?" Josh asked in his usual irreverent fashion.

"We sent him on a meaningless errand so we could use his office."

"For what?"

"For your initiation. I want you to meet your kindred spirits, the Holo Men, short for Holographic, because like you, they have become accustomed to life in the radically different world we inhabit now. Like you, they are adventurers; like you, they hunger for change, like you, they are changing, evolving mentally and physically into the men and women of the future. Brothers!" the transparent man in the president's chair stood and shouted, "this boy has passed all the tests, has demonstrated to me that he is worthy of induction into our cell. Welcome him!"

The monks divested themselves of their robes, which were actually elaborate cloaking programs designed to shield their identities from the uninitiated or from anyone else for that matter. Ethan Allen was still dressed in his 1770s outfit, and Mao was wearing a Mao jacket, but the rest of the group didn't bother to maintain the revolutionary figure motif. They were an eclectic bunch, some with drab faceless icons, one dressed as a bohemian, another as a dandy from the Victorian age with a coat of flocked velvet, lace and frills, yet another in the post-punk chic of shaved head, tattoos, and pierced body parts popular in the last years of the twentieth century.

"This is—Abbie Hoffman—I believe you said?"

"I'd prefer to use my own name. My namesake Joshua ben-Nun was a revolutionary too. He blew down the walls at Jericho."

"Very well. Joshua it is. Meet your peers."

The group closed in on him, enveloped him in their unity. They massaged him with tactile programs, a thousand starfish arms touching him with tingling tentacles, a thousand downy feathers caressing him. They linked in daisy chains of sensual abandonment, replicating like strands of DNA, double-helix intertwined. It was unexpected, exciting, and a little frightening, like having sex with a total stranger, but it wasn't sex exactly, more like the mingling of a school of fish or a pod of whales who touch each other for reassurance and to communicate. Joshua noticed the sensitive swollen areas of his brain around the 'trodes were pulsing peculiarly as they responded to the subtle intervention. Then, just as suddenly as it had begun, the group grope was over and the figures separated into their distinct identities. Ethan Allen approached him, and Joshua grinned, remembering the game of iconic transformation they'd played at the last meeting. The ersatz colonial figure also smiled.

"You're one of us now," said Ethan. "No need for me to scurry away."

"Do I get a secret decoder ring or somethin'?" Joshua asked, because he still wasn't taking the whole thing too seriously. The smile disappeared from Ethan Allen's carefully drawn icon.

"We've noticed a certain disrespectful quality about you. This is one of your appealing traits, and we don't seek to suppress it, indeed, it's one of the reasons we selected you to join us. However, we would appreciate it if you would show more formality when you address our leader, K-M." Ethan Allen indicated the ghoul behind the desk who had fetched him. Joshua turned toward him and hummed a few bars of "Hail to the Chief."

"No prob. What should I call you?"

"I prefer the title Comrade."

"Makes sense. 'Hackers of the world unite.' "

"Soon enough all the world will know my name, but for

now, the old Communist greeting maintains a certain necessary anonymity among us. When the Net is ours—"

"Huh?" said Joshua. "The Net's supposed to be for the people."

"We are the people. The Net is controlled by Corporate interests, and monitored by Netwatch. We're going to liberate the system and run it ourselves."

"Chill," said Joshua, though he didn't believe they could do it. Corporations like Arasaka and Militech were too big, too powerful, and the Netwatch sysops were in their pay. Then again, here he was campin' out in the Oval Office, so maybe these Holo Men were serious. He'd find out.

The next few days were happy ones for Joshua. He did some serious all-night living in marathon sessions of interactivity. He left the Net only once, when his landlord banged on the apartment door to threaten eviction if Joshua didn't come up with rent money in the next five days. Joshua ignored the warning. In a few days he'd be a permanent resident of the Net, he thought, then there'd be no need to deal with a greedy landlord, meddling parents, or anybody else who bothered him in the real world. Occasionally he felt a twinge of regret over the way his relationship with Sally had ended, but then something else the Holo Men revealed to him would catch his interest and he'd forget about her again.

It was a revelation to Joshua how many of them there were. He was happy to find others like himself. He enjoyed the camaraderie, the shared vision. He didn't feel alone anymore, as he had in those first few days after Sally left him. In the first meeting he'd met only a dozen or so, but the circle had expanded since then, though Josh suspected that the core group consisted of those few revolutionaries he'd first encountered. He saw no more of the mysterious K-M. He'd asked one of the others about the meaning of initials, and was told that they stood for Karl Marx, the proto-Communist, but Joshua figured out on his own that they could also be short for Kilo Mega, a notorious criminal who had escaped from a maximum security prison just hours before his planned execution in 2019 and hadn't been seen since. Kilo Mega's story was legend among Net players. He'd been convicted of murdering the assistant chief of security at Militech when the agent found him deep within the protected confines of Militech headquarters. Some said he'd sneaked in through the phone lines, since there was no known way to penetrate the inner lockdown zone where the Militech Corporates worked. Others conjectured that he hadn't actually been there, and that all they had locked up was an electronic image of himself that he'd somehow rendered so realistically they took him into custody, and that he'd simply shut off when it no longer served his purposes. His empty cell had been found with the door still electronically locked.

The Holo Men had programs he'd never dreamed of, insanely clever. They'd devised a subterranean method of traveling through the Net using unassigned logicals, a Heisenberg principle of maneuvering; you weren't quite certain where you'd end up but if you cycled through a few variations you'd arrive at a destination close to where you wanted to be. The interim stop-off points were meaningless, and the result was that you reached your destination much faster than if you'd simply set a straight course—it disproved the old notion that the shortest distance between two points was a straight line; in the Net the shortest distance, in time, turned out to be a succession of random access jumps. They introduced him to the wonders of running in MicroNets, and hinted at a MacroNet that they weren't yet ready to reveal to him, or he wasn't ready to see.

Two of the Holo Men were especially friendly to him. One was the Ethan Allen character, who was his chaperon because the Holo Men didn't really trust him yet, even though they'd welcomed him into the group. Every time Joshua turned around, Ethan Allen was there in his corny Rev War getup, prattling away about how the Holo Men were going to do this or that. He was a fanatic. Joshua distrusted him instinctively. Ethan knew how to find him at any time, though Joshua had tried a few basic dodges to shake him, because sometimes he just wanted to wander around, but aimless Net thrashing wasn't part of the Holo program, they were too earnest for that.

The other was a Japanese *otaku* named Taro Takahashi, a data nut who liked to pop trivia questions on Joshua when he was least expecting them, and who was about as committed as Joshua to the revolutionary dogma of the Holo Men—he was interested but still checking them out. Taro dressed in black t-shirt and jeans and combat boots like a typical *otaku* post-punk info-freak. His black hair was shoulder length, ropy, and probably greasy, though Joshua had never touched it with any tactile programs. He was a real Japanese, not a Japanese-American. He logged on from a tiny apartment in the basement of a cinder-block worker's hive in Ikebukuro, beneath a convenience store, where he'd worked out an agreement with the shop owner to provide him with the basics of life, soda and microwaved junk food, through a hole in the ceiling so he never had to leave his apartment. He was even more of a Net junkie than Joshua. The two of them hit it off right away, maybe because they were the junior members of the group at nineteen, the others being at least twenty-three, and K-M rumored to be an old man of thirty. Taro'd been busted for posting the code to a new software program before it was even released, effectively killing the market for it, because he believed that all software should be freeware. Right after the bust, he'd moved into Ikebukuro and eliminated all traces of himself in Japanese security records. In essence he had vanished, and only his closest friends, and now the Holo Men, knew that he was still alive.

The day after Josh's induction into the Holo Men, he received a message from Taro inviting him to come along on a little Net-rove.

"What about Ethan?" Joshua asked, because he knew that as soon as his icon appeared into a known Net location his warden would show up nearby.

"We'll ditch him," said Taro.

"I've tried," said Josh, but he was afraid their conversation was being monitored so he didn't say more.

"Meet me at *****," Taro replied. The place he named was encrypted. Josh had no trouble decoding the encryption routine, which identified a local hacker's hangout in Night City, but he suspected that Ethan wouldn't find it difficult to unscramble either, so he ran a second routine on the name and discovered that it too was a code, actually an elaborate cultural pun that directed him to another location. In English the name was innocuous enough—Mr. Ed's—but you had to know a lot about old-time American television from the early 1960s, almost sixty years ago, that it was really referring to a sushi bar called Wilbur's that was famous for its horse sashimi. On a hunch he showed up at Wilbur's, and there he found Taro waiting for him and grinning a crooked smile. "Hey! I knew you would figure it out."

Josh stared at his companion for a minute. He couldn't help noticing that Taro's face was covered with acne, his teeth were rotting, and his eyes were weak and one wandered, giving him a lopsided, homely appearance. "Most people like their icons to look better than they do in real life. How come you don't pretty yourself up?" Josh asked.

"How do you know I haven't?" Taro answered. "Maybe I'm even uglier than this!" The two teenagers laughed and set off on Taro's mission of the morning, which was to hack at the Media Fort north of Night City. Taro was into collecting the statistics of pop stars, and he used every means available. Joshua had discovered that Taro knew incredible amounts of useless information about singers like the radical eco-punk bytegyrl and movie stars like Homero Blanco, who had just appeared together in a holovid megahit called *Maglev Disaster.*

"Do you have a girlfriend?" Josh asked his newfound friend as they flew toward their destination, backstroking lazily across the grid-lined sky while their travel programs propelled them northward.

"Uh, no."

Joshua was surprised. "Have you ever gotten laid?"

"What's that?"

"You know, had sex."

"You mean, like, with another human being?" Taro asked quizzically.

"Well, yeah. What other kind is there?"

"The Net kind. Sim-sex. Holovids, slasher porno, that's what I'm into. It's—cleaner. You oughta try it sometime. You're a natural for it."

Wow, thought Joshua, *this dude's way more hardcore than I am.* The image of Sally, naked and writhing under him, flashed through his brain for a split second. No more of that for him now, but the idea of yanking off while watching holovids of other people doing it didn't appeal to him. In the future he'd avoid asking such personal questions of Taro. Joshua thought the Japanese would have been more reticent about his personal life, but he was wrong—the web of strictly defined social relationships that governed Japanese society was obliterated in the Net. Anybody could be anything, and no one would know. Even now, Joshua couldn't be sure that his acne-scarred new friend wasn't really a middle-aged Japanese housewife with a vivid imagination, or someone not even Japanese! but he doubted it.

"It's like when a rich person owns a dog," said Taro. "The vet takes care of it, the maid feeds it, the dog walker walks it, all the rich person has to do is enjoy it."

Josh knew that Sally, for one, wouldn't appreciate being compared to a pet. He tried to move the conversation to more neutral ground.

"Let's talk about something else," he said. "Like, what kind of deck do you run?"

"Ah, you know, it's completely custom-built. My pad's full of stuff I've ripped out of it; I gotta hold a garage sale one of these days," Taro said with a smile. Obviously he wasn't going to tell Joshua too much about his rig.

"How about cyberware? You got SmartEye?"

"Uh-huh."

"Pit Bull?"

"Sure, and Guard-Dog."

"Hellbolt?"

"Hellbolt 3.2, and a version of Hydra that isn't on the market yet." Taro then rattled off a dozen programs Joshua'd never heard of, Japanimation black market shit that wasn't available in America.

"Let me show you a picture of my place," said Taro. Before Josh's eyes flashed an image of a ten-by-ten room, barely larger than a prison cell, with the guts of computers spilling over everything, crashed drives, chips, and keyboards piled everywhere among the plastic and paper remains of uncountable fast food meals, a chaos of confusion

that made Joshua's messy apartment seem positively pris-
tine by comparison. Posters of sexy young Japanese pop
idol (*idoru*) singers—male, female and androgynous—
lined the walls, fighting for space with printouts of lines of
code.

"You live there?" said Joshua, wondering how Taro had
taken over his visual display for that instant and superimposed the still of his Tokyo microflat.

"No, I live here. That's just where I eat and sleep and
shit."

Josh was getting a glimpse of himself through Sally's
eyes. This must be how he appeared to her, a ghost from
the machine who'd vacated his body for the other world of
the Net. And why not? For Taro, there was space, room to
move, freedom like he could never enjoy in the real world
of Tokyo, where he'd be an outcast, a reject, forced to
work some mindless Corporate job producing bank state-
ments or insurance code, always the guy in the last row
where desk position meant everything. Now they'd found
the Holo Men, and their future was even more promising,
they might even end up running the Net.

As they approached the Media Fort, Joshua was amazed
to discover that the building was on fire, a phenomenon
he'd never witnessed on the Net. Black ice was dripping
like Halloween candle wax down the sides of the structure.
Flames shot into the artificial sky, flecks of ashes and soot
drifted by, and Josh could swear his tactiles felt the heat
emanating from the blaze. It was impossible, of course, but
he still shielded his face from the inferno.

"This way," said Taro. They swooped around the Fort to
the back side. The fire must've just started, because the
Netwatch goons hadn't shown up yet. Beneath the ice
patches of firewall were showing up, the older and more
traditional defense against hackers, long since breached.

Taro picked a spot and dove through. Joshua followed. They both passed through the wall like crystal monokatanas through polyunsaturated oleomargarine. Behind the firewall the data elements were lined up like safety deposit boxes in an old bank vault, row upon row, but Taro didn't stop here, he continued to penetrate walls, and Joshua quickly found that the fort was a palimpsest of hundreds of nested routines, each layer wrapped around the preceding like the skins of an onion. Taro was headed for the core. Each time they plunged into another sheath Joshua's programs ran slower and more memory was eaten up, but Taro was breaking trail so he followed in the Japanese teen's electronic footprints.

"Is it really on fire?" Josh managed to shout to his companion's heels.

"Nah, that's just a distraction," Taro replied over his shoulder, his hair streaming behind him as he continued his dizzying descent into the interior of the Fort. "They'll figure it out pretty soon, but we'll be gone by then."

The inner workings of the Fort were like jeweler's watch movements in three-dimensional sphere form, millions of curved wheels spinning in a unique representation of data storage that Joshua had never seen. Each tiny cog represented a bit, and the way they meshed determined the sequence of information that was stored. The surfaces of the spheres were in constant motion as the gears shifted, separated, and rejoined with others. Inside one was another, its surface also made up of circular gears rotating and coalescing. It was extremely dangerous! Their icons could easily become entangled in the merging, shifting patterns, but Taro undoubtedly had been here before, because he continued to pick his way through the maze, unerringly moving deeper and deeper into the heart of the Fort. At its inmost center was a hollow space, like the eye of a spherical hurricane. They burst into this emptiness and floated there while all around them the data flowed in unending transformation on the inside curvilinear plane of the innermost sphere. It was like sitting behind a waterfall or under the glassy tube of an endlessly breaking wave.

"Don't you just love it in here?" Taro asked Joshua, who made no reply, his eyes were dazzled by the sight. After a few minutes though, he began to wonder about Taro's ultimate goal.

"What are you hacking?"

"Nothing. I could take anything I want, but sometimes I just come to chill in the core."

Joshua admired his companion's daring, but he questioned the safety of remaining inside this electronic maelstrom. If the Net crashed, they'd be trapped here, and if the Netwatch crew found them, there'd be no escape.

"Don'cha think we oughta be getting goin' soon?" he said worriedly.

"I suppose you're right," said Taro. He stretched his hands above him as if praying to the gods of information, then began to retrace his path to the surface. Joshua chased him, sometimes falling behind, grabbing at Taro's heels to pull himself through the next outer section, then, about fifty layers from the surface, it happened, he didn't get through between two turning gears and his icon was trapped! Pinioned between the cogs, he felt no pain, but he knew that at any moment his icon could be frozen and isolated by the Fort's automatic security defenses, which would summon the Net police, and that would be the end of his Running days.

"Taro!" he yelled to his friend, who had disappeared ahead of him. "I'm stuck!"

The Japanese teen came flying back through the next sphere. "Don't tug," he shouted, "that's what sets off the alarms," but it was too late, flashing lights and audible bleeps signaled that the Fort had discovered an internal disruption. The surfaces of the spheres began to spin faster and crazier. It would be nearly impossible to pass through now. The spaces between the spheres were collapsing as the entire structure compressed itself, one of its defense mechanisms, like a porcupine rolling into a ball. Taro pulled Joshua free, but by now they were forced to slither sideways along the ever-constricting passageway between the two layers, and they were still many concentric rings inside the object.

"We're going to have to blast out!" Taro yelled above the noise, which was a deliberate attempt to disorient them. "Hold on!" Taro folded his arms, assumed an Indian mudra position, and held his breath until his icon turned blue.

"What are you doing?" Josh shouted.

Taro expelled two lungfuls of air. "I'm psyching myself up," he said. "I've never tried what I'm about to do."

"What!?"

"Icon Meld!"

Josh wanted desperately to know what that was, but there was no time left for discussion, in a few more seconds the Media Fort would be completely converted to compressed file format and the two of them would be sandwiched inside, easy pickings for the Netwatch police.

"Hold on to me," Taro commanded. Joshua's icon wrapped his arms around Taro's waist. He heard the young hacker chanting, thought maybe it was Sanskrit, not Japanese, but then there was no thinking, only a hollow, rushing sound like the moment before a jet powers up to full throttle, then a sudden jolt as accelerators kicked in and the pair went screaming through the upper layers of the Fort. Joshua had the sudden sensation that he was slipping inside Taro's brain, and a confused, exotic place it was too,

racing in Japanese thought through rapid calculations,
dodging left and right to find creases in the surface of spinning cogs, crashing through where there was no opening.
They hit the inside of the firewall and bounced back, then
struck it again and tumbled through, still linked in tandem,
Joshua babbling in Japanese, Taro breathing heavily, and
Joshua saw himself, or at least his Joshua icon, through the
eyes of another. He laughed. His robes were tattered, his
beard singed, and the famous trumpet dented and bent, but
they were free!

"Split, man!" Taro shrieked, and Joshua saw his friend
clawing at his head in an effort to expel him, but he lingered just long enough to touch the memory centers, because this was a special moment, really, the two of them
were almost one, he'd never been this close to anyone, not
even Sally, it was like he knew everything about Taro, his
secret hopes and fears, his dreams and his neuroses, and he
also was completely exposed before Taro, there was nothing he could hide from his friend, but Taro wasn't looking,
he was struggling to extricate himself from the Icon Meld.
Finally Taro broke free, and they stared at each other, sep-
arate entities once again but never to be truly apart, for
each knew the other completely, like twins, there was nothing left to pretend about, the barriers were removed that di-
vide all but the most passionate lovers, and mother and
children, and men at war.

"That's what the Holo Men want," Taro whispered.
"Total unity."

Josh didn't know what to say, because he still didn't
comprehend the enormity of the experience, it was like a
dream had overwhelmed his waking mind, but then he
jumped up and tugged at Taro's sleeve, "Get up!" as a
squad of Netwatch police rounded the corner of the Media
Fort and came charging at them with electron guns drawn.

A wreathy web of fine optic fibers twirled above their heads and dropped down on Josh and Taro. Josh reacted quickly and somersaulted out from under it, but Taro was still shaking off the effects of the melding and failed to react quickly enough. His icon was ensnared in the filmy netting.

"Got one!" the lead policeman crowed, but Josh brought his trumpet to his lips and sounded a curious series of notes, and the spidery lines melted away.

"Get us out of here!" he screamed at Taro to startle him out of his daze. Instantly the Japanese grabbed Josh by the arm and the two flew skyward, followed closely by the police, but it was no contest, once they'd lost the element of surprise the lawmen were no match for the electronic gymnastics of the youthful hackers, who toyed with their pursuers before leaving them behind in a blaze of baffling transformations far out over the ocean. Once they were certain they'd won the chase, Josh and Taro floated gently down to hover over the rocking waves, somewhere in Wilderspace.

"What happened back there?" Josh asked. "For a minute we were Siamese twins bonded at the brain."

"I told you, the Holo Men gave me that routine. It's still in beta test, I'm one of the debuggers on the project."

"Yeah, well, it works, that's for sure. I mean, I can speak Japanese with a language chip, but for a minute there I *was* Japanese. I was you."

"And I was you. And Josh, pal o' mine, I love ya, but I wouldn't want to be ya."

"The feeling's mutual."

They laughed. "How'd you break their hold on me back there at the Fort?" Taro asked Joshua.

"Oh, that. Just a little macro I wrote. I call it 'Fade

Away.' Works on the gridlines too, if you ever need it to. Copy it over onto your deck."

"No need. When we melded you got everything I had, and vice versa. Take a look and see."

Joshua shifted to analog and scanned his files. Sure enough, all the programs Taro had boasted of were now loaded in his ROM. He was about to open a couple of them when they were buzzed by a slow-moving, low-flying dirigible icon that flashed messages on its side like a blimp over a sporting event. In this case the communication was for them, from the Holo Men: "PLAY PERIOD IS OVER. TIME FOR LITTLE BOYS TO COME IN."

"I hate it when they talk to me like that," said Taro. "Like, they're cool and all with their tech stuff, but I'm no baby." Josh and Taro entered the icon and zoomed into the underhanging gondola of the blimp, where they found the inner council of the Holo Men seated in overstuffed leather observation chairs, as though there was really something to view out the windows of the icon other than the endless uniformity of the ocean projection. The room was a carefully reconstructed version of an early twentieth-century drawing room, with walls of veneered wood masking the dirigible's metal superstructure. Velvet drapes lined the spacious windows. The furniture was Edwardian: heavy, impractical, stolid. The men were smoking cigars and sipping brandies from oversized snifters. K-M was not among the assembled. Chairman Mao was chairing the meeting, which was called for the purpose of reprimanding the two young renegades, as Josh and Taro soon found out.

"We can't have you messing about in databases to no purpose."

"I had a purpose," said Taro.

"Yes, but it was not ours," intoned the Chairman. "If you are truly to be a Holo Man, you can no longer act out boyish fantasies. Your every movement must have intention, must further our cause. And you, young Joshua, who have just joined us, we had hoped that you would be a positive influence on Taro-san, not the other way around."

"We were just playing," said Joshua.

"Precisely. But now that you are a man, a Holo Man, you must put away childish things, and concentrate on the tasks we assign you."

"You haven't given us anything to do," Taro complained.

"Not yet. You haven't proved yourselves worthy. But when the time comes, both of you will have important roles to play in the coup d'état—"

Joshua was startled by the Chairman's not-so-veiled reference to an overthrow of the government. Che tugged at the sleeve of Mao's Mao jacket and whispered a few words in the Chairman's ear. Mao nodded, glanced out the window at the ocean drifting beneath them, and turned back to the group.

"On the advice of counsel, I'll say no more. You have sinned. What would be a suitable punishment?" Chairman Mao asked idly.

"The Scrambler!" someone shouted. The suggestion was greeted with approving laughter from all except the two who stood in judgment.

"For how long?"

"Two minutes!" one Holo Man spelled out gleefully.

"Four!" said another.

"Come come, they only triggered a Netwatch alert, not a full-scale repression."

By consensus, it was decided that Taro and Joshua would spend ninety seconds in the Scrambler. Joshua wondered whether this was a physical machine or a reference state. He didn't have to wait long to find out. He felt his icon becoming weighty and slow, as if he'd landed on a huge planet with heavy gravity, and soon found himself incapable of movement. Out of the corner of one eye he saw that Taro was suffering the same fate. Neither of them tried to resist, which would have been useless, but also because both were curious about the Scrambler. It sounded like a futuristic amusement park ride.

Then, it was as though the atomic glue that bonded molecules together was being dissolved. Back in his apartment, Joshua jerked to and fro in a vain attempt to free himself from the disorienting effects of the Scrambler. He was coming apart at the seams, the fabric of his being was shredding, disparate parts floating away in the wind, and worse, elements were recombining in senseless disorder, his thoughts regurgitated in a blenderized mash of alphabet soup. Blithering dithering smithereened creamed, he'd been Scrambled, man, his thoughts were ooops hey yeah got no train, rattle in the brain pan, loose widgets, sticky wickets, calisthenics, calculus, roger a-okay over and out. No control, slow to a boil, sit and simmer, he's a swimmer, a dimmer switch gone bad, plaid, simply crimping up like a crumpled hump, wait, caught a line there, hooie, kaflooey, no hold on, tryin' to catch his mental breath. So uneasy, nauseous, like vertigo, nothing solid under his feet, like mmmm, after an earthquake, fearing the ground on which we tread, take it for granted, but you can't not now or ever, it shifts, it might jump up and knock you down.

After a few minutes his senses returned to him, one by one, the Turkish hash-high two-dimensional mosaic of colored patterns he'd been staring at blindly with such intensity resolved itself into the strands and fibers of the carpet on the floor of the dirigible where he'd plunged facedown, the muddled cacophony of sounds separated themselves into distinct noises, the scraping of chairs and the clinking of glass snifters, the mulligatawny stew of odors into the heady vapors of cognac and the thick sweet scent of Cuban cigar smoke. It was over, he was un-Scrambled. Josh turned his head and saw Taro lying next to him, equally discombobulated.

The Chairman addressed them: "Ninety seconds can be a very long time, *n'est-ce pas*? Had you remained in the Scrambled state for five minutes, the effects would become permanent, irreversible. There are several individuals residing in state institutions today as a result of this treatment."

"But how?" Joshua gasped, naturally curious despite his bedraggled state. "I mean, you're only hitting my icon, not me."

"Ah, my young friend, now you are touching upon one of the essential discoveries of the Society of Holo Men. We have learned how to reverse engineer our way back into the mind of anyone signed onto the Net and using an icon. With this functionality, we can not only tamper with their Net attributes, but fundamentally alter their very beings—" Once again the Chairman was given the high sign by the Che character not to reveal too much to new initiates. "I'll speak no more. Suffice it to say that we want you to behave yourselves, to use your many talents for the cause, not for frivolous and trivial pursuits. Do we have your agreement on this?"

"When do we learn how to Scramble people?" Taro asked. His unabashed enthusiasm for the prospect brought more laughter from the senior members of the council.

"When you prove yourselves worthy. Though we've accepted you into the Society, you remain in the probationary stage. Like the knight-bachelor of an earlier order, there are trials you must undertake to prove your worthiness to sit at our table. We assign one to the two of you now. Take this—" The Chairman produced a glassy sphere like an old-time fortune-teller's crystal ball from thin air and handed it to Joshua, who turned it over in his hands and passed it to Taro. "We want to know who made this, and why. Your task is to find this information and report back to the council."

"What is it?" Taro asked.

"It's a program. When you run it, you'll understand why the Society would be interested in meeting its maker." The Chairman raised his hand to forestall more questions from the two initiates. "Go," he said, "and sin no more." The blimp disappeared, and once again Josh and Taro found themselves floating in the make-believe sky above the make-believe ocean of the Pacifica grid.

CHAPTER 4

NASTY NASTURTIUMS

Sally sat amid the wreckage of Phil O'Dendron's Nursery
and read the note again: "A pox on your phlox, your pop-
pies floppin', sadness on your glads, your begonias be-
gone, your lillies gone silly, your iris dire, disorder in your
shrubs, the madness of a garden gone to seed, a world gone
a rye." Someone with a bent poetic mind had taken perverse delight in systematically ruining the shop—pouring
salt in the soil, spiking the water-drip irrigators with battery acid, snipping the best buds and callously stomping
them to green mush. Phil and Sally had discovered the vandalism early in the morning, but despite heroic efforts they
had not been able to prevent total collapse of the fragile
greenhouse ecosystem that had supported so many forms
of plant life. If they hadn't moved the most expensive blossoms, the orchids and roses, to a secure location the night
before, Phil would have been bankrupt. As bad as it was,

he was able to remain open for his mail-order customers and the special delivery orders, while Sally began the melancholy task of clearing the nursery of dead plants. They still hadn't any idea who would want to ruin Phil. But the trashers had left clues, calling cards, spray-painted tags boldly marking their rampage through the greenhouse: VIR-TUAL RITUAL—CYBER IS FINE—STAY ON—NET WAY IS THE BEST WAY. Once again Sally thought of Joshua. He had the motive, she'd walked out on him. He had the opportunity, he knew her schedule and the password to the nursery. But she still couldn't imagine him doing this, he was such a simple, sweet kid, if a little misguided. She was going to have to contact him, though, no matter how painful that might be for her. The weird slogans sounded like his computer mania.

That afternoon, after sweeping up the mess on the floor, repotting in fresh soil anything that could be saved, and flushing out and purifying the water supply, Sally returned to the apartment where she'd spent a few months as Joshua's lover. She expected him to be home, he always was, and she knew he'd be jacked in to his deck, but she hadn't anticipated the terrible deterioration of his physical state. She found him slumped in his chair, asleep in cyber-space, unwashed, smelly, bleary-eyed, and starving. She shook him awake.

"Hey, Josh, it's me, Sally."

"Oh. Hi. What're you doing here?"

"I just stopped by to visit." Sally'd realized immedi-ately there was no way Joshua was the culprit of the nurs-ery bashing, he was too far gone into his imaginary existence, he was a lost soul.

"Oh, you're not coming back then?"

"To what? To you lying in your own shit, wasting away?"

"I'm not wasting, Sally. In fact I'm growing by leaps and bounds." Joshua straightened up, ran a hand through his unkempt hair, and tried to make himself presentable. "I'm going to be important someday soon, you wait and see. These guys I've hooked up with, they're real visionaries, they—" Joshua faltered, he was sworn to secrecy, he couldn't tell Sally too much, and anyway, what would she understand of his new life as a member of the Holo Men? Wait till she saw him on the Net, runnin' the show, then she'd regret her decision to leave him. But there she was, talkin' again.

"Somebody destroyed the nursery. They sprayed these all over the place." She handed him a piece of paper on which she'd copied the graffiti. Joshua squinted to read the letters, it'd been so long since he'd read anything other than code. He was surprised to recognize a couple of the Holo Men's catchwords among the jottings.

"Why did they do this?" he asked her.

"I was hoping you could tell me."

"No idea. Is Phil some kind of Neo-Luddite or something?"

"He's a gardener, a nurseryman. You know that. He's about as sweet and harmless a man as I know, and so were you, until you started spending all your time inside that box."

"It's not a box, it's another world," Joshua protested, but they'd had this argument before, it led nowhere except to fighting and tears, so he fell silent.

"So, you don't know anything?"

"No," Joshua lied, and Sally knew he was lying, but she didn't say anything, she just picked up her things and left, like the last time, and Joshua stood in the doorway and stared out at the puke-green cement wall that separated their apartment building from the next one, and finally said—"Frack it!" and crash-dove into the Net again. Why would the Holo Men have any interest in a silly old man like Phil? It didn't make sense. He'd ask his friend Taro about it. They'd agreed to meet in the Night City grid (on the Net, of course, not in the real place, Taro remained seven thousand miles away in Ikebukuro, and Joshua never left his crumbling apartment) at a noodle parlor in Little China, where they could both pretend to slurp chow fun and sim-drink Tsing Tao beer while they talked. Taro'd taken the glass ball to run some preliminary debug tests on it. Josh took a seat at the counter of the narrow restaurant, which was authentic to the max: rude waiters, flies buzzing in the air, window displays of calendars with Oriental beauties in one-piece bathing suits, shiny gold and red Chinese characters in cardboard dangling from the light fixtures for luck, menus hand-scrawled in both English and Chinese pasted to the walls, a Buddhist altar in one corner with moldy oranges in a brass bowl. The place was a favorite of Pacific Rim gangs, Malay and Hong Kong thugs scrapping over the latest import-export scams. Reputable Net-goers never came down here, and even the Netwatch police were reluctant to interfere with the "benevolent" Tongs, which made it a perfect place to meet Taro. Joshua ordered a bowl of Szechuan barbecued pork noodle soup and waited for his friend to appear. The waiter brought him a glass of lukewarm tea and practically threw the food at him, but that was all part of the charm of the place. Josh'd hooked himself up to a Bodyweight bio-feed station that supplied him with water and nutrients because he expected this to be a long run, so he wasn't able to simul-drink and eat in his apartment and could only enjoy the olfactory hallucination that he was sniffing the odors of roast pig and ginger.

Taro's arrival coincided with the outbreak of a fight between several other patrons. Knives were drawn, curling Malay daggers and ornate Chinese blades of jade. No one could actually get cut, but there was a good deal of face on the line, like whose icon was the swiftest, who'd programmed the niftiest moves into their martial arts routines, and the outcome of these confrontations was accepted as seriously as if the gangs had met in the alley and really let some blood. Pecking order was established, turf won or lost, deals consummated, all on the basis of these bloodless battles. Joshua wrapped his arms around his bowl of soup and watched as Taro picked his way through the leaping, kicking combatants, dodging flying chairs and shards of smashed porcelain. He was carrying the glass sphere wrapped in a silk *furoshiki* decorated with a pattern of diamonds and circles, a flimsy covering for an item apparently so valuable, Joshua thought. He would have at least put it in a box, but the Japanese favored these pretty coverings for their symbolic value. His friend sat down and placed the object between them significantly while the hand-to-hand struggle raged all around.

"We've got to get rid of this unholy thing!" were the first words Taro uttered.

"What are you talking about?" said Josh. "We're supposed to find out who made it."

"I wouldn't want to be within fifty parsecs of the guy who programmed this. Wanna see what it can do?"

"I don't know, do I?"

Taro removed the cloth cover. "Rub it," he told Joshua.

"What's going to happen?"

"Just rub."

Joshua placed his hands on the globe and gave it a ginger massage. Instantly the warring gangs fell down as if dead. The waiters, cooks, and other customers in the restaurant also lost their iconic animation, as if they were frozen. They hadn't been logged off, they were still visible, but they were paralyzed, immobile. Joshua stood up and walked over to one of the Cantonese gang members, examined him carefully, stole an ice pick from his clenched hand, and drove it between his eyes, where it remained stuck like an inverted unicorn's horn.

"Why doesn't it affect us?" Joshua asked, his voice loud in the sudden stillness.

"Because we're holding it. What you see here, that's not all it can do, but come on, let's blow this joint, I don't know how long the effect lasts."

On the way out they smash-mouthed a couple of other gangsters just for the fun of it, though neither of them was really into the old ultra-violence thing. The globe glowed weirdly until they tucked it under the *furoshiki*. Next they dropped into a bazaar icon crowded with cyber-shoppers who could order the goods displayed by the bustling vendors and have them delivered to their actual homes later that day. Even the lowliest fishmonger was equipped with a fax modem and connected to a delivery system that functioned effectively, as long as your credit was good or your e.b. were new and crisp. Ducks and geese in cages were displayed according to a strict rating system that allowed only the appropriate symbol to be used to represent them, so that a fat greasy duck appeared so and a scrawny rabbit or a stinking day-old flounder was downgraded to its equivalent depiction on-line. Corporate housewives from Beaverville liked to shop at these ethnic outposts, which gave them the feeling that they were participating in the modern multicultural world when in fact they were safely sealed away in their isolated sterile suburban homes. Joshua and Taro were uninterested in these amenities. They were looking for another place to hide out and talk now that the noodle parlor was shot. Taro suggested a sym-

opium den in a basement of the bazaar, but Joshua had a better idea—he wanted to visit the Toy Box, a store run by the venerable Hing Chin, who had been selling toys to generations of children in Little China since well before the cyberpunk age. Hing Chin had allowed himself to be cloned for the Net, so that he could extend his sales to the children of other communities. Joshua thought he might be able to provide some insight into the unusual properties of the glass ball, since its appearance was that of a toy. Taro agreed it was worth a visit, so they popped out of the bazaar icon and dropped into the Toy Box. Hing Chin was inside among the kites, whistles, nested boxes, marbles, and other simple antique toys that made up the bulk of his wares. Of course they weren't talking to the real Hing Chin, but a computer-generated version that was programmed to respond exactly as its model would have done. The store was a jumble of overflowing bins stuffed with paper fans, hats, streamers, tiny windup devices in the shapes of miniature animals or tiny shoes and false teeth that clattered and chattered across tabletops. Nothing in the brightly-lit store was electric, robotic, or computer-oriented. Many of the objects were made of wood instead of plastic, like the monkeys that did somersaults on sticks, or the hand-painted clowns that balanced perilously on strings strung above the heads of the customers and teetered back and forth in a precarious mechanical highwire act. The electronic simulation of the venerable Hing Chin sat on a stool in the center of this delightful chaos, wearing a Taoist magician's robes and a conical priest's cap. He smiled and nodded in typical automaton fashion and occasionally stooped to pat the head of a child, but he reacted quite differently when Taro and Joshua raised the globe into his line of vision.

"Please leave my store!" he declared. "This is a place of

peace, a place for children and their dreams. That which you hold is an instrument of destruction."

"We came only to ask—"

"Please go. I can tell you nothing. Netwatch has been notified of your presence here."

That should have been enough to send Taro running, but he was surprisingly calm, perhaps because he thought the power of the ball would protect him.

"Hing Chin! Who made this?"

"I cannot tell you. Go!"

Taro persisted, "Who can tell us?"

"Ask Dr. Lee, if you must."

"Wu Chii Lee? The herbalist?"

Hing Chin nodded, then his expression froze. Someone had shut him off.

"Netwatch must be getting close. Come on."

They left the toy store icon and shifted over to a coordinate where they could enter the icon for Wu Chii Lee and Son's Apothecary & Yeh Ching Yah School of Martial Arts. The ground floor was the herbalist's stockroom, like the Toy Box crammed with displays from which Net-goers could order goods to be delivered in the real world. Glass jars were stacked on countertops all along one side of the store, each containing ginseng in many different shapes and sizes, from tiny roots the size of peas to hefty turnip-sized pieces. One wall of the shop was completely lined with hundreds of neatly labeled cherry-wood drawers with brass fittings, each of which could be opened by the counter help to reveal different ground powders, dried plants, and animal parts, from crusty starfish to mottled comblike shark's fins. The opposite wall was illustrated with charts and models showing the acupuncture points on the human body, as well as advertisements for the latest in herbal therapy. An automaton version of Dr. Lee waited on special customers at the back of the store, while several assistants in white lab coats took care of ordinary orders from behind the long counter that ran the length of the narrow store in front of the display of drawers. Taro and Joshua headed toward the rear but found their way blocked by Dr. Lee's son Bryan, who owned the martial arts gymnasium upstairs. His role was to screen clientele so as not to tax his father's stamina. Bryan Duncan Lee was a well-known figure in Night City. He'd been a renowned amateur martial artist until an automobile accident in 2017 killed his mother and cost him his eyesight. In the last few months he'd finally received cyberoptic implants, and had resumed teaching in the gym above his father's shop, as well as doing unspecified Solo jobs for the businessmen of Little China. Though Bryan Lee was Chinese, he had adopted the Nipponese method of training. He called his gym a dojo, and his students *kohai*, and they called him *sensei* instead of the Chinese term *sifu*, and they wore white cotton karate *gi* instead of black silk kung fu pajamas. Though Bryan Lee was proficient in Shaolin kung fu, it was in karate that he had been an Olympic contender, before the tragic accident that had ended his hopes for a medal. This version of him was a simulacrum like his father and Hing Chin, but it was quite capable of carrying out its mandate in Net fashion. He stood before Taro and Joshua with his arms crossed lightly on his chest and smiled blankly.

"My father is very busy. What do you want?"

"We seek not herbs, but the venerable doctor's advice," Taro said in a formal way that caught Joshua by surprise. The ancient animosity between the Japanese and Chinese was known to him, and also the fact that in many ways Japanese culture was based on the Chinese, in everything from their use of the Chinese ideographs in their written language to the styles of art and poetry. Taro was playing the role of supplicant. What surprised Joshua was that a teenage data-punk like Taro even knew the proper formalities, Joshua sure didn't know them, but they seemed to do the trick, because the Bryan Lee icon unfolded his arms and placed one fist in the other cupped hand in the Chinese hand gesture of salutation and stepped aside to let them address his electronic father.

"Dr. Lee, it is I, Taro Takahashi, your humble student." Once again Joshua was surprised. Taro had given him no indication that he knew the ancient apothecary, much less that he was a student of the arcane profession of dosing with herbs. It seemed out of character for the young computer genius.

"Ah, Taro-san, how may I help you?" There could be no doubt, the two were known to each other.

"I have brought an object for your inspection." Taro removed the *furoshiki* and showed the sphere to Dr. Lee, who gazed at it with the weak, watery, but still discerning eyes of a very old and very wise man.

"Does this article have a counterpart in the physical world, or does it exist only here in Heaven?" Dr. Lee asked, and Joshua suppressed a laugh. He'd never heard the Net referred to as Heaven before.

"I do not know," Taro answered. "If I were to guess, I would say it exists only here, as a program. It has significant powers. It immobilizes icons, for one thing, and it also can effect at least three of the Seventy-Two Transformations."

"Huh?" said Joshua. "You lost me." But they weren't talking to him, they were dealing directly with each other.

"Who made this?" Taro asked.

Dr. Lee did not answer immediately. He held his hands open in front of him and Taro placed the round transparent object in his palsied hands. It began to glow and turn of its own volition. Taro and Joshua instinctively backed away a step, but the Dr. Lee icon laughed and waved them closer. "The one who created this is a criminal," he said. "He violates the holy. This is a profane item. Destroy it, and do not attempt to manufacture another."

"Who designed it?" Taro asked again.

"You know them."

"Who?" Josh asked, but the Oriental druggist would only repeat his assertion that the persons responsible for the globe were known to them. Pretty soon the two tired of the game and left the virtual reality automaton talking to himself while they left the drugstore icon and hung above the Night City grid.

"What did he mean by calling the Net Heaven?" Joshua asked.

"In Chinese mythology, Heaven is simply the real world moved to the realm of the immutable, the eternal. Heaven is simply all of organized civilization, its bureaucracy, its politics, even its streets and cities, moved into the invisible other world. What better description of the Net than that?"

"And what are the Seventy-Two Transformations?"

"Taoist magic. The alchemical, on which much of Dr. Lee's medicine is based. Things like being able to revive dead men, and turn lead into gold."

"And which three can this—" Joshua started to ask, but Taro wasn't listening anymore, he was backflipping into the air like the hero in a crazy Hong Kong cyber-fu movie, somersaulting impossibly into the sky to avoid the oncharging Netwatch goon who had appeared out of nowhere. Joshua followed his friend's example and rocketed skyward, his heels just escaping the outstretched grasp of the security icon, then both of them ascending away from Night City toward the comfortable emptiness of the ocean and Wilderspace.

"That was close!" Josh shouted as they sailed through cyberspace, the city receding behind and beneath them in perfect spatial relation. "Where did he come from?"

"I don't know. Some of my detectors and alarms didn't function. I gotta go off-line and check this out. Take this—" Taro handed a surprised Joshua the cloth-covered orb.

"What am I supposed to do with it?"

"You gotta hold on to it until I can run some tests in my pad. I mean, it's like a virtual object, I can't take it with me."

"That's what they say," Joshua joked, but Taro either didn't get the allusion or was too whacked by events to care.

"If we don't find out who's responsible for this we could end up dead, and I don't mean just Net-dead," Taro warned.

"Who could it be?" Josh asked Taro. "Maybe somebody from Japan? One of the *otaku*s?"

Taro shook his head. "Nobody I know there has the skills or the programs. Josh, we're in deep now. I don't like it. Don't show that thing to anybody, and don't try to use it without me."

"Don't worry, I won't," Joshua pledged. Taro logged off. Joshua floated above the waves by himself, far from Night City, in the nether reaches of Wilderspace. This should have been a completely empty quadrant, but as Joshua drifted aimlessly across the next gridline he heard a crackling, hissing sound like when an insect hits an electrified field. He'd touched off somebody's defenses, though this was a public sector that shouldn't have been rigged for detection by anybody. Within seconds the air was filled with buzzing as a dozen icons wearing black ninja outfits surrounded him. At first they were content to toy with him, trying to force him into the cyber-water below, probably to slow him down so they could seize him, but when Joshua proved elusive (after all, he was Runnin' with the best deck other people's money could buy) they became increasingly hostile, finally mounting a full-scale attack with electronic throwing stars. If one of these whirling disks struck him it would send such a jolt through his system he might crash. Bouncing and pinging across the empty sky like a pachinko ball, Joshua managed to avoid the first round of throws, but the pattern of the ninjas' assault was becoming increasingly complex. He would soon be pinned like a specimen against the background field of the Net by one of the pointed barbs hurled at him. He had no choice, though he'd promised Taro he wouldn't use the globe, it was his only hope to avoid capture by these unknown assailants. He quickly threw off the cloth *furoshiki* and gave the sphere a quick rub. The effect was instantaneous—the ninjas dropped from the sky like shotgunned black crows, splashing dramatically into the sea. Joshua zoomed across two gridlines and dipped into the ocean, transforming himself into a fish icon to mingle with the artificial schools of bottlenose bluefish and tuna placed their by Net designers for authenticity. Only problem was, underwater the magical glass glowed like something radioactive and boiled the water around it, creating a little round cloud of steam like a miniature earth with its own vaporous atmosphere, and Joshua had lost the *furoshiki* in his haste to flee the ninja ambush. He sent out a frantic call to Taro, but he received no response—his Japanese friend must have been working off-line on his holo-disk. He couldn't stay here, the sphere was like a beacon to anyone patrolling the waters from above. For the first time in his Runnin' life, Joshua was afraid. Sure, he could ditch the

orb and sign off, sit in his apartment and wait for Taro to
call, but he knew what would happen—somebody else
would find the thing, and use it for who the frack knew
what purposes. Even now he could hear the unknown ninja
gang searching for him from afar. The Net program was
cleverly designed to transmit sounds across vast distances
just as they would under real oceans. Who were these
guys? They might have been Arasaka renegades, spinning
off their own grandiose dream of Japanese domination of
the world, or they might be *yakuza* gangsters using the Net
for illegal operations, or, again, they might not even be real
ninja, just some bunch of shits capitalizing on the image to
scare other Runners. If they caught Joshua, he'd find out,
but then it would be too late, because they'd open him up,
force him to give his real address, and pay him a personal,
physical visit.

There was only one thing left to do—he was going to
have to swallow the ball. Inside him or, rather, inside his
icon, it would no longer be visible, but what would be the
side effects from taking this program into his construct?
All Joshua knew was that if he continued to hold it, he was
asking for trouble, he was probably the most visible thing
around for hundreds of grids. If he was in Night City he
might be able to find a place to stash it, but not here, where
the ocean's sandy bottom extended in all directions, the
water was transparent, and the sky empty blue except for
the faint lines demarcating each new grid.

The ninja were flying above him now, he could see
them, distorted through the water's opaque density. The effects of the globe must be temporary, Josh noted in the
back of his mind. They hadn't spotted him yet—oops, now
they had, one by one they dove toward him. Without another second's thought Joshua enlarged his icon so that the
sphere, in ordinary Net perspective about the size of a

grapefruit, was now about the size of a pea. At this dimension Joshua was about forty feet tall, a difficult icon to maneuver in the confines of Night City-sim, but easy enough to control in the wide-open spaces of the ocean over the Pacifica grid. His sudden size shift caught the ninjas off guard for a minute, until they too changed into winged monsters with raking talons, rows of vicious teeth, and slashing tails with spikes like prehistoric reptile birds. Joshua was no fighter, he was completely out of his element in holographic battle. They looped and strafed him feet rigid for slashing impact, while he ducked and cowered near the ocean's surface as if that pure vacant body of water would protect him. Then suddenly the attack was over, and the ninjas-turned-birds were fleeing in a panicked rush of squawks and ruffled plumage, leaving behind a trail of fluttering loose leathery feathers.

What had scared them off? Joshua looked around and saw nothing that would have frightened them, then glanced down and received a shock—his icon had transformed into a dragon hundreds of feet tall, a godzilla-like creature with massive claws for feet and hands, scaly skin and a jaw drenched in saliva that jutted out far enough for Joshua to be able to see his own teeth, now turned into immense ripping sabers. *One of the Seventy-Two Transformations*, he realized with a start. Then he absorbed a jolt of pure terror when he found himself unable to shrink back to human proportions, followed by a second wave of blank-mind horror as he realized he couldn't undo the transformation. He was contemplating permanent existence on the Net as a two-hundred-foot-tall fire-breathing dragon when Taro appeared in front of him, a miniature speck the size of a fruit fly.

"I told you not to use it!" he shouted, then leapt back as a stream of simulated flame spewed from Joshua's nostrils.

"Help me, I'm stuck in this shape and size," Joshua lamented.

"You're a sorry excuse for a monster," Taro said with a laugh. He reduced Joshua by degrees, a few feet at a time, also effecting the return to ordinary icon shape in stages, so that Joshua felt himself evolving, a strange and not altogether pleasant sensation. His scales fell away, his tail shrank to a tailbone, and his claws retracted into common fingernails. His few seconds as a mythical beast were over. Once again he and Taro faced each other in flight above the water. Taro's face was tight and drawn, an expression Josh'd never seen him use.

"What's up? What'd you find out? Hey, is that thing still inside me?"

"No. I dissolved it. And you aren't going to like what I discovered."

"Who made it?"

"They did."

"They who?"

"Them. The Holo Men. I wouldn't be surprised if that was them that jumped you in ninja garb."

"You saw that?"

"Sort of. The globe was like a crystal ball too. When I tapped into its program attributes I got a transmission line of everything that was happening to it, including as it passed down your gullet."

"But why? Why would they want us to search for somebody they knew didn't exist? Why would they attack me?"

Taro shrugged. "Another test, I guess. They're playin' with our heads, Joshua, and I don't like it, but on the other hand—"

"They're really powerful, aren't they?"

"It's awesome. If they show me more tricks like I

learned today from analyzing that globe, I'm going to be dangerous, man!"

The two friends drifted back toward Night City. Before they reached the limits of Wilderspace, they saw the now familiar icon of the Holo Men's ship, which must have been placed in their path, as Josh and Taro had been meandering back in no hurry to reenter the urban grid.

"Should we go in?" Josh asked.

"Why not? We've done everything they expected of us."

"Let's flip 'em out a little," said Joshua, and he turned himself into a pygmy-sized replica of the Taoist dragon they'd made of him. Taro copied his form so the two of them were twin demons. As they entered the inner sanctum of the Holo Men, which was configured this time as a lavish medieval banquet hall, they wrestled playfully with each other, scattering the Society members, who had been seated decorously on heavy high-backed wooden chairs around a colossal sim-feast of platters of roast meats, huge crusty loaves of bread, and jugs of honey-colored mead. Chairman Mao picked himself up from the stone floor and pounded on the massive table with a pewter flagon.

"Joshua. Taro-san. Welcome and congratulations. You have passed the final rite of initiation. No more tests. We accept you as full-fledged members of the Society."

Josh and Taro immediately altered themselves into their standard icons, Joshua as the bearded warrior-prophet, Taro as the geeky Nipponese *otaku*. The Holo Men were once again arrayed as historical revolutionary figures. K-M materialized in a glittering white suit and snappy fedora, like he'd just stepped out of a Havana nightclub. Something had changed, Josh observed. The other Holo Men, who used to be near equals, were now quite deferential around their charismatic leader. This showed itself in the distance they kept their icons from his, and the way they scurried to make him the center of the tableau as they lined up to offer their congratulations to Joshua and Taro. The adulation and acknowledgment of rank were signs of his increased power. There was also an element of fear, Joshua sensed. K-M was reputed to be a skilled killer—perhaps he'd displayed some of his talents to the Holo Men.

"Well, my fine young cannibals, you've shown yourselves to be adventurers of a high order. It's time for you to apply those attributes to a meaningful goal. The Holo Men are in the last stages of preparation for a venture that will change the face of the Net forever. You are to play an integral part in the action. Are you ready to enter into the holy of holies, the most secret covenant of the Society?"

"Yeah, sure," said Josh offhandedly, trying to be cool. Even through his icon his voice trembled with excitement.

"Ours is a holy mission. The dictatorship of the proletariat. So often it has been talked about, attempted, crushed. 'Let the people lead, and the leaders will eventually follow.' Always the leaders have controlled the communications, they were the ones who posted the clay tablet proclamations, printed the books, monitored the radio and television airwaves, ruled the Net. Now, the people are going to take their place as the rightful rulers. The Corporations are going to drown in their own swill, while the true voice of the common man gains ascendancy. And we, the icons in this room, are the ones who will make this happen. We are the Select, the Destined, the Chosen. Behind us are the millions, the billions who now live as mutes, voiceless, without representation or choice. When the Net is ours—"

Joshua glanced at Taro, whose *otaku* icon was agape at the boldness, the audacity, the glorious thrill of it all—

"When the Net is ours, they'll have a voice, our voice, they'll speak through us, and we'll tell the Corporate jackals what to do!"

The room exploded into cheers. Joshua and Taro were swept up in the excitement of the moment. It was like being at the birth of a new movement, like the few landed gentlemen at Philadelphia must have felt, or the first Communists in their secret cells, or the Cuban guerrillas in their jungle redoubts. Everyone danced for the sheer joy of it, to commemorate their impending triumph that seemed so near and so sure. In the midst of the chaotic celebration, K-M stood serene and powerful, presiding like a proud, stern father over the jubilant outpouring of his children's emotions. Joshua caught Taro's eye as they spun in the clumsy ring dance that had developed, icons linking again into that daisy chain of collective energy they had experienced once before. They had made it—they were Holo Men!

CHAPTER 5

CATHEDRALS OF MEMORY

Once the human memory was the repository of all knowledge. If no one remembered a fact, a story, a place, a face, it ceased to exist. Schools of philosophy were based upon the wondrous powers of recall. Systems for remembering were developed. Loci were assigned to attach a physical location to a fact like an anchor, a fixed point of reference. Just as prisoners of war play rounds of golf on their favorite course in their minds, or wander throughout their homes touching each remembered object in extraordinary detail, men of antiquity could summon up storehouses of information by wandering through cathedrals of memory. In the chancery, perhaps, were facts on armor, in the side chapel, equestrian lore, and so forth. Then came the written word, and the edifice began to decay. Then came the printing press, and the foundation was further eroded. Then came the computer, and mass storage of data, and the human memory became a weak thing, hardly worth exercising, as all of its functions were duplicated and enhanced in computing devices. Now came the Net, and suddenly the human memory was important again, because how was one to catalog and navigate without it? One couldn't, after all, make a map of a map of a map. To wander in this virtual world one had to remember, to note one's way with mnemonic tricks, to use the gimmicks of association and correlation that charlatans employed to confuse and astound the gullible. It was like the heady days of the Renaissance, when new worlds were being discovered at every moment, worlds filled with new species of flora and fauna, who could remember them all without systems, and so new classifications were created, whole new sciences sprang up, botany replaced the folksy realm of the herbalist, zoology superseded the bestiary; the Net was like that—new streets, new cities, new creatures, were a minute-by-minute occurrence. The entire surface of the earth was mapped to the square yard. The oceans were charted, coastlines plotted, bays, rivers, and deltas drawn to scale and altered as they altered year by year. The stars had been probed to unimaginable distances, galaxies plotted, the sky segmented into quadrants, but no one held the map of the whole Net. It was growing like the universe in the seconds after creation, expanding in all directions at just under the speed of light. Only the Holo Men knew where squatters were inhabiting some of the largest invisible portions of Wilderspace. It was like Tokyo or Scottsdale, Arizona, in their heydays of growth—streets and whole neighborhoods springing out of the barrens without street signs. Pioneers and outlaws roamed these nether regions. Opportunities existed for the making of quick fortunes, or for sudden death. But to succeed, to thrive, to be naturally selected, one needed the Darwinian advantage of a fabulous memory. This was the secret of the Holo Men. A phenomenon of conscious evolution was manifesting itself within a few individuals. Their brains were responding to the rapid kinetic stimulation at the 'trode holes by enlarging, swelling, adapting to the new input. One in a million, one in ten million, was displaying this new feature, always accompanied by a parallel facility for navigating the Net. These were the individuals targeted by the Holo Men. Josh and Taro were two of their prodigies. There were others. It was the Nazi dream of the superchildren come true, naturally, without drugs or surgery.

Kilo Mega, the real K-M, not his dapper Net icon, stood in his office, an abandoned plumbing supply warehouse in the urban backwaters of Night City, musing on these and other thoughts. Contrary to his dazzling iconic representation, the real K-M was dressed down in a garage mechanic's overalls, a style he favored for its simplicity and comfort, also for the many pockets it afforded as places to conceal weapons, and paradoxically because it reminded him of the prison jumpsuits that had been his only mode of dress for most of his life. His hands hung loosely from his sides, and he appeared harmless enough, but he was well armed, oh, yes, my friends, he was loaded for bear, he was bristling with murderous devices strapped to his ankles, up his sleeves, and in those many spacious places of concealment on his clothing. His face was that of a man who trusts no one, hard and squinty about the eyes, which were constantly shifting beneath black brows, yet when he brought his stare to bear few could look him in the face for long. His mouth was cruelly curled at one corner, the result of a knife slash in the prison yard. His opponent had not survived the encounter.

The room he was in was a combination office space and living quarters. Computer equipment lined the walls, and there were several chairs, but K-M was alone with his thoughts. Where had he learned so much about memory? As a prisoner, of course, not a hero of warfare but a common thief and low-life gang-banger who'd spent so much time in solitary confinement for beating up on other inmates that gradually he'd begun to study his consciousness systematically as he stared at the patterns of cement on the opposite wall from where he lay, day after day, uselessly dreaming of retribution on this guard or that lifer. Another man might have turned to religion, many did, or drugs, which were cheap and readily available, but K-M turned his formidable mind upon himself and became a genius at remembering. He started by reliving many of his past escapades, rapes and robberies, thrashings and trashings, and when he tired of that he ordered books from the prison library and memorized them, reciting verbatim whole passages from technical manuals on how to assemble aircraft engines and other complicated treatises, but it all might have amounted to nothing more than a way to pass the time between brief violent stretches of freedom if he hadn't stumbled onto Rache Bartmoss's *Netguide Number Three*. Suddenly he saw a way to turn his prison-honed skill into a new level of criminal brilliance.

It was pitifully easy. Many there were who hungered for a leader, and he, K-M, most willingly obliged. The wide-open Net was perfect for his talent. In a few months he was able to create an organization that existed only virtually. As in the old Communist structure, many of its members had never met, they knew each other only by their icons, but this didn't stop them from conducting numerous outrageous scams: electronic check kiting, account switching, Ponzi schemes, pyramid ventures, phony stock swindles, all directed and facilitated by the prodigious intellect of K-M, who exactingly skimmed off thirty percent to support the organization. It was all done in the name of revolution, but none of the inner circle were political, they were merely criminals who found it expedient to hide behind the banner of social change while they exploited the talents of youthful converts like Joshua and Taro.

The Net police knew of the existence of K-M and the Holo Men, but they were incapable of stopping him. Today, for instance, he had already pocketed (if one can use that word to describe the movement of a few blips of data) several million e.b. on the International Exchange by forcing the yen into a nosedive and selling his holdings short. It was no more than any legitimate money speculator would do, in fact many of them had piggy-backed on his trading that morning, with the difference that K-M himself had caused the currency to decline by threatening (in several key Net bulletin boards) Holo Men's terrorist activity against the Bank of Japan. Unlike King Midas, K-M couldn't run his hands through his gold, couldn't feel his earnings grow, but he had the satisfaction of viewing spreadsheets of his secret Swiss accounts as they inflated, and every once in a while he converted one of them into bullion and had it shipped to secret locations where he buried it just like the greedy monarch of legend. Today he was contemplating his next action. The stakes were increasing, and somewhere in the depths of his devious mind K-M had begun to actively consider whether or not he might pick the whole world as his plum. No one had stopped him yet. He had the young prodigies of the planet in tow, with their evolutionarily swollen 'trodes, the best minds of their generation, working toward his ends. Why not? Why not K-M as dictator, to rule those Corporate toadies who'd caused him to live so many years in prison cells? He was beating them at their own game, it was revenge at its sweetest. Why not go all the way and seize control of their financial empires? They were helpless without the Net to implement their international monopolistic designs.

They'll regret the way they treated Kilo Mega, locking him in darkness, he said half aloud to the empty room, talking in the third person as egomaniacs are wont to do. A buzzer at the outer door alerted him to a visitor. Casually he flipped a switch that converted the spreadsheet display into a television picture of the back street. Satisfied that he recognized the new arrival, K-M pressed a second button that opened the door, but the guest was still not permitted into his chambers, and instead was forced to wait in this portcullis (where in castles of old boiling oil could be poured on trapped invaders through slits in the ceiling) between two sealed gates (the outer door swung shut and locked behind him) until he submitted to a second, more thorough search that included a low-level X ray for weapons. The man seemed to be taking all this in stride as though he had endured these indignities many times before.

"Enter!" came K-M's voice over the intercom system, though he was sitting scarcely a dozen feet away on the other side of the wall. The second, inner door opened automatically to allow the visitor entrance to K-M's sanctuary.

"Good morning! How did the action go last night?" A careful observer might have seen the similarities between the facial expressions of this person and the Net icon he used to represent himself. It was Ethan Allen, in reality a disgruntled Michigan farmer named Marlon Dime who'd spent time in prison with K-M for his involvement in the terrorist activities of radical right-wing civilian militia groups. He lacked K-M's fearsome aspect, indeed he would have been considered jovial, fatherly, by those who didn't encounter his paranoiac streak. A big, loose-boned man with a small head, narrow-set black eyes, and a shiny bald pate, he too was dressed in overalls, farmer style rather than grease monkey, but obviously aping his leader K-M.

"Let's just say the yen isn't what it used to be," said K-M brusquely. "Never mind that. I want a full report on the two newest recruits."

"Aw, K-M, we cleared 'em both a while ago. Hell, we put 'em through more rigorous checks than anybody we've admitted yet. They're nothing but a couple more punks with swelled heads, an' that's no figure of speech." Both men laughed, but K-M pressed Marlon, a.k.a. Ethan, on the point.

"I don't trust them," he said. "Keep them under surveillance. Continue disruptive actions against their friends and families. I want to see if they revert."

"Okay, K-M. It's a fracked-up sick world when you can't trust the kids, isn't it? 'Member up in Ypsilanti one time we staged a riot in the mess hall, and it was the young inmates who sided with the guards?"

"I remember," K-M said irritatedly, because he didn't like to be reminded of his past, especially by those who had been there with him. He made a mental note that Marlon Dime would have to be purged when his usefulness was at an end, and when K-M made a mental note it stayed in memory permanently, or until he cleared it. "Are we ready for the next Net broadcast?"

"Yessir, we are." Marlon Dime slapped his hands together exaggeratedly to show his approval. "Gonna put the fear of God into those General Motors-Arasaka-Militech bastards. It's gonna be American Revolution Number Two, and we're gonna rid this country of anybody who doesn't love freedom the way we do. Ya oughta tell 'em, if ya wanna live here you're gonna have to speak English, salute the flag, and kiss a Holo Man's ass," Marlon chortled, a snuffing sound like a pig rooting. K-M paid little attention to the man's political ravings. He had his own agenda. When Marlon Dime suggested specific text for the speech, however, K-M's mood shifted from annoyance to anger. K-M's eyes assumed a hooded aspect, like a snake about to strike or a bird mantling over downed prey. As Marlon Dime turned his back to K-M briefly it looked as if the leader was going to make a meal of his most loyal follower, but instead he relaxed and merely made a shadow motion of pulling the trigger on an imaginary gun. Marlon must have felt something, if not the virtual bullet splattering his brain matter across the room, because he turned around quickly in some confusion, but by then K-M was once again seated with his arms crossed.

"Did you ever do any duck hunting up there in Michigan, Dime?"

"Sure, K-M, all the time. I have a prize collection of duck decoys, fills the whole swimming pool, and a gun collection too, Remingtons, Winchesters, Colts, the old stuff, quality, I keep 'em greased up and ready to use. Why? You wanna go up there sometime for target practice or something?" Marlon asked, slightly nervous at the prospect because he'd just felt himself the object of K-M's stalking mind.

"No, Dime, but I always wondered, why do the ducks go to the decoys? Can you answer that?"

"Well, K-M, it's because they think it's safe down there if other ducks are sitting on a pond," Marlon explained. "You know the old expression, 'ducks on a pond.' "

"I don't think that's it, Dime. See, I think ducks have better vision than that, they can tell a real duck from a wooden decoy, I think their hearing is better than we give them credit for, and they can distinguish between a phony duck call and a real one. No, that's not it at all. I think the ones who go down for the decoys want to die. That's what I think." K-M gave Marlon Dime a murderous look that sent the American ultra-patriot scurrying for the door.

"Uh, whatever, you might be right. Listen, I gotta go. See you at the studio this afternoon."

"Think about it, Dime. They're just asking for it."

"If you say so, K-M," said Marlon Dime, though as a hunter and back-country man he knew it was absurd. He also recognized that it was unhealthy to argue with K-M, especially when he was in a funk like now. Better Marlon should take out his frustrations by beating up on some hapless passerby, some fracking immigrant with no right to be in this country, than to confront K-M over a bit of trivia. Besides, Marlon told himself as he exited through the portcullis, waited to be released into the street, and felt himself come under the intense scrutiny of K-M's fearsome gaze through the vid-cam, *K-M was only speaking in parables, like Jesus, he wasn't really talking about ducks at all, that was his way.* He wondered what his leader had meant by the anecdote, and shivered slightly at its implications.

K-M had already dismissed (not forgotten) Dime from his mind. He crossed the stark, cell-like room and unlocked a door that led farther into the recesses of his lair. The inner chamber was a hothouse, artificially heated and humidified, and lined with rows of fancy orchids from Phil O'Dendron's Nursery. In addition to tricks of memory, K-M had picked up this second hobby of tending flowers in prison. With a delicacy that belied his murderous nature, he pruned and watered, like Hitler painting still-lifes of roses in his mountain aerie at Berchtesgaden.

CHAPTER 6

TEUTONIC MNEMONIC BUBONIC

Net broadcasts were issued from the Netwatch sysops. It was a stroke of genius for the Holo Men to appropriate the frequency for their own purposes. Joshua contributed a little trick he knew for accessing Netwatch functionality, and one Monday afternoon, everyone who was logged onto the Net or watching television suddenly heard the mysteriously powerful intonations of K-M instead of the standard Netwatch announcer, and saw floating before them the ghastly skinless man K-M used for his image when he appeared in iconic form. Once again the backdrop was the Oval Office of the White House, once a mythic symbol for all that was powerful, now something less than that but still resonant of majesty and authority. K-M wasted no time in long introductions, but launched into his theme immediately.

"This is the voice of the future. Pay attention. In the next few moments we will describe to you how your lives will change in the coming revolution."

All over the Net, tourists searched the sky for the source of the omnipotent voice. Panicked Netwatch sysops rushed to throw cut-off switches, but they were electronically jammed.

"A plague upon your fatuous Industrial Age machines and their predictable repetitive behavior. Where are the geniuses of old, leaping over antiquated theorems in their haste to create new ones, discarding the accepted in favor of the incredible, what frontiers are left for men like these, the true revolutionaries of the epoch? Who can stop them, for their weapon is their imagination. This is the credo of the Holo Men: life in the new age will be creative, unpredictable, far-flung. If we need resources, we will seize them, and no one will stop us for we are the cybernauts, the boundary-breakers, the true innovators of our era."

K-M paused briefly. Joshua wondered how he could continue to broadcast, as the Net sysops would be able to trace any transmission longer than sixty seconds back to its source—at least he, Joshua, would have been able to do so—but K-M resumed his diatribe. There was something fearful and arrogant in his eloquence. The art of oratory, like that of memory, was nearly lost, but K-M roused the listener, incited him, cajoled, soothed, stimulated, massaged, energized him. It was like listening to Hitler at Nuremberg before the war, a million Nazis enthralled at his feet in the dazzling torch-lit arena ringed by powerful searchlights pointed straight up to form columns of light. The scary thing was, his message was not that different from the Fuhrer's—'We are better than you, we know where we are going and you don't, follow us or die!' The Holo Men had no designs on real power, as far as Joshua knew, their only ambition was to rule the Net, but in this world, so dependent on information, that would be a kind of domination.

"How much easier it is," K-M continued, "for those who have charts and graphs, books and papers to refer to, for those who can spread before them the work of accountants and engineers, how much simpler for those to whom the task is merely one of building upon the labor of others. We have no such luxury. Ours is the blank page that must be started, the empty canvas that must be drawn upon, the file of zero bits that must be created line by painful line. No map to guide us, no history to inform and persuade us, we sail uncharted waters, seeking the New World, which we will discover, because ours is a holy quest!" Joshua trembled. Even he, who had steeled himself against the propaganda barrage, found the hairs on his neck rising with excitement, and his mind threatened to be swept along by this stirring vision. K-M pursued his grim theme.

"—A world that could exist eternally, because it would no longer depend on human folly for its sustenance, that whimsical, perverse, misguided engine of disaster that has led us to the state we find ourselves in today, overpopulated, underfed, fractured and fragmented, in danger of poisoning ourselves to extinction with our own waste. Consider what we offer instead—oneness, holistic unity, a realm of tender intertwinings like the spongy unity of moss. Prepare for us, welcome us, or be subsumed by us, for we are here, pervasive, irresistible. Our power knows no bounds. We can take control at any time, but we wait for your invitation."

The clandestine broadcast was abruptly terminated. The ghostly image of K-M disappeared from Net screens all over the world. Joshua was surprised. He sent out a question to the group: "Who shut us down?"

"Nobody," came the response. "It was supposed to end that way."

Joshua wasn't so sure. Why had the Holo Men put out this teaser, this tantalizing glimpse of K-M? What purpose did it serve? Wouldn't it only cause Netwatch to hunt them more aggressively? Or was that what K-M wanted? The more resources he sucked into a chase, the fewer the Sysops people could devote to maintenance and security functions. It was a classic guerrilla war tactic—draw your enemy into a series of small and wasteful skirmishes—never a decisive battle, win by attrition, by sapping and diverting the enemy's strength, by stringing out his defenses and overextending his supply lines. A chill crept into Joshua's heart. These people were serious. They thought they could control the Net! K-M was a megalomaniac, to be sure, but like they say, "It ain't boasting if you can back it up." Later Joshua modemed up Taro on a secret channel they'd established so they could talk without being overheard. Taro had watched the broadcast from his ten by ten in Ikebukuro.

"What'd ya think of the show, bro?" Joshua asked.

"Awesome. K-M's got 'em stung. They don't know whether to pay now or pay later."

"Pay what, dude?" Joshua wasn't catching his drift.

"It's blackmail, choomba, pure and simple."

"You don't think he really wants to run the Net?"

"Nah. The guy's a criminal. It's a lot easier to be one from the outside than the inside."

"What the hell you mean? Washington and Tokyo for that matter are full of politicians who're crooks."

"Sure, but they're masquerading as honest men. He's an out and out bad guy. What could he do once he got the master key to the Net control room? Nothing he can't do now. Nah, he's shaking 'em down for something."

"I'm not so sure. I think he really wants ta do it."

"Either way, do you want him to succeed?"

"No."

"Neither do I. I like the Net the way it is, nobody really controls it, it's just out there, growin', changin'; if K-M and the Holo Men get their way we wouldn't be hackin' anymore."

"Nah, we're just his tools. This is bad, choomba."

"What're we gonna do?"

"Become counterrevolutionaries."

"Wish we'd figured it out before we took the pledge," said Taro wistfully.

A line had been crossed. The two new Holo Men had realized that they didn't support the goals of their organization. It was a dangerous decision; like trying to resign from the Mafia, it just wasn't done.

"So, what'cha gonna do?" Joshua asked.

"I dunno. I guess we could try to lay low for a while, see if they leave us alone."

"And if not?"

"Then we gotta confront 'em, tell 'em we can expose 'em if we have to. It's bad, Josh. We're in deep."

It was worse than they knew. Their allegedly secret channel was being monitored by a Holo operative who taped their conversation and reported everything back to Ethan Allen, who dutifully conveyed the information to K-M. The leader was surprisingly calm in the face of treason within his coterie.

"Don't kill them," he said. "We must make an example of them, for all the others of their kind. Yes, this will promote loyalty in the ranks. See that they never disturb us again, but don't kill them. Let them live, but take away the one thing that has made them special in the world. Yes, let them be ordinary citizens, and see how they like it." That was K-M's sentence, and it was shortly carried out.

CHAPTER 7

ALL THE SQUARES
GO HOME

A flutter, a flash of green, bright sunlight slanted into slats, a whiff of roast partridge, a golf ball clicking off concrete, timbales, *eau-de-vie*, pince-nez, skidmarks on a guardrail, endless blue sky, life, the world, breathless, infinite, trivial, an exhale, heroic, a reflex, passionate, banal, awkward, poignant, tasty. *Help me, O mother, to feel this pain. Like clouds passing by, my life is passing by.* Joshua was falling down the rabbit hole, stepping through the looking glass, bopping to free jazz. He'd just logged on the morning after K-M's speech when everything corroded, dissolved, broke up into meaningless patterns. He was paralyzed, hypnotized, immobilized. He was under attack.

Another jolt hit him, he was like the condemned man gulping cyanide-infused air, each inhale an agony of constriction, the keyboard a soft machine just beyond the reach of his grasping fingers, his seat an electric chair. He gasped and clawed for air. He was being hung, shot, drawn and quartered, crucified. Then the world went black.

When it was over, he awoke in front of his blank term. He was sick. He soon learned how bad it was. He'd been infected with a virus whose effects manifested themselves like dopamine for hackers—if he tried to log on he felt queasy to the point of nausea. It was impossible for him to enter the Net, he began to vomit as soon as the screen warmed up. It was cruel that they'd left the deck in his apartment instead of smashing it up or taking it away. Everything that had been his life before was denied to him: Net access, the roaming, roving life of the Runner. He couldn't even write lines of code without rushing to the bathroom to heave his guts into the porcelain bowl. There was nothing for it except to venture into the real world. His landlord had boarded up the windows to his place as if he wasn't even there anymore, and there was a FOR RENT sign on his door. He tore it off angrily, and stumbled down the stairs into the street. The sky was a dismal gray, and the moon and sun weren't visible together as they were in the gridlined cerulean majesty of the Net. People's faces looked lumpy, splotchy, and bruised after the shiny perfection of Net icons. There was no magic, none. Everything was so ordinary. He tried to walk through a wall and bam! it thwarted him with its boring solidity. He couldn't fly, he couldn't change his shape or appearance. He stumbled along, rubbing his face and scratching at his dirty hair. Garbage was piled on street corners in stinking mounds, the remnants of a strike by Night City civil servants. There was no trash in the Net, Joshua remembered ruefully. Anything that wasn't part of the construct was swept up by those beautiful clever dolphin programs, ah, how he missed them already! He absentmindedly touched the place where his brain had swollen and received a terrible shock—the swelling around his 'trode holes was subsiding, he was turning into a normal person again. Everything that had made him special was dissipating: his excessive devotion to the Net, his subtly changing brain configuration, the knowledge of the virtual world that he had built up in the past few years of Running was seeping out of him. He was nothing but a miserable, broke teenager with no job, no home, and no future. They'd taken away everything that was important to him.

How could he fight back? He couldn't even confront them, he wasn't even allowed on the field of play. Worse, he knew nothing of the Holo Men outside of the Net. The Chairman could be anybody. Ethan Allen, Che, he knew them all only by their icons. Only the leader K-M was a known entity with a face, but he was a diabolical criminal; everybody from the CIA to Interpol to Militech security forces had been looking for him for years without success. What was the likelihood that a teenager from the streets of Night City was going to find him, especially without the tools that had made Joshua special among young men his age? Ah! He couldn't even contact his friend Taro, he realized with an ever growing feeling of hopelessness. Tokyo was only an hour away by near-orbiter, but it might as well have been on Mars, for all the chance Joshua would have of getting there. He wondered if Taro had received the same fate as himself. Probably—they were responsible together for the counter-revolutionary acts that had hindered the Holo Men from achievement of their goals.

His brain was clogging up like a hovercraft windshield in tule fog. He started singing the song "Kill World," by pop icon bytegyrl Calla-lily, changin' the lyrics to fit himself into it:

"It's a pill world, a chill world
A tough and rumble kill world,
I Joshua sans trumpet
Ain't quite cuttin' it."

He thought about throwing himself off the Night City Bridge, but what good would that do except he'd be dead. This kill world wasn't going to get him so easily. He'd hole up in his apartment till the district rent cops came to evict him, then he'd go live in a squat, maybe, sell his deck for a few weeks worth of kibble, that way at least he could avoid prison for a while. Yeah, that's the other thing the Holo Men had done, the bastards, was to inform the authorities about some of his little pranks on the CorpZoners before joining the Society, so that even if he managed somehow to overcome the nausea and the loathing that crammed his craw if he even thought about anything Net-related, he'd be as much of a wanted man on the Net as Taro, not that that bothered him, he could deal, it was just another minor irritation in his ruined life. Frack it! On top of everything else, the wrong guys were going to win. If the Holo Men took over the Net, they'd suck the thing dry for their own uses, and everybody else'd be left to play with stick figure line drawings and old-fashioned text files, no graphics, if there was even that much of the Net left, because the Holo Men were so crazy they might even do something suicidal like eat up the operating system RAM and crash the whole thing permanently, forty years of careful building up a worldwide web of interrelated data, it could all go down in a blaze of bad looping and CPU-sapping negative energy, like a black hole visited upon the system, it could, Joshua knew, and if that didn't happen then those berserko fascists would tell everyone what to do, make rules, set limits, Wilderspace would be closed down, they'd control it all, it'd be worse than if Militech or Arasaka took over—those were lumbering Corporate entities, any respectable hacker could keep ahead of them— but the Holo Men were future gurus, out there anticipating change and diverting it to their advantage, there'd be no stopping them once they owned Sysops—and Joshua stopped right in the middle of the street as he realized that he'd just stated the unspoken goal of all the Holo Men's activities thus far, all the disruptions, feints, forays, the wild goose chases he and Taro'd been sent on, everything pointed toward a takeover of Sysops itself. God, why hadn't he seen that before, he'd been blinded by the pseudo-political slant, the revolutionary names, the popping in and out of the Oval Office, but the Holo Men didn't want the White House, they wanted the Black Ice fortress of Central Sysops, that was their target. But who could he tell? Who was in a position to stop them? Who'd believe him, without arresting him?

So here he was, suddenly adrift in a world of gangs, cyborgs, Fixers, CorpZoner SOBs, a little boy among men. A minor-league Solo strutted by, decked out in cybergear and pumped up with artificial muscles and body-sculpting. Even Joshua could see that this guy was a nobody, a primping fool who would probably be dead within the month, but Joshua cringed and stepped into a doorway to let the heavily armed soldier pass by. The world was a frightening, threatening place. Where could he go to hide? Who would protect him? His parents would take him in but Joshua could see all the way down that path—severe restrictions on his personal freedom followed by regulated schooling and assignment to a minor professional position as a bank clerk or insurance company drone. No, even if he starved to death he wasn't going to go crawling to his folks.

He continued to wander the streets. Light and shadow were infinitely more complex here than in the Net—it was difficult to synthesize and order reality. There was a certain symmetry to the Net world that was missing in the real world, which was all odd angles and jagged edges. The most complicated depiction of reality in the Net would miss the thousand quirky details of a real world scene: random, chaotic intrusions, unidentifiable hums and bumping noises in the background, lights twinkling, wisps of fog, leaves stirring, trash blowing across the ground, textures, shadings, variations from moment to moment and day to day. It was all so simple, really, in the Net, and so much more difficult here. He missed the clean, pure aspect of Netrunning, where it was easy to identify people, glean their motives from the shape of their icons, size them up from their Running style. Here in the real world there was no such certainty. A Net character might hide behind an icon that didn't represent him, but you could always find out who it was—in real life people changed their identities and motives with alarming frequency, sometimes for no reason.

This real world was rough, crude, cruel. The Net was safe. The Holo Men knew his home address. If they wanted to, they could send paid Solos or rent a gang to smash up his place, but why should they, the equipment was useless to him as long as the virus made him violently ill each time he tried to log on. Lost in thought, Joshua wasn't watching his step and bumped into someone passing in the other direction.

"Hey, look, a fracking cyber-geek. Hey, chumper, don't you know when to step aside?" a crazed-looking gang-banger yelled at him. This creep was dressed in full-body replacement mode like a Gemini full conversion humanoid, but that wasn't real Exoderm® on his surface, it was just a latex suit, and he wasn't a real borg, only a gangster who wanted people to think he was a full-fledged metal head. It was like a mannequin dressed up as a human playing a puppet, but the effect was still scary. Two or three of his buddies congregated behind him, similarly outfitted.

"Sorry," said Joshua, trying to step around the pseudo-cyborg, but he wasn't going to get off that easy.

" 'Sorry'? Yeah, well, that ain't good enough, data-brain. Ya prob'ly thought ya could walk right through me, din't ya, ya chiphead? Like I was some phony icon in the Net."

"No, I—"

"This is rock-solid reality, asshole. Out here you gotta look where you're going, or you get hurt. Got it?"

"Yes."

"Yes what?" the gangster gave him the military line. Joshua'd never served but he'd seen enough old war holopics to know the drill.

"Uh, yessir?"

"That's right. Now frack off, ya little creepoid." The faux Gemini nailed him one with a combat boot in the rear as Josh turned to go, and sent him tumbling into the cement sidewalk, which was as hard as advertised. The gangsters howled with laughter that followed Joshua down the street like a cold wind. By the time he returned to his apartment he was thoroughly depressed and paranoid, slinking along the walls to avoid contact with anyone. Another human obstacle was sitting on his stoop, dressed as the legendary Netrunner Flight Sim Fred, but Joshua didn't believe that's who it was, not for a second. This character didn't seem so tough, and Joshua wanted nothing more than to crawl inside his barren hovel and lay there, so he risked confrontation and tried to sidle by the fake Fred, but the stranger would have none of it.

"You Joshua Victor?" he asked. Joshua didn't know how to answer. The weirdo blocking his way might be someone sent from the Holo Men, or a Netwatch dude, a government operative, or somebody from one of the Corporations finally catching up to him.

"No," he said.

"That's funny. You look like him, minus the beard and the trumpet," the man said, referencing Josh's Net icon appearance.

"Listen, I'm sick, I gotta go lie down," said Josh.

"That's why I'm here, to help you," said the man.

"And who are you?" Joshua asked wearily.

"Gee, I thought a pro-Runner like you would have recognized me."

"I can see who you're trying to look like," said Joshua cautiously.

"Gettin' so you can't tell the genuine article from the clone, eh? That's a sign of spending too much time on the Net."

"Yeah, well, I don't have that problem anymore. Listen, I really gotta sleep."

"You sent me a letter," said Fred. That got Joshua's attention.

"I sent a letter to the real Flight Sim Fred—"

"In Last Chance, Colorado—"

"That's right—"

"And here I am. I tried to contact you on the Net, but you didn't answer, so I flew up here. I still like to take those F30s out for a spin every once in a while."

"Holy hell! Are you really?"

"The one and only."

"Gee, Mister, uh, Fred, I'm sorry. I'm so confused right

now—" Joshua was near tears. He shook Fred's outstretched hand and stumbled up the stairs. "Come on in, I mean, if you want to, I haven't got anything to offer you, but—"

"We can talk. I'll buy you dinner later, you look like you need it." Joshua led Fred into his apartment. The two of them sat in the kitchen and drank glasses of water, the only amenity Josh had to offer his guest, while he relayed the story of his involvement with the Holo Men. Fred was one of the original designers of the Net—Josh could see the onetime aviator's outrage growing as he described the Society's grandiose designs on the system, their intrusive, manipulative style, the diabolical vision of their leader K-M.

"So now you say you can't use your rig?"

"Makes me puke just to think about it."

"They've infected you awright. I don't suppose you've been to a doctor?"

"Can't afford it."

"How did you used to pay for everything?"

"Well, uh, I had a girlfriend who had a job, and uh—" Joshua was embarrassed to admit that he'd been a Net prankster, selling bits of information gleaned from his hacking, but Fred saved him the discomfiture.

"You were a semi-pro hacker, right? It's okay. As long as you knew who the enemy was, and respected the sanctity of the system, I have no problem with that. I was quite the cowboy in my time too. Just a few months ago I almost bought it from an operative who was after a couple of cyberpunks I was helping out back in Last Chance. This guy trashed my whole rig, with me in it, but I managed to escape. I'm still putting together a new deck, though, which is why I'm not quite ready to jump in and disinfect you."

"You could do that?"

"I sure as shit hope so. I wrote the code, baby. Anything those Holo Jerks can do, I can do better, quicker, deeper. But that's going to have to wait. First I want to take you out for a good meal, then we'll map out a course of action. When do you think they're going to try this takeover?"

"Soon, Fred. K-M's in a hurry. He'll go before he's ready, take a risk, that's his style, blitzkrieg, ya know?"

"Yeah, well, we're not Poland or Czechoslovakia. We'll put up a fight. And we have allies. You won't have to do it yourself." Flight Sim Fred stood up, brushed the dust from his flight jacket, adjusted his shades and his aviator's cap, and thumped himself on the chest.

"I can't run so hard anymore, the old brain cells can't take it, but you can. We'll team up. I'll do the code, and you'll make the Runs. But first, dinner." Fred located a restaurant in Josh's neighborhood that Josh'd never seen before, a trendy bistro serving what they called "industrial cuisine" to local techies who worked in the urban sector. The ambiance was retro diner, with Formica tabletops, plush fake red-leather booths, and miniature jukeboxes at each table for playing ancient tunes over crackly speakers, but the food turned out to be very fine Norte California fare, heavy on simply served expensive fresh fruits and vegetables. It'd been a long time since Josh'd sat down in a restaurant for a meal, outside of the Net, where he usually confined himself to kibble or diet soda and junk food, the ubiquitous programmer's diet, even when he was sim-feasting in exotic Net locales. He studied the menu but couldn't make up his mind and finally let Flight Sim Fred order for him as if he were a little boy or a convalescent patient out of the hospital for the first time in months. Fred selected a steamed artichoke with garlic aoli appetizer, fresh pasta with sun-dried tomatoes and fresh herbs for an entree, and a plate of sliced papaya for dessert. Throughout the course of the meal, the explosion of flavors startled Josh's senses.

"This meal must be costing a fortune," he whispered to Fred across the Formica table with its curvy deco legs when the heaping, steaming plate of pasta arrived, brilliant yellow strands of noodle topped with bright red and green sauce.

"Don't worry about it. You've got sponsorship now. Think of yourself as a highly specialized athlete whose training expenses are covered as he prepares for an important competition. Enjoy. I bet you haven't had a decent meal since that girlfriend of yours left you."

"Yeah, true," said Josh.

"Where is she now?"

"Dunno." Joshua shifted uneasily in the booth. He really didn't want to talk about Sally, but Fred pressed him on the point.

"Maybe this would be a good time to look her up, now that your head's not ostrich'd into the Net all the time. She might even take you back, what do you think?"

"I doubt it. She thinks I was harassing her after we split, but it wasn't me, it was those Holo creeps, they went after her boss's business, screwed him up bad."

Fred was puzzled. "Why?"

"Beats me. He's a florist."

"I'll look into that. But you should call her. Tell her what you've learned from this whole experience. And what have you learned so far?"

"I dunno. It's too early to say. I'm still in shock, man. I've lived the last year almost continuously on the Net—"

"That's part of your problem, isn't it, young man?"

"I suppose so," Joshua answered halfheartedly. "But hey, Fred, like, what are you doing this for? What's in it for you?"

"D.I."

"Say what?"

"Data Integrity. My personal watchword. See, the Net's kinda like my baby, and as a parent, I don't like to see my child corrupted, violated. It makes me damn angry. Way back in the way back, a few hundred of us had a vision, that there could be a world shared by all, free information, free software, free exchange, no boundaries, no controls. The Net was going to be a peaceful, open place, a space to learn to grow. Of course the Corporates took it over and put an end to all that, turned it into one big advertising bill-board, that's why I'm a renegade cowboy instead of on the board of directors today. The Net's still big enough and new enough that there's room for us free spirits out there in Wilderspace. But if a small group of control freaks like the Holo characters take over, who knows what might happen? The Arasakas and Petro-Chems of the world might pull the plug altogether—"

"If they could," Josh interjected.

"I don't think the Society of Holo Men could fight the Corporate Alliance," said Fred.

"Not head on, maybe, but these guys are guerrilla fighters, they don't do big pitched battles, they eat away at the structure. I've seen 'em in action, Fred, they're good. I thought I was a hotshot hacker, but these guys got tricks I never dreamed of." Joshua told Fred about some of the programs he'd been given on his initiation, all of them now inaccessibly locked in the deck he couldn't use. Fred asked him a few questions, he was especially interested in the properties of the glass ball, then turned in the booth and waved at the waiter for the check.

"Okay, I'm convinced. These jokers are a real threat. Here's what's going to happen next. You're going to get a good night's sleep while I try to figure out what they've done to you that makes you barf at the sight of cyber. It must be some kind of crossover virus that affects both you and your machine. The fact that your trode holes are shrinking is a clue, I'll start there. By the morning maybe I'll have you back on-line."

"Gosh, you think so, Fred? That'd be on!"

"I'm not making any promises. First you've got to get yourself together, you look like a goddamn 'dorph junkie, all pale and pasty. And I want you to call that girlfriend of yours—"

"Ex—"

"Okay, ex-girlfriend."

"Why don't you call her, Fred? She can tell you herself about the crazy shit the Holos did to her and her boss." The waiter arrived with the check. Fred paid it without glancing at the total. Joshua wondered briefly if Fred did what he did and buried the accounting in some Corporate backwater, or if he had his own methods for circumventing the billing system. One thing Josh was sure of, Fred wasn't paying out of his own pocket.

"You've got it bad, don't you?" said Fred, catching Josh off guard.

"What?"

"You love this girl, but you're too far gone to do anything about it. Maybe I shouldn't reconnect you, maybe what you need is a few months out here in Solidville to get your head back on straight."

"No, Fred, I mean, yeah, I love Sally, but I screwed up with her. I put everything into the Net, I didn't pay her enough attention. I know that's wrong now, but I still need to get back there to stop the Holo Men. If only she knew how I felt, maybe she'd come back, but I can't tell her, I don't know what to say." Joshua was still focused on one goal, he was like a junkie, still fresh from kickin' it, he was

craving the Net and would do anything, say anything, to
get back on-line. Fred eyed him with a mixture of pathos
and disgust. He'd seen it before, this cold turkey sweatin'
and slaverin' that Net junkies went through during with-
drawal, but he needed to put Joshua back in the deck-seat
if he was going to combat the ugly threat represented by
the Holo Men.

"Okay, pardner, I'll talk to her for you, but don't expect
miracles. Now go home and get some sleep. I'll be by in
the morning."

"Where are you staying, Fred?"

"I gotta friend in Night City who owes me a few favors."
Fred planned to crash in the RV once owned by Digital Librarian Winfield Owens and now used as a research and
study lab by Maglev "byteboi" Tolstoi, the first cybermonk
of cyberpunk. byteboi was currently overseas on a schol-
arly expedition to view some of the last remaining illuminated Celtic manuscripts still housed in Irish monasteries.
The RV was parked behind the Night City Art Museum,
and byteboi had given Fred the code to gain entry. Fred and
Joshua parted in front of the restaurant, and the world,
which had looked so bleak to Joshua only a few hours ago,
now shone a ray of hope on him.

When Joshua returned to his flat, though, it had all
changed again. The FOR RENT sign was back up, and the
door to his flat was open. When he entered the place, he
found his computer equipment crushed and broken, pieces
strewn across the living room floor like so much kulch in
a Philippine landfill, electronics pulverized, motherboards
detached from their housings, monitors imploded, drives
crashed and smashed. Joshua sat down amid the pile of
shattered devices and cried. He didn't know if it was his
landlord, the Holo Men, or passing, random looters, but the
pride and joy of his life was destroyed. The Holo Men

wouldn't have done this, they knew he was powerless to
use the stuff, unless they'd already learned of Flight Sim
Fred's visit to him and the help he was promised, then they
might have trashed his place as a warning, yes, it had to be
them, now that he thought about it, the landlord would
have hocked the stuff and thieves would have fenced it!
The Society was determined to break him, and they were
doing a good job of it, he thought as he lay sobbing amid
the ruins of his former life. It was all *gomi* now, junk,
worthless clutter.

Fifteen minutes later the Housing Authority goons
showed up and whisked him out onto the street, barely giving him time to stuff a clunky valise with what remained of
his possessions. They placed an electronic seal on the door
so that he was permanently barred from reentering, and
told him to get the frack off the stoop, he wasn't allowed
to sit there. He was lower than bourgy, he was a prole, a
homeless, jobless, useless cipher. He spent the night on the
street, wandering, and hiding from the real street people,
the ones who'd flatline him for the few e.b. the contents of
his suitcase would bring in a back-alley bazaar. This was
it, the bottom, the abyss. To think he used to be a Gold-
enkid, one of the up and coming, he had a future paved like
a maglev track, friction free, all he had to do was play
along and life would have been a piece o' cake, but instead
he'd gotten into Running, and this is where it'd taken him,
to the Edge, not out there where it was chill and chipped,
but the brink of the pit, and he was halfway fallin' in. A
near stranger was his only hope. Josh had to hang around
so that when Fred came in the morning he wouldn't give
up on Josh. If Fred didn't come and find him, then maybe
Josh'd reconsider that bridge, one long swan dive to obliv-
ion. At least it wasn't raining tonight, the acid rains in
Night City could be fierce, even lethal. A couple of blocks

away from his apartment building, Josh found a nearby squat that'd been boarded over loosely, pried away one of the planks and struggled into a crawlspace between the floor and the foundation, just big enough for him to curl up in, then propped up the unattached wood to hide his break-in. With two pieces of cardboard for blankets and his suitcase for a pillow, Josh made himself as comfortable as he could and cried himself to sleep.

Sometime later he was awakened by the sound of automatic weapons fire. He thought he was safe underneath the abandoned house, but seconds later the firefight descended on the very squat where he'd found shelter. From what Josh could tell, two gangs were warring over turf, and the object of their strife was the ruinated town house where Joshua had camped. Bad choice! Stray bullets plowed into the dirt around him. Heavy booted footsteps tramped over his head, as the two factions exchanged possession of the entryway several times. Hand-to-hand fighting ensued, accompanied by grunts of pain, the thudding sound of fists on flesh, confused shouting—

"Stick the frackers—"

"Hey, Johnnie, over here!"

"Watch out! Watch out!"

—and a loud "ooof!" when one of the unseen gangbangers took a whack to the head and pitched forward, his face inches from the hole where Joshua lay cringing and cowering. The gangster opened his eyes, blood dripping from a head wound, dazedly saw another human being, and silently pleaded to Joshua to haul him in. There was barely enough room for Joshua alone, but he pushed aside the planking and dragged the bleeding gang-member in on top of him, then covered the opening again. The unknown gangster passed out lying heavily on top of Joshua, who tried to stanch the bleeding from the man's cracked skull.

The other side must've won, because soon Joshua heard them above him, boasting of their victory and wondering where "that fracker Raspis" went to—

"I chocked him out good, he shoulda been lyin' out there—"

"They musta dragged him off—"

"He won't be frackin' with us anymore—" and at the mention of his name Raspis stirred and groaned. Joshua quickly clamped a hand over his mouth and pointed toward the floor above. The gang member's eyes widened slightly, but then he slumped into unconsciousness again, pressing down ponderously on Joshua, who couldn't shift position in the narrow confines of the crawlspace. The night dragged on, the victorious gang drinkin' and druggin' themselves into a frenzy of celebration, playing earsplitting heavy speed metal rock from a boombox, stomping around in combat boots on the uncarpeted floor above Joshua's head. No way he could sleep, but Raspis was passed out on him, still bleedin' but more slowly now, every once in a while issuing moans of pain that Joshua had to stifle, though that was less risky now that the music covered everything in a blasting backwash of sound. At dawn the party began to wind down, but there were still whoops of primitive joy until well into the morning, and Joshua didn't dare venture out, though he knew he might be missing his appointment with Fred, two blocks away at his abandoned apartment. Joshua wrapped Raspis's head in a bandage torn from his own shirt and finally managed to lay the man sideways against the foundation so that he could sleep a little, but it seemed like as soon as he nodded off Raspis was nudging him roughly to wake him. The morning sun had risen well into the sky. Josh was fracked. Flight Sim Fred would have come, found the place trashed and locked, and written Josh off as an irresponsible kid. He was probably already on his way back to Last Chance, Colorado, which might as well be the moon, for all the good it did Josh.

"Time to go," the gangster whispered in a voice that was, well, raspy.

Joshua glanced upward. "What about them?" he mumbled, still half asleep.

"They split. We gotta do the same." Joshua cautiously slid the board aside and peered out. The street was deserted. He scrambled outside on his hands and knees and looked around, rubbing his eyes. It seemed like he and Raspis were the only two human beings on the planet. This corner of Night City was evacuated—everybody'd been scared off by the violent night.

"Okay," Joshua called, and Raspis came out grunting and groaning. When he stood up Joshua saw that he was at least six and a half feet tall, and probably weighed three hundred and fifty pounds. No wonder he'd been such a load! The giant swayed unsteadily on his feet and clutched at his head. Joshua offered him a supporting shoulder, but was pretty useless as a crutch. Raspis staggered around for a minute like a drunken Samson, then got his bearings and stared at Joshua.

"You gotta help me."

"Listen," Joshua began, "I already probably missed an important meeting 'cause of you, and I already helped you—"

"You gotta get me to the Slammer down on the Upper East Side," Raspis insisted, naming a bar on the seedy side of the city, an area controlled by roving gangs. "After that my boys'll take care of me."

"Jesus, that's halfway across town," said Josh. "You'll never make it."

"My bike's parked in an alley in the next block."

"Okay, I'll bring you to your bike." Joshua guided the shaky giant to his motorcycle, a savage-looking thing painted all black right down to the spokes. Raspis stood next to the cycle and shook his bandaged head wildly, trying to clear the fog. Josh was about to slip away when the gang leader grabbed him and hauled him up so that his feet dangled off the ground.

"You gotta come with me, make sure I don't pass out and dump the bike."

"Alright. Put me down, man. Is that any way to treat a guy who saved your life?" Raspis considered this for a long dull minute, then set Josh down roughly.

"Get on," he said. "Punch me if I start to lose it."

The ride across town was terrifying. Raspis was still weak from loss of blood, and the two of them were covered in it, which gave them a gory appearance that caused others to swerve out of their way. Raspis was barely conscious, and Joshua found that only by twisting the dazed behemoth's ears could he keep him from falling off the seat and dumping the cycle at a hundred miles an hour as they raced through the streets of Night City.

The Upper East Side used to be a nice CorpZoner section, safe and secure due to its proximity to the police entrenchments around City Center, but creeping urban decay had set in and the area was now an uneasy mix of gangs and Corporates still hanging on because office space was cheap. Boostergangs traded ripped items openly on the street, and sometimes found buyers among Corps softies looking for a sweet deal. One of the most powerful gangs on the Street was the Raptors, headed up by Raspis Raptor himself. Like his bike, he was black from head to toe save for the strip of bloodstained shirt Josh had wrapped round his head. He wore motorcycle leathers with silver studs running down both arms and pant legs, long black hair

with a death-warrior goatee, and he disdained the law re-
quiring mandatory helmet. Heavy cycle boots sans buckles
completed his wardrobe. There was nothing fancy about
him, no frills, no color, just a load of muscles and bulk atop
a noisy bike. Except now he was splashed with crimson
gore, his own and others'. As soon as they turned onto
Rucker Street they were swarmed by a pack of Raptors on
similarly drab and dingy-colored bikes, roaring around
their wounded leader worriedly. If they weren't so scary-
looking they might have been comical, like the phony motorcycle gangs in old Disney movies, but these characters
weren't wimpy Hollywood extras, they were real thugs,
prison rejects, hardcore gangers, with tattoos, fu manchu
mustaches, muscles bulging from workouts in the cell
yard, and loads of heavy weaponry on display.

Raspis waved his hands to indicate he was okay and almost dumped the bike. He skidded to a halt and shouted
over the backfiring revving of the cycle engines: "Hey!
This punk kid saved my skin! I wanna give him honorary
colors! Whaddaya say?"

A roar of approval rose from the throats of the fellow
Raptors, who pummeled Josh enthusiastically, then, not
satisfied with that, hauled him off the bike and tossed him
in the air a few times. A spare black leather jacket was
brought out bearing the logo of the Raptors, a sinister
lizard seated on the standard ebony motorcycle, driving
with one hand while waving a Militech 25mm pistol-
grenade with the other, a slutty female Raptor clutching
him around the waist from behind. Josh donned the jacket,
which was several sizes too big for him, and raised his
arms over his head in the victory sign. This initiated a second round of cheers and battering until Josh was more
thrashed than if he'd encountered the Raptors in a street
fight. He crawled away from them and motioned weakly to

signal he'd had all the congratulations he could take. He
started to limp off, but Raspis Raptor grabbed him.

"One o' the Raptors give ya a ride home," he said.

"I don't have a home," Josh answered bitterly. "Anyway, I'll walk. I'm in no hurry."

"Alright, choomba. 'Member, you got a friend in the
Raptors. You get stuck, you call us."

"Are you on the Net?" Josh asked, though he had little
hope of ever Runnin' again himself.

"Nah, we're strickly a street operation. Out here is
where it's happening, not inside some phony machine."

Right now, today, Josh couldn't argue with him, though
yesterday he would have passionately defended the virtual
life. He waved good-bye to the king of the Raptors and
shambled down the street in aimless fashion. Idly he
checked his pockets, but there wasn't any e.b. in there at
all, he was stone broke, not even enough money for a hard
roll and a cup of cheap java from one of the street vendors
dragging their dented wagons around. Where should he
go? There wasn't any point now in returning to his old
neighborhood, Fred would have come and gone long ago.
He thought about calling Sally like the electronic aviator
had suggested, but some vestige of pride wouldn't let him
go begging to his former girlfriend. No, he had but two
choices, to debase himself altogether and go home to his
parents, or, the bridge. He wasn't far from it now, if he cut
through City Center it would be waiting for him at the very
end, the end of High Street, his end. With growing convic-
tion he started across the plaza at City Center, past City
Hall and the Night City Justice Court, that Brutalist archi-
tectural landmark that loomed like a nihilist version of the
Pantheon over the rest of the buildings in the area. Behind
the Court was the Night City Art Museum, and there, in
one corner of the parking lot, Joshua spotted the RV Fred

had mentioned last night. It was a long shot, but Joshua decided to knock on the door and see if by some stroke of luck Fred was still around. He had to scale the security fence of the lot, but frack, what was the worst that could happen, they'd throw him in jail at the Court next door, at least he'd get a few free meals after the cops beat him up. Maybe they'd take pity on him, given that he was already covered in Raptor blood.

No audible security alarms sounded as Josh hopped over the fence. He soon saw why—a second, more formidable fence with obvious electronic monitors separated the parking lot from the museum itself. Josh guessed they figured anybody stupid enough to enter a deserted (except for the RV) parking lot deserved all the trouble that would come their way. On days the museum was open, this lot would be manned by several Militech guards checking for tickets and hassling people for no good reason, but it turned out to be Monday. Josh had no idea what day it was until he saw a CLOSED MONDAYS sign, for him the day of the week had been meaningless in the twenty-four-hour-a-day seven-days' Runnin' environment of the Net. The RV was parked in one corner of the lot, and from the looks of it hadn't been moved in some weeks. It was covered with leaves and needles from nearby trees, and layered with a patina of dirt and dust. Josh looked around to make sure he wasn't being observed, then scrabbled across the open area between where he'd jumped the fence and where the vehicle was parked. He pounded on the door, desperately hoping that Fred was there, but instead the RV began to talk to him.

"Stand back. You have violated a security perimeter. Remain motionless or you will be zapped with one million volts of taser energy."

Joshua obeyed the mechanical voice and stepped backward, then stood still. He knew what was happening now—the machine was scanning him for weapons and explosives.

"State your business for the record."

"I'm looking for Flight Sim Fred. He's supposed to be staying here."

The artificial intelligence pondered this statement for a few seconds, parsing the logic and comparing it to a list of appropriate responses. Finally it blurted out a monotone mechanical answer.

"The person you seek is a guest of the owner of this vehicle. Neither the owner nor the guest is on the premises. Please leave your name and a number where you can be reached."

"Sorry, don't have a number."

Again the AI deployed its wits to try to come up with a logical rejoinder, but the best it could do was to repeat a warning not to enter and for the intruder to leave. This was almost like dealin' with a Net AI, Josh decided, so he tried his hand at a few commands that might trigger a better action from the electronic guardian of the RV.

"AI, what is your name?" Josh probed.

"Breughel," the resident intelligence answered swiftly. Josh thought that an extremely queer name for a watchdog, but he passed over it.

"What is your mission?"

"To protect and serve the one known as Maglev Tolstoi, his possessions, and his visitors."

"Very good. You're resident in a data term inside the RV?"

"Correct."

Josh knew that as long as he kept asking nonthreatening questions the AI would answer.

"Why don't you let me in?"

"You are not on the list of authorized personnel."

"Read me the list." This command was borderline, and both Josh and the AI knew it.

"You are not authorized."

"How do you know? You don't know what my name is."

"What is your name?" the AI countered, but this was the opening Josh was looking for in the analytical chess game he was playing with the AI's digital brain.

"My name is encoded. You're not authorized to know it. Run a matching stack on the following sequence against all references in your database." Josh fed the AI a set of numbers he had memorized from the Net that were the access codes for the main Sysops locations.

"Master," the AI responded after a time. The AI, which was Net-driven, as Josh had suspected, had assumed from the numbers Josh had fed him that it was dealing with a high-level systems operator who could override any local command structure.

"Place the name Joshua Victor in the master list."

"Done."

"Memorize my voiceprint."

"Done."

"Open the RV door on my verbal command." Josh held his breath. There was the slightest hesitation, then the aluminum hatch to the vehicle swung outward. It was a minor victory for Joshua. He may not be able to access the Net, but he still retained the ability to use his cyber-skills in the right setting.

"Sleep until I summon you," he told Breughel. The obedient AI fell silent. Josh stepped into the RV. Josh shucked off the Raptors jacket and collapsed onto the carpeted floor, barely glancing at the cluttered surroundings. It had been a long day's night, losing his Net privileges and half his mind, Runnin' with the king of the Raptors. Almost as soon as his head hit the cushion, he fell into a hard dreaming sleep, full of disturbing dreams. His namesake Joshua visited him, the leader of seven armies, who, contrary to popular myth, never blew the trumpet himself, but ordered it to be sounded by the priests who accompanied him into battle. The prophet was brimming with righteous anger.

"You have sold your birthright for a mess of pottage," the archetypal figure scolded him.

"No," Joshua protested, "it was taken from me."

"You didn't fight hard enough. Observe." As Joshua watched in his dream, the armies of Israel swept across the plains of Jericho and knocked down the legendary walls.

"But I was all alone!" the modern, dreaming Joshua cried, and had anyone been watching, they would have seen him futilely raising an imaginary trumpet to his lips in his sleep, from which no sound issued, because it was only the dream of an illusion, and even that was lost to him.

CHAPTER 8

LIVIN' IN OBLIVION

The next two days Josh hung out in the RV, afraid to go anywhere. He perused the many books of art and history that crowded the shelves, and he examined the paintings that took up every inch of wall space that wasn't occupied by volumes of books, but he avoided touching the elaborate deck setup, 'cause just lookin' at it made him queasy. Each day the parking lot filled with Beaverville tourists come to look at the last remaining vestiges of classical civilization as portrayed in the Night City Art Museum, but Josh, penniless, never left the RV, anyway there was all the art he needed to see right here in the cozy confines of the roving library once owned by a Digital Librarian. The refrigerator and larder were simply but amply stocked. If he had to hole up, this was the place to do it. Anyway, where else could he go?

On the morning of the third day the vid-phone rang.

Joshua listened as the AI awoke from its electronic slumber and handled the incoming transmission.

"Breughel? Is Maglev back?" It was Fred! Joshua clambered to his feet and rushed to intercept the call.

"Breughel, transfer the vid-phone to the on-line speaker port."

"Done."

"Fred, it's me, Josh."

"What the hell are you doing there?"

"I got kicked out of my place by the Housing Police—"

"So I saw. Why didn't you wait around for me?"

"It's a long story. Fred, come back, will you?"

"Sorry, can't right now. I'm on a special project. But I can still help you. What you need is an antidote. Go see Dr. Lee."

"But, Fred, I can't get on the Net—"

"Not on the Net, in person."

"I've got no money, Fred."

"He won't ask for any."

"If I leave here I won't be able to get back in—"

"You have to leave anyway, Maglev's due back any day now. See the herbalist. Then go see your girlfriend. She's waiting to hear from you." The screen went blank. Fred had given him some clear direction, a path to follow, but it was difficult for Joshua to abandon the RV. In some ways it was like the Net for him, a shelter, a haven, the size of a bus instead of a box, but still someplace safe, where gangs and guns and all the rough edges of the physical world could not harm him. During his stay at the RV Josh'd gotten to know the AI Breughel, who resided in the RV as a disembodied spirit, or as the soul of the RV itself. He'd confessed his trickery to the machine, which lacked the weak human qualities of resentment and jealousy, and so forgave him without a second thought, if one can use that word to describe the functioning of an AI, partly because AIs have no second thoughts, no subconscious. The AI's name derived, as the AI explained pedantically, "from the family of Flemish painters of the sixteenth century, particularly Pieter Breughel 'the Elder,' a devotee of Hieronymous Bosch, whose influence can be seen in Breughel's *The Fall of the Rebel Angels*. My master Maglev says that if he were to descend again into the world of the streets, he would name his gang the Fallen Angels after that painting."

"Very interesting. Do you paint, Breughel?"

"No. This activity requires creativity, of which AIs have none. I can generate some amusing fractal images, but they are not art. My master Maglev has made that clear to me."

"Where does creativity come from?"

"If I knew the answer to that question I would enhance myself with it. It comes from the Void, according to some, but what they mean by that I do not know. It is clear they do not mean vacuous nothingness. Perhaps they refer to an idea more like the Buddhist conception of the Great Emptiness as the source of all things, not merely the creative impulse."

"You're quite the professor, aren't you, Breughel?"

"I had a very good human teacher, Winfield Owens, a Digital Librarian. He has passed this vehicle, and all that goes with it, including me, on to Maglev Tolstoi, once known as the punk byteboi. I am teaching him. I could teach you too."

"You already have."

"Thank you."

Joshua was picking up allies: Fred, Raspis Raptor, Breughel, but would they be enough to combat the treacherous strength of the Holo Men?

The real Little China was much dirtier, more crowded,

noisier and smellier than the Net version. If he'd had any money, Josh would have been fearful of pickpockets in the jostling mob that spilled over from the sidewalks into street gutters filled with duck and pigeon feathers, tiny bits of plastic wrapping, and exploded shreds of firecrackers. The stink of steaming crab, boiled shrimp, and fried sand dabs filled the air. Still flopping fish on ice-filled crates were slowly rotting alive in the humidity of midday. None of those sea creatures was fit to eat if they were caught in the polluted waters of San Morro Bay, as they almost certainly were, but this didn't deter either customers or vendors from carrying on a brisk trade in bottom-feeding flounder, squid, and ugly gasping sea bass. It was a particularly sweltering day; cobbled stones from the original pavement rose up through the melting asphalt and stuck their hard heads out. The air was searing with a slightly sour acidic taste that constricted the lungs. Joshua spent his last few e.b. on a steamed lotus bean bun and a cup of tea at a Chinese bakery. The one time he'd visited Dr. Lee it had been with Taro, when they were in possession of the glass sphere. Dr. Lee had correctly surmised that the Holo Men themselves had made the thing, though he told Josh and Taro only elliptically. What reason would the herbalist have to help him, Josh wondered as he munched on the gooey bun. He had no e.b. to offer, and no connection other than his fleeting earlier meeting. Still, it was the only path open to him, his only hope. He hurriedly finished his meager breakfast and rushed down the street to the apothecary's shop.

The Net's olfactory function hadn't been able to capture the complex melange of odors that permeated the shop, rich in musty fungus and pungent spices, with an overlay of salty brittle tang of dried starfish, all dominated by the sweet cloy of ginseng. Dr. Lee's son Bryan greeted him just as he had in VR, and for a moment Josh experienced the disorienting sensation of deja vu, but Taro was missing, and the feeling passed. Once again the doctor's blind but now cyber-sighted son barred Josh's way to his father.

"You don't look like the great warrior who slew the armies of Ai, Makkedeh, Lachish, and Eglon," Bryan scoffed. His artificial eyes made small buzzing sounds as the servomotors made constant tiny adjustments in focus and tilt. When he looked at Josh, the young hacker felt like the laser beams were burning right through him, as well they might, but there was no window into the martial arts master's soul through these eyes, the effect was oddly lifeless. It was Bryan Lee's finely tuned body that suggested the depth of knowledge, emotion, and intellect behind the glittering but dead orbs.

"I need your father's help. Flight Sim Fred sent me."

"Ah, the legendary Fred. So, you no longer run with the wolves of the Society?"

"You know of them?" Josh asked in surprise.

"The Holo Men are not as secret as they might wish themselves to be. When you cause the kind of turmoil they have, you must expect to attract notice. My father believes they may have been responsible for the accident that killed my mother and robbed me of my natural sight."

"Then you must want to see them brought down as much as I do!" Josh exclaimed.

"Come with me," Bryan ordered him, and turned abruptly away from him.

"But, your father—" Josh faltered, because down the aisle he could see the venerable pharmacist at work behind his table.

"Will see you in a few moments. First, follow me." Bryan ushered Josh upstairs to the gymnasium, a bright, spacious room with mirrors lining one wall and a polished hardwood floor swept immaculately clean. No other students were practicing at the time. When Joshua lingered at the edge of the room, Bryan Lee motioned for him to move to the center of the empty space.

"You study the martial arts?"

"Not at all."

"You're not a warrior like your icon, then?"

"No," Josh admitted. "I'm just a hacker."

"Ah. I'd hoped to engage you in kumite, partner practice, to feel your essence and ascertain your true motives."

"Sorry, I don't do much of anything physical. I've been sitting behind a Net deck for the last three years."

"Mind and body are one. You've fallen out of balance. If you're to take on the Holo Men, you must begin to prepare yourself. I'll teach you."

"I can't pay—" Josh started to say, but Bryan Lee waved him off with a derisive gesture.

"This is not about money." Bryan was only a few years older than Josh, but the difference in their physiques was dramatic. "Take a fighting stance," the kung fu master ordered his reluctant student.

"I don't know—" Josh began to protest, but suddenly Bryan Lee leapt at him. Josh jumped back and retreated a few steps. In the Net his icon had known the whole bag of tricks, karate, kung fu, chi gung, capoirea, fast style tai chi, judo, aikido, he could back-flip and side-kick with the best of 'em, but it was a whole different game to try to make his muscle groups work in coordination to perform the same movements in real time. He was slow, clumsy, and out of shape. Still, he wasn't going to let this opportunity pass by, he had no other hopes. He tried to visualize himself as his icon. The next time Bryan Lee surged at him he attempted a *gedan-barai* block. It was ineffective, and if Bryan Lee had really been punching him he would have broken

Joshua's jaw, but the teacher grunted his satisfaction that Joshua was at least trying, and led him through several kata that Josh knew only as strings of commands to his icon. He was always late and frequently missed the mark, but there were memories in there of the endless times he'd practiced these moves with his icon in the game format. He tired quickly and was soon left gasping and sprawled on the gym floor. Bryan Lee stood over him.

"If you're going to defeat the Holo Men you'll need all those skills and more," he said. "They won't limit themselves to the Net in their attacks on you."

"May I see your father now?" Josh asked.

"Yes. You'll come back tomorrow for your first lesson?"

"Yeah. Sure. As long as you know I can't pay you."

"Don't make your teacher repeat himself. This is not a matter of money. This is revenge." A terrible glint issued from the blazingly blue synthetic eyes of Bryan Lee. Joshua bowed and stumbled down the stairs. Dr. Lee greeted him warmly.

"So, my son has acquired a new disciple," he commented sagely. "He is a fine teacher. You will learn much from him."

"Fred told you about me?" Josh asked to make sure Dr. Lee knew the reason he was here.

"Only that you needed my help. As I recall, the last time you were here, in the divine realm, you were in the company of another young man."

"Yes, Taro. I don't know what's happened to him. We've lost contact, because I can't access the Net where we used to communicate."

"Yes?"

"I have a virus," Josh explained. "It seems to have spread from my machine right into me."

Dr. Lee scowled. "This is very serious. Many people

participate in that imaginary world. The possibilities for an epidemic are great. This must be stopped."

"Can you help me? If you can cure me I can fight them."

"No. I cannot cure you. You will be infected forever. I may be able to mask the effects, but you will never be free of this disease. It has entered your blood, your brain."

Joshua was stunned. He was sure that Dr. Lee was going to give him some potion that would free him of the sickness, and now the doctor was telling him that his case was hopeless. He was near to tears, his throat was constricted, and his whole body was trembling. "Am I going to die, then?"

Dr. Lee smiled, and held his hand in front of his face to hide the laugh that was forming there.

"No, young man, you are perfectly healthy in every respect except one—you are now allergic to electronic transmissions. But such allergies can be treated, through diet and exercise. Your lessons with my son will strengthen your nervous system. I will fix you an elixir that will further improve your constitution."

"How can I pay you? I have no money and no place to live," Josh blurted out, not that he expected Dr. Lee to take pity on him, but simply because he was honest.

Dr. Lee frowned, his Oriental face a mass of wrinkles behind a wispy beard. "My potions are fabulously expensive, you know. What can you offer me in trade?"

Joshua thought for a minute. What did he have to offer? Nothing. That's why he was here. He hoped Dr. Lee could cure him of the debilitation of his one marketable skill, his extraordinary deftness on the Net.

"I could clean the store for you every day," Josh proposed doubtfully. His suggestion was not met with enthusiasm.

"Look around you. I have many employees. I have no

use for you. But my son might agree to take you on. He has few students now. They won't come back until they learn that his martial art is greater now than before his unfortunate mishap."

So it was that Joshua Victor became Bryan Lee's *deshi*, his all-around servant and gofer. Over the next days and weeks Bryan worked him mercilessly, both on the practice floor and outside the dojo. The son was far sterner than his father, whose feelings had been softened and mellowed by the passage of time. There was an urgency, a focused energy and passion to Bryan's movements. He was eager to build up a body of students again. He had flyers printed that Josh distributed all over Night City. The dojo, which had gone unused for three years, was spruced up with a fresh coat of paint and a new sign, both applied by Josh. Bryan-*sensei* showed Josh how to clean the dojo floor properly, on his hands and knees with a wet towel. Their morning regimen included a five mile run through the streets of Little China and beyond. At first Joshua could only trot a few hundred yards before collapsing and straggling in many minutes after Bryan was already back, showered, and waiting for Joshua to serve him his congee breakfast rice soup. Little by little Josh increased the length of time he could keep up with his teacher, though Bryan always disappeared in a final sprint that left Joshua gasping and shaking his head.

Slowly, Josh discovered a new confidence in himself. Bryan Lee required him to cut his hair short and dress neatly. For the first time in many years he was eating a healthy diet, consisting mostly of rice, vegetables, and tofu. Every day he boiled and drank to the dregs Dr. Lee's elixir, a bitter mixture of bark, roots, and herbs that stank up the small apartment off the dojo where Joshua lived. There were still days when he felt the loss of his powers on the Net like a big empty place in his brain, and he wondered what he was doing, if he wasn't wasting his time while the Holo Men were continuing their preparations for a takeover, but mostly Bryan kept him so busy that he had little time to think about the Net or the Society. Three times a day they practiced for two hours, sessions that left Joshua's body so sore he had to crawl to the bath, but somewhere within him he realized that this was a magnificent opportunity to study with a master, so he accepted the pain, and Bryan's constant criticisms and corrections, and the menial tasks he was asked to perform, and the unfamiliar food and the strangeness of living in the Oriental quarter. At the end of the sixth week he glanced in the dojo mirror and saw quite a different fellow staring back at him, not a slouching, acne-faced teenager with scraggly hair and bleary eyes but an erect, trim, lithe figure with his weight carefully balanced on the balls of his feet, ready for the world. He hardly recognized himself, and shook his head in wonder at the changes that were taking place inside him.

The next day he ran into Sally while running an errand for Bryan in his old neighborhood. She was walking slowly, with her head down, carrying a potted plant that she'd been tending at home like a convalescent case until it was strong enough to bring back to the nursery. Josh was jogging (Bryan required him to run everywhere, even if the matter wasn't urgent) on the other side of the street when her saw her. His heart leapt up, but then he wondered if she'd even talk to him. He followed her for a block or two before he got up the courage to approach her.

"Sally!" he called.

She turned and peered through the leaves of the plant she held, but seeing no one she recognized, she continued walking.

"Hey! It's me!" Josh said with a laugh as he bounded up beside her. She almost dropped the pot in surprise.

"Josh! Is it really you? You look fantastic! What's happened to you?"

Josh took the plant from her hands, set it on the sidewalk, and put his arms around her. "I lost my apartment and I don't have any money or a real job," he said. Sally looked confused. "But I've been rescued by a karate master in Little China. I'm his personal slave." Sally broke away from Josh and stepped back to examine him. The physical changes were so striking she could hardly believe it was him, but his words were troubling to her.

"Are you into another cult thing?"

"No, no," Josh assured her, but Sally was skeptical.

"What happened with you and that Society?"

"I still have to deal with them. I'm waiting till I'm strong enough."

"It sounds weird, Josh. But you look so wonderful." Sally began to cry.

"What is it? What's the matter?" Josh asked.

"I don't know. It's so strange to see you so different. I guess I'm happy for you," she trailed off. She didn't know what she was feeling.

"Sally! After this business with the Holo Men is settled I'm going to do something good with my life, get a job, teach maybe. I want us to be together again, but first I have to stop them, they're still planning to control the Net, I can't let that happen."

"Oh, Josh," she said, "I don't know."

"What? What don't you know?"

"It's all so sudden, to see you again, to see you again, so changed. It makes me feel funny."

"Hey, it's not like I went in for full body-sculpting surgery or turned myself into a cyborg or anything. Look, the swelling around my 'trode holes is going down, I'm actually revertin' back toward normal. The Holo Men infected me with some virus that keeps me from Runnin' on the Net. Dr. Lee's treating me."

"Who's he?"

"My teacher's father. Listen, why don't you come around to the dojo tomorrow and you'll see it's a good thing I've gotten into. I'm growin' up, finally. I thought you'd be proud of me," Joshua said with a trace of bitterness, because this wasn't what he'd fantasized about meeting Sally again.

"I am, Josh, I am. Just give me a little time to adjust."

"Yeah, sure. Well," he faltered, "I gotta go. Come see me in Little China."

"I will, Josh."

"Tomorrow?"

"Maybe. You know, I'm still working and all."

"Oh, yeah. How's Phil? Did Flight Sim Fred ever contact you?"

"Who?" Sally looked puzzled.

"I guess not. He's a guy who saved me, and he said he was going to help you and Phil, but I guess he didn't. I'll call him."

"Oh, so you can still use a phone," Sally said.

"What do you mean?"

"All this time, you never called me. I went by your place, it was all boarded up, I didn't know where you'd gone, I was worried about you." Sally was crying again.

"But, Sal, you left me," Josh pointed out.

"That's not the point," she said. Josh shuffled his feet and looked away. He didn't understand women. They talked for a few more minutes, then parted, Sally with her recuperating plant in her arms, Josh with a heavy heart. He'd promised to come by the nursery the next day—

strange events were still happening there, outbreaks of suspicious plant diseases, break-ins in which nothing was stolen, vandalism that didn't seem random, though there was plenty enough of that in the heart of Night City. Josh began to trot back toward Little China and the suddenly comfortable world of the Cantonese ghetto.

Not everybody in Little China appreciated that Bryan Lee had adopted Japanese karate as his martial art of choice. Resentment lingered from the era of Japanese domination and cruelty in the years before the Second World War. The current revival of Japanese imperial ambition, the new Asian Co-Prosperity Sphere, was widely seen as a front for the ambitions of Arasaka Corporation to take over everything. Beyond all that, there was still the martial artists' competitive "my master's kung fu is better than your master's" thing goin' on, so Josh wasn't surprised when a couple of Asian thugs in tight T-shirts and baggy black pants stepped into his path as he cut through an alley on the way back to the dojo.

"Hey, *guailou*, you white devil. What you know?"

"Nothin'," Josh answered noncommittally, but with his new awareness he placed himself equidistant from his two challengers with an alley wall behind him so he couldn't be surrounded. From this position his antagonizers could attack him only one at a time.

"That's right. You don't know nothin'. Shit. Japan's nothin' but a rip-off. Rip our language, rip our art, our culture, our kung-fu. They're just imitators."

"So?"

"So, why don't you tell your teacher to be Chinese, not some stooge for the Nips."

"Why don't you tell him yourself? You know where his dojo is."

The bigger, burlier punk stepped into Josh's aura space.

It was the classic threat step—Josh couldn't retreat any farther, his back was already against the wall. He sidestepped and took a *kibodachi* stance—knees bent, legs parallel, back straight as if he was mounted on a horse with his feet in stirrups.

"See, that's what I'm talkin' about," said the menacing punk. "It's not a damn dojo, it's a *mi-yao*."

"My teacher believes all martial arts are equal, just like all men."

"Bullshit. In our Chinese culture it's year four thousand seven hundred and eighteen. Japan, they go back maybe half that far. And you fuckin' white boys were barbarians livin' in caves when our emperors were ruling half the world from palaces of jade."

"True. But look who's on top of the heap now."

"Now the world's a heap o' junk, 'cause you made it so."

In the midst of this ugly confrontation, Joshua happened to glance up at the first stars in the twilight sky. Often it wasn't possible to see them through the polluted atmosphere above Night City, but tonight, there they were, each one an immense furnace larger than our sun, boiling away in nuclear reaction light-years from planet Earth. Why did these cosmic thoughts come to him now, as he faced possible death at the hands of two punks obsessed by a cultural struggle that had almost nothing to do with him? As he looked down from the firmament, he saw that the second dude had edged closer to him. Josh brought his hands up to *chudan* level, ready position. Following traditional karate principles, he would almost never attack first, hoping to lure his opponents into a first punch that would leave them open to counterattack. He didn't have to wait long. Uttering a high-pitched cry, the more aggressive thug tried to reach him with a fancy kick, but Josh remained poised and fended it off easily with a *gedan-barai* block. Now the two of them took turns trying to reach him with kicks and punches, but Josh had the advantage of superior defensive position and the knowledge that he needed to no more than keep them at bay to win, while they must continually attack to attempt to penetrate his shell, which is more tiring. Soon they'd exhaust themselves, and he'd be able to break out of the alley.

"Ah shit, let's get it over with," the smaller assailant finally said as he withdrew a pistol from the waistband of his pants. In a flash Josh realized these weren't rival martial artists at all but paid assassins who'd been sent to eliminate him, they didn't give a shit about kung fu versus karate or Chinese nationalism versus Japanese imperialism. They were probably in the hire of the Holo Men. All this he comprehended in the infinitesimal pause that signaled his shift from defense to offense, as he launched himself at the man with the gun. *It's just like on the Net*, Josh found himself thinking, *except it's real.* As he grappled with the gunman there was a deafening explosion near his right ear. Fragments of brick flew off the wall and struck him and his attacker, causing some minor bleeding, but neither of them was struck by the bullet.

The other attacker had backed off when the gun came out, and now he called out to his companion, "Leave it, Chew. The cops'll be here any second."

Another shot resounded, another miss, more splinters of red-baked rock and stone flew off. Joshua somersaulted, not in the air like on the Net but low and close to the ground. Once, twice he rolled, another turn and he'd be at the corner where the lane opened onto the street. A third shot reverberated in the tight space, but Joshua felt nothing, and somewhere far off he could hear the wavering erratic sirens of the Night City patrol car closing in. The two thugs fled down the opposite path and out onto the street, where they quickly mingled with the passing crowds. Josh stood up, dusted himself off, wiped a smear of blood from his forehead, and ran into the street himself to evade the oncoming police. When he related his actions excitedly to Bryan Lee, his teacher only grunted and told him to be more careful, that he shouldn't have let himself be trapped in an alley, that a really aware student would have sensed the attack coming and avoided it, but Joshua saw that his *sensei* was secretly pleased with him.

Joshua continued his studies. Satisfied with Josh's progress in free-hand movements, Bryan Lee began to instruct him in the use of weapons—the *boh*, the six-foot staff of oak, the *kendo*, the sword, and the *joh*, the short stick, all of which, at close range and in the right hands, were as deadly as any gun. At times it seemed that he had forgotten all about his former life as a hacker, and the malevolent conspiracy that still threatened the Net, but then he would remind himself that his friend Taro might still be alive somewhere and needing his help. There was so much to learn, he'd never be able to absorb it all, but his teacher was patient. It was a cram course only possible because Josh's mind had learned many of these moves in the Net before his body practiced them. Each day his body became harder and yet more flexible while his mind calmed and grew more controlled. The process of devolution continued as the unusual nodes around his 'trode holes shrank, a healing he attributed to Dr. Lee's powerful twig and bark tea, which he dutifully brewed and consumed daily. New students were attracted by the revitalized dojo and by Bryan Lee's almost mythical status as a blind (though now cyber-sighted) martial artist in the tradition of the blind swordsman/masseur Zatoichi. One day Bryan asked Joshua to lead the warm-ups for the beginner class, an unmistakable mark of his progress. As he observed the eager

faces of the new students, Joshua saw a whole new life of
teaching open up before him, if only he could put to rest
the haunting knowledge that he had major unfinished business from his previous existence. That evening he approached his *sensei* as Bryan worked out alone in the dojo,
practicing advanced sword movements Joshua could still
only dream about. The old Josh would have run up to him
and tugged at his sleeve; the new Joshua waited quietly in
seiza off to the side of the dojo floor until Bryan finished
his many kata and acknowledged his *deshi*'s presence.

"Bryan-*sensei*, I have to leave the dojo. There are people who need me, and others who must be stopped from
evil actions." Joshua feared that Bryan would be resentful
or disappointed, after all the training he had given to his
sole student for many weeks, but instead his teacher only
smiled and said:

"You have been ready for many days now. We were
waiting for you to come to us."

"But, am I better?" Josh asked. "I mean, has your father's treatment had enough time to work? Will I be able to
run the Net again?"

"Why don't you ask him yourself?"

Joshua bowed and rose and rushed downstairs. Though
it was late, the store was still open, a few clerks helped
last-minute customers, and a light was on in the back
where Dr. Lee concocted his formulas. The elderly Chinese man was still hard at work, grinding seeds in an ancient mortar and pestle, with a precise circular movement
that suggested magic, though it was nothing more than
stone against stone. He looked up and smiled as Joshua tip-
toed toward him. Before Joshua could formulate his question, Dr. Lee gave him a grin that if it wasn't on the
wizened face of an Oriental sage might have been de-

scribed as shit-eating, and said, "I hear that you have cured yourself."

"What?!"

"You should be able to resume your activities with computers, at least to some degree. I congratulate you on your resolve."

"But—the elixir?" Joshua asked.

"A placebo. Tree bark, but not medicine. No, it is you yourself who have cured you. There is nothing I could give you that would treat the malady you have. Your own efforts have led to your improvement."

"But it was so bitter—" Joshua protested weakly.

"Convincing, neh?" Dr. Lee smiled, and if Joshua hadn't been living in Little China long enough to break down some of his stereotypes he would have called the expression on the pharmacist's face inscrutable. "There is an old Chinese proverb that says one needs to eat bitter to reach enlightenment."

"So, I'll never be well?"

"You are healthier than you have ever been, only you can't use computers for extended periods of time. Is that so terrible?"

"The Holo Men—"

"Are still a threat. You will have to lure them out, fight them on your ground now."

"I don't know what they look like. They go by these icons of historical figures, they could be anybody."

"Would they recognize you?" the sage herbalist asked.

"No." Josh grinned, remembering the full-bearded prophet that was his Net image.

"So, you see, you are at equal advantage. When you summon them, they will come, if only to try to destroy you. But they still think of you as the helpless adolescent. Do you still think of yourself in that way?"

"No."

"Test your old skills. But don't forget that you have learned new ones." Dr. Lee bowed and withdrew behind an iridescent blue silk curtain adorned with startlingly white images of elegant storks wading among bamboo reeds.

"But wait!" Josh cried out, remembering that he didn't even have a cyberdeck on which to confirm his recovery. Impetuously he flung back the curtain to find—nothing! Dr. Lee had vanished. A solid wall and impervious floors gave no evidence of any trapdoor or secret escape. The old herbalist had proved to be a magician as well. Joshua backed out of the shop. He knew it would be fruitless to ask the clerks how Dr. Lee had disappeared, they'd deny having seen him, or else they'd feign an inability to understand Joshua, though he'd spoken to many of them in the past few weeks. Though he'd been told he was cured, and though he'd announced that he was going to leave, Joshua didn't depart from the dojo immediately. He returned to the empty space above the pharmacy and continued his practice of the "empty hand," *kara-te,* whose root is the same as *kara-oke,* "empty orchestra," the sing-along entertainment machine in bars and homes, but whose meaning is infinitely more profound. Josh knew better than to ask Bryan about his father's mysterious disappearance. His teacher would reject all suggestions of the supernatural. He'd merely shrug and say "more practice" or "lower your koshi." By now Josh had realized just how much of a beginner he was. He'd learned perhaps twenty basic katas, but there were hundreds. He could successfully defend himself against one or two attackers, but Bryan gave demonstrations in which he fended off the strikes of eight and ten men. Josh had begun to apply himself with the same fanatical devotion to martial arts that he had once given to deck-running.

A few evenings later he was alone in the gym, working out with the *boh* on his *morite-tsuki*, when Bryan stuck his head in, studied his student's form for a minute, then called out, "There's someone here to see you." Josh rushed downstairs from the gym, hoping that it was Sally, or maybe even Taro who had somehow come to the States and found him, but when he reached the street there was no one there. A beat-up pickup truck carrying a camper shell with Colorado plates was parked in the otherwise deserted street. As Joshua turned to climb the stairs again, he heard someone call his name.

"Joshua! Hey, boy, looking good. Where's that scrawny kid I left a couple of months ago?" It was Flight Sim Fred! He hopped out of the driver's seat and crossed around in front of the truck. Joshua raced over to shake his hand.

"Fred! What are you doing here?"

"I came for the chop suey," Fred joked. Joshua winced. They didn't serve chop suey in the authentic restaurants of Little China, that dish was a phony American invention like the pizza, the French fry, and the Polynesian puu puu platter. "Hey, step up into my home away from home here, I have something to show you." Joshua followed Fred into the oversize shell, which was much smaller than byteboi's RV. The inside of the camper was a roving communications station, lined with all kinds of electronic equipment from mini-sat dishes to consoles with holovid terms and weird keyboards without any keys.

"I brought you a little present," said Fred, pointing to a rig that sat on the all-weather carpet in the center of the shell, not connected to the maze of wires that linked much of the other equipment in the truck.

"What is it?" Joshua blinked, because his heart was creeping up his throat. He knew what it was.

"Take a look."

The deck was a complete custom job, in a style Joshua had never seen before. Extremely compact, streamlined, aerodynamic even, it was the ultimate in state-of-the-art cyberspace Runnin' gear. Joshua studied its components with a mixture of fear and fascination, like an addict starin' at his first fix after a long dry stretch.

"Go ahead, put it on," Fred urged him. Instead, Joshua turned and faced the cybernaut who had participated in the building of the system that once ruled Josh's life.

Joshua deliberately turned his back on the cyberdeck and spun around to face Fred. "I can't be that person again," said Joshua. "I mean, I'll go on-line, I'll find the Holo Men and expose them or whatever it takes, but I'll never be a true Runner again. There's too much else to do in this world."

"Of course there is. That's one of the things I hoped you'd learn from Bryan Lee."

"But, you sent me to his father for a cure."

"I sent you to the father, but called the son. You see, you're like byteboi in many ways. You got yourself all wrapped up in the future, but what you really needed was a dose of the past, to slow down your mind, steady yourself. The karate-do did that for you, yes?"

"Yes," Josh admitted gratefully.

"Now when you run the Net, it won't be as a renegade data hoodlum, but purposefully."

"Fred, there's one thing. Taro—"

"Ah yes, Taro-san. Check your E-mail, I believe you'll find some communication from him."

"I still have no money, Fred."

"I'm bankrolling you, fronting you this deck, on the speculative notion that when you defeat the Holo Men you'll capture secrets that'll make us all rich." Josh took a minute to digest all that, then slowly twisted around to look at the deck again. Could he do it? It seemed like nausea was clawing at his innards and waiting to seize him if he dared to log on, but he'd learned this much from karate— he who hesitates is lost. He grasped the lightweight device and strapped it on.

He let out a low appreciative whistle. "Slick!" he said to Fred.

"Fire her up," Fred urged him. Joshua reached around behind the unit, found the on-off key, but didn't flip the switch.

"Doesn't it need to be plugged in?" Josh asked. Cyberdecks were notoriously power-hungry, most couldn't operate on batteries for more than a few minutes, because battery technology was one of the last areas where science had not achieved real miniaturization and portability. Units still required relatively bulky external power supplies, but Josh saw nothing like that on this deck, it was so small he could wear it around his neck.

"There's been a breakthrough. Between the new batteries and wireless modems, hell, you could put the whole thing in a soda can if ya wanted to. Come on, take her for a spin." Obviously Fred wasn't expecting Joshua to have any viral reaction. Joshua tensed himself and clicked the switch over to the ON position. The rainbow explosion of colors that signaled the start of a Net run flashed before his dazed pupils. He felt his stomach constrict, and a light-headed sensation caused him to stagger momentarily, but soon the familiar outlines of the Night City grid presented themselves to him.

"I'm in," he told Fred, though he could no longer see him. "Wait, Fred, won't the Holo Men know I'm back now that I've logged in?"

"I've been tweakin' your icon for ya, kid. You're cloaked. Feelin' okay?"

"Yeah. I guess so."

"Great. I'm gonna leave you here and go grab some chow." Joshua used Flip Switch 2.0 to give himself a real-space view without leaving Netspace. He told Fred where to go and what to order, so that he'd have a good meal, then locked the door behind him after he left. He took a deep breath and plunged into the world he'd left behind many weeks ago. Following Fred's suggestion, the first stop he made was the Post Office, where electronic mail was delivered. Of course one could simply ask to see the list of incoming messages, but it was a Net convention, a cozy anachronism, to enter the P.O. icon to pick up one's mail if not in a hurry. Josh'd hardly ever been here, after all, he was a hacker, he didn't just announce himself wherever he went, but Fred had assured him that he was protected by stealth. He checked into the Net News. The Holo Men had been active in his absence, he discovered. They'd made a couple more clandestine broadcasts, and they'd seized the backbone of the system for seven minutes, causing havoc with world stock-trading programs. Only a heroic effort by Arasaka programmers had prevented a complete collapse of the exchange system. The damage to the structure was still being analyzed, but it was believed that the Society had stolen and deposited vast sums of e.b. in hidden accounts during the seven-minute blackout. Other criminals, ever watchful, had piggybacked on the terrorist act and taken advantage of the confusion to conduct more electronic thefts of securities and treasury bills. The whole Net community was jittery, which helped to explain why Joshua saw an increased security presence, more Netwatch police on patrol in every icon he entered, but they paid no notice to him, either he was invisible or he was sending out such innocuous signals that they wrote him off as a nonthreat. The Post Office icon was a replica of a stolid civic building of the mid-twentieth century, all faux-marble and granite, with clever echoes simulating footfalls in an empty hall when you walked down the pointlessly long corridors to collect your mail from rows of glass-plated mailboxes. Josh had a little trouble remembering the combination to his box, but finally guessed it out. Inside was a sheaf of curled-up papers. Several of the messages were from the Holo Men—mocking, testing memos, where was he, why didn't he come back to see them, as if they didn't know. Josh supposed that read receipts were issued on each of them to alert the Society if he ever picked them up, but he also assumed that Fred had this covered. Only one of the messages interested him—he was sure it was from Taro, though there was no name, just three words: "Come see me!" and an address written in English and Japanese. No greeting, no electronic chitchat, none of the goofy personality Josh expected from the eccentric young Japanese hacker, just the cryptic plea and the address. He sent the text to the printer in Fred's truck, then closed the mailbox and spun the dials to reset the lock. As he turned away from the wall of pigeonholes, he was shocked to see his own face among the old-fashioned Wanted posters tacked above a table stocked with various mailing forms. He wondered if Fred had changed his appearance when he "tweaked" his icon.

Josh knew that he had to go to Japan, even if he was broke and still wanted by the Netwatch police and hunted by the Holo Men. The letter was dated a week after Josh'd been infected by the virus and catapulted off the Net; that was almost eight weeks ago now, but it seemed like longer, he'd changed so much. He'd have to find a way to travel overseas—Josh realized if they'd afflicted him they'd probably hit Taro too. He tried sending a quick message and immediately received a system message—"USER ID

NOT RECOGNIZED—TRY AGAIN" but he didn't need resend, he knew it meant that Taro was off-line or, worse, flatlined. Josh was more alone in the world than ever. Though he'd made some new friends, his teacher Bryan, Fred, the AI Breughel, and even Raspis the king of the Raptors, it was Taro he was most concerned about now. He'd fly to Tokyo—other than Night City the punkiest place on the planet, you could reach it in two hours by near-orbiter—and he'd rescue his friend if that was still possible.

Something was nagging at the back of his mind, some connection he hadn't made, a thread of thought that should have connected to other ideas and formed a new paradigm, but was missing, like an old memory, a face without a name, a song without a title, it was maddening really. Just then he passed a mirror in the Post Office that showed him the icon Fred had created for him to manifest on the Net, he jumped back as others were likely to do, because his image was that of a beast with the head of a cobra, hairy apelike arms with eagle talons for hands, a lion's hindquarters and tail, something like an upright griffin with different animal parts substituted. It was a frightening vision, even among the oddities that populated the high end of the Netrunning spectrum. Somehow the sight of himself as a mythical creature jolted the notion he'd been seeking into the forefront of his consciousness—it was Sally, and Phil, and the goings-on at the nursery. After he ran into her on the street, he'd meant to visit her the next morning, he'd told her he would, but somehow the days had slipped by until it had been almost two weeks since he'd seen her. He was fearful that she no longer wanted him even though he'd started to become the kind of person she hoped he'd be: responsible, organized, levelheaded. She'd asked for his help, and he'd let her down again. So had Flight Sim Fred. Why hadn't he called her? As Josh was thinking on these things, absentmindedly wandering inside the Post Office, the horizon began to tilt and rock. Josh tried to hold himself rigid but the queasy sloshing motion increased until he hung his head between his knees to counter the nausea-inducing vertigo. So, he wasn't cured. The virus reacted as soon as he lost his concentration even the tiniest bit. It was there inside him, waiting for him to show fear or inattention. When Fred returned, carrying a white paper carton of leftover Chinese food, Josh confronted him.

"You said you were going to get in touch with my ex-girlfriend, Sally. Why didn't you call her?"

"I did call. I left a message."

"She didn't say anything about that."

"Maybe the Society has her phone bugged too. Maybe they erased the tape. Those creeps are capable of anything."

"There's something going on at the nursery, it's part of the Holo Men thing—"

"So why don't you go there and investigate?"

"I will. Plus, I need a plane ticket to Japan. I gotta help Taro."

"That can be arranged. How'd it go, the Run?"

"I got sick, but only when I let my mind wander. I think I can handle it."

"That's good news. Ya didn't meet any Holo Men, did ya? Yer new icon's supposed to protect you from them."

"I didn't talk to anybody. I saw myself in a mirror, though. What kind of weird shit is that you've got me Runnin' in?"

"Special first-class iconics. Guaranteed t' scare off the casual tourist, and cloaked to prevent recognition by Holo Men, Netwatch sysops, or anyone else who shouldn't know who you are, like any Corporate goons still after your ass."

Later, after the debilitating dizziness wore off, Josh ventured one more Net session. He accessed the protected files of the Holo Men, who, as he suspected, were so sure he'd never again be able to log on that they'd left his recognition routine in place. Before his exile, he'd been accepted as one of them, with entry to all the secrets of the Society, but he'd never done much more than dabble in the database they maintained. Now he zeroed in on the information lattice, working quickly just in case Fred's shielding programs weren't as effective as he claimed. He started by requesting any records on Sally Thrower. He expected to find an entry or two, perhaps only as keywords in his own file, but was surprised when the search revealed a substantial number of documents. The dossier compiled in laborious detail Sally's movements, Phil's shaky cash flow, and, most significantly, the Holo Men's intrusions and deceptions, all catalogued precisely. No longer was an army of clerks required to maintain files on individuals—the Net provided a ready means of organization. It was the banality of evil exemplified. Sally wasn't an important player in the unfolding drama, and certainly Phil O'Dendron was not, yet their files if printed out would make a stack of papers two inches high. Josh knew that if he opened his file, or Taro's, or Fred's, he'd find an even more thorough accounting. What fantastic misdirected energy was being poured into this effort, like the absurdly meticulous records the Nazis kept of victims already destined for the ovens of Auschwitz. It was madness, frightening, and wildly out of control despite its apparent order, like the obsessive repetitive movements of a schizophrenic.

"Shit!" was all Josh could find to say in the face of the ludicrous, childish tricks they'd played on the poor nursery owner and his innocent helper. Clearly the Society was much more powerful than Josh had suspected, if they had the time to devote resources to such insignificant pranks. One note maddened him particularly. It read: "Removed one dozen pink-blossomed moccasin flowers for K-M's hothouse." Apparently the great K-M was a lover of orchids. He was stealing from Phil, or having his toadies heist the flowering plants for his private collection. Once again Joshua logged off, leapt over Fred, who was sleeping in a cot at the back of the truck, and rushed off to warn Sally. He was too late. The nursery was boarded up, its windows covered over in black. Josh scraped away a little paint but all he could see were empty tables where rows of plants used to stand. A FOR RENT sign was posted on the door—it was all depressingly similar to the way he'd found his apartment after his ejection from the Net. The Holo Men certainly were thorough; when they wrecked your life they did so completely. Joshua sprinted toward Sally's apartment, hoping not to find a repetition of the same dreary scenario. The place looked inhabited, but Sally wasn't home. Josh decided to wait, no matter how long, until she returned. He was still hanging around at midnight when Sally came shambling down the sidewalk in her hunched, preoccupied gait. She didn't notice Joshua until she almost stumbled over him as she mounted the stairs of her stoop.

Sometimes an opening isn't an opening, as when an airport jetway connects to empty space instead of a plane. Sometimes a closed door isn't really closed, as when lovers' hearts are uncertain. Sally smiled her pleasure at seeing Josh again, but then she remembered she was supposed to be angry with him. "Where have you been? You promised to help."

"I'm sorry, Sal. I wanted to get over here, but it was hard—" Josh stopped. He knew so much more than he could express, about why it'd been so difficult for him to

see her, and so many other things, but how could he make
her understand when she still saw only the irresponsible
teenager he had been, and not the true warrior he'd become, so much more than the Net-running joker she'd
lived with?

"Yeah, well, you're too late. Everything's gone to shit.
They shut down the nursery and confiscated all the
plants—"

" 'They' who, Sally?"

"They said they were from the police, but they didn't
even bother to show us badges, so I don't know. All I know
is I don't have a job and a good man, Phil, is ruined, and
it's all your fault." This time Sally didn't cry—perhaps she
was too bitter for tears.

"You're right," said Joshua. He told her about getting
back onto the Net and what he'd found in the files on her
and Phil.

"But why?" she asked, puzzled.

"Sheer perversity. Evil people are crazy—they hold
grudges longer than ordinary human beings, they don't
know how to let go."

"What are you going to do now?"

Josh told her of his plans to find Taro, and how the two
of them would battle the Holo Men together. Sally looked
at him like he was still the starry-eyed dreamer she'd left.

"What can you and your friend do against these Hollow
guys? They sound dangerous to me. Why don't you just
contact the Net police and—"

"Listen, Sally, for all I know the Society may be made
up of disaffected policemen. It wouldn't surprise me. At
root the police and the criminals are playing the same violent game, you know what I mean? Lots of thugs who
might have been crooks end up with uniforms on. Anyway,
I'm still wanted out there for the Corporate prank stuff I

pulled, the Holo Men saw to that. Maybe if I bust them I can clear my record, it's worth a chance." Joshua edged closer to Sally, put his arm around her. "You and I should be together—"

"No, Josh." Sally pushed him away and curled up on the stoop.

"Let me finish—"

"No. I'm not ready for that." Sally showed a flash of her old Irish temper. "You can't just show up twice in two months and suddenly expect I'll be ready to take you back, start up where we left off. I don't even know where you've been, what you've been doing, except you look better, your body's changed somehow, and your eyes are clearer, they don't have that fuzzy redness they used to get when you were jacked in all the time. Now you're talking about going back into that world—"

"Only temporarily—"

"So where does that leave me? Will I be cleaning up after you again, waiting around while you leave your body behind and send your brain into hyperspace? No thanks!"

She got up to enter her apartment, thinking she'd leave Josh behind. The old Joshua, wrapped up in the silvery strands of the Net, would have let her go, but he'd learned some things from living in Little China, among the raucous Chinese families, always shouting as if they were angry at each other but really showing their love, and from watching the filial piety shown by Bryan toward his father, so different from the family he grew up in, his bored mother and his preoccupied father. He raced ahead of her and barred her way.

"Listen to me. My life is going to be completely different after this is over. I'm going to be a teacher—"

"What, teaching kids how to make trouble on the Net?"

Sally asked skeptically, but she liked it that he cared now, that he just didn't let her walk away.

"Martial arts. I've got a lot of years of study ahead of me. I could do it, if I had somebody like you who believed in me. But first, I've got to finish what I started. I'm the only one, well, me and Taro, and Fred, and this goofy AI named Breughel, we're the only ones who know just how bad the Holo Men could make it for people if they grab the Net for themselves. You've seen what they did to you and Phil. They've got to be stopped." Then Joshua kissed Sally hard on the mouth, and she melted into his arms and Joshua wouldn't have been surprised if the skies over Night City had exploded into dazzling fireworks but then it probably would just've been a terrorist attack or an industrial accident or something.

They slept together that night but in the morning Joshua returned to Bryan Lee's. Sally and Josh had agreed not to see each other until Joshua's trip to Japan was over, partly for Sally's security, so that she wouldn't be associated with Joshua if anything happened. Joshua continued to live and study with Bryan Lee while he made preparations to visit Japan. Fred turned up once a week for the next three weeks, the first time to give Joshua a passport and ID in a phony name, a second time to deliver tickets in the new name for a near orbiter flight ten days hence, and then a few days before Josh's departure with another present he brought out when Joshua visited him in his camper-shell compartment.

"Here." Fred handed him a slim carrying case for the deck, with foam cutouts for holding the battery pack. "You're on your own now, Joshua Victor. There's nothing more I can do for you." That wasn't true of course, but both of them knew that Josh had to venture out on his own. Eight weeks ago he would have doubted himself. Now he gripped the handle on the attaché case tightly with one hand and gave Fred a firm handshake with the other.

"If I can just find Taro, the two of us'll frack up the Holo Men good."

"Many people are depending on you, son," said Fred. Joshua speculated silently as to who this Fred character really was and whether he was really as much of a rebel as he said he was. Sometimes Joshua got the impression that Fred was really connected to some super-secret government agency, and that the whole renegade thing was just an image, a front, like so many other things in life, both less and more than what it seemed. But it didn't matter to Josh if Fred was the Mad Hatter or just a plumber, he'd helped Josh raise himself from the depths, and he was against the Holo Men.

"Thanks for everything, Fred. I won't let you down."

Just before his flight, Joshua found one more reason to hate the Holo Men, as if he needed one. When Joshua had first arrived at the Chinatown dojo, Bryan had suggested ominously that there was a cause for revenge between him and the Holo Men, but Joshua hadn't caught the full meaning of that remark. Now that he was back on the Net, he checked for a Holo Men's file on his teacher and his teacher's family. It was sealed in a deeper layer of security than his own and Sally's, and this in itself was significant. Joshua soon cracked the code, his hacker skills were flowing back into him, though he'd never again allow himself to be so involved that his brain stem swelled and his life outside the Net diminished. As soon as he opened the Bryan Lee file an alarm went off, a hidden trigger Josh had overlooked, so he could only glance at the contents before backing out hurriedly, counting on Fred's cloaking mechanism to cover his tracks. What he saw confirmed his worst suspicions about K-M. This wasn't a Holo Men's political foray, it was a personal vendetta. Bryan and his father had resisted the infiltration of criminal elements into Little China, gangs attracted by the lucrative tourist trade and the *pai gow* gaming clubs that serviced the indigenous population. A tagged entry in the file showed that the automobile crash that had blinded Bryan and killed his mother was not an accident but had been deliberately staged by a Holo operative. How pervasive they were! Everyone they touched was hurt in some way. There seemed no end to their malign influence. It was no accident that Fred had sent him to the Lee's. He was being used by Fred and whomever he worked for just as he had been induced by the Holo Men, but to combat them instead of fostering their evil intent. For Bryan and his family, for Sally, for Taro, Joshua would fight the Holo Men, but when this was all over he vowed never to allow himself to be manipulated again, by anyone.

CHAPTER 9

AROUND THE WORLD
IN EIGHTY MINUTES

The near-orbiter took off from a distant corner of the Night City Airport, where the magnificent thunder of its engines wouldn't shatter windows or roast onlookers. Passengers were required to undergo a mild medical exam to ensure their hearts could withstand the brief period of stress caused by the acceleration necessary to achieve orbital velocity. After the exam, the fortunate few who could afford it were placed on a bus to be shuttled out to a remote runway that pointed out to sea. The orbiter resembled the space shuttles of the late twentieth century, with a blunt nose and stubby wings, and massive rear where the engines resided. Advances in technology had allowed the booster rockets, which used to mandate a vertical blastoff, to be shrunk and strapped to the fuselage so that the plane could effect a rolling takeoff like an ordinary airplane.

From the air, golf courses and cemeteries look similar: swatches of green with curving lines of trees. Joshua stared out the plexi window at the densely populated corridor of the Night City area between the sea and the first line of coastal hills. Night City, that den of Corporate thieves, that punks' paradise, city of Runners, Net and Edge, the creation of a single mind, a planned urban development laid out by Richard Alix Night before his death in 1998, the "City on the Edge of Tomorrow." Only, tomorrow had come and it wasn't pretty. The vehicle circled once before heading out over the ocean for the flight to Tokyo. The ride began as an ordinary plane trip, but quickly rocketed into something else, as the massive thrusters of the solid fuel boosters kicked in and shoved the aerospace plane into a shallow orbital angle that revealed the penumbra of the Earth's edge against the emptiness of space; a sight Joshua, for all his futuristic leanings, had never seen. The space vehicle resembled a common jetliner inside, except for deeply padded seats and additional belt restraints to keep passengers from floating off during the brief period of zero G.

The trip might have been more enjoyable except that Joshua found himself seated next to a wild-eyed American who kept saying, "Isn't life magical?" in a loud voice, like he was on drugs or something. The other passengers, conservative Japanese and Western businessmen, ignored him, but since Joshua wasn't dressed in a suit this character seemed to feel that meant Josh would be interested in his ravings, which were of the quasi-cosmic, "Wow, look at the Earth from space, we're all one big happy planet" variety. Though obviously American, probably a Californian, and maybe even from Night City like Josh, the lunatic was dressed in a gown fit for the bedroom, a flimsy flannel thing, and sandals. Josh wondered how he'd even gotten onto the flight, but then the man turned to him and said conspiratorially, "Your secret is safe with me."

"Huh?" said Josh, who hadn't been paying much attention to his seatmate's inarticulate pronouncements. Instead of continuing in the secretive mode, however, the semideranged traveler winked slyly, satisfied that he had gotten Josh's attention, and ushered in a new topic, one that was dangerously close to his concerns.

"Helluva thing about those renegade Net-nicks, huh? Imagine tryin' to take over the Net, the nerve of 'em, after all, it's a free market, open architecture, all that capitalist bullshit, yeah?" He raised his head to see if the other passengers were taking note of his comments, but he didn't seem disappointed that they were all engrossed in reading or operating their handheld computers. Joshua was his main and captive audience.

Josh, meanwhile, was examining the man closely. His bristly haircut suggested someone who had recently been institutionalized, either in prison, hospital, or asylum, yet here he was on an expensive trans-oceanic suborbital flight. Why? His eyes were in constant motion yet focused on nothing. His hands churned the air rapidly in an excess of demonstrative gestures, yet these movements were unconnected to his speech.

"What's your name?" Josh asked.

"What's yours? Is it Isaiah? Ezekial? Abraham?" naming other Old Testament figures and clearly implying that he knew who Josh was and why he was on his way to Japan. Josh was suddenly frightened and claustrophobic. *He must be an emissary of the Holo Men,* Josh thought. There was no escaping his unwanted companion until they landed at Tokyo Aerospace Port-Chiba. Josh could only assume that somehow the Holo Men had found out about his planned trip and had sent someone to conduct surveillance on him, but why this unusual figure, who even more than in America would stand out grotesquely on the streets of Tokyo among the black-haired, black-eyed throngs.

"Leave me alone!" Josh said angrily, and turned his face to the window, but his tormentor wasn't so easily shaken.

"Ah, loneliness, it's such a universal state, the existential dilemma, we wish to be alone yet we can't bear it when our loved ones spurn us and society rejects us." His next words were obliterated by a sudden increase in the whooshing roar of the jet's engines as the near-orbiter plunged into its descent. Everyone on the plane was forced into their seats as gravity took hold of them again, pressing them into the molded contours of the chairs. Joshua forced himself to turn to look at the man next to him, and discovered him grinning spasmodically at Josh, his lips forced back by the pressure into a horrible death's-head grimace. Josh hoped to lose his annoying associate in the aerospace port, but the passengers were channeled through a narrow series of gates at Customs, then trundled directly onto the Shinkansen bullet train into downtown, and it seemed that every time he turned around there was his ghoulish comrade, winking, blinking, and nodding in a frenzy of meaningless expression. Finally the high-speed train pulled into Shinjuku Station and Josh bolted out the door, nearly knocking over an elderly woman and drawing disapproving glances from his fellow travelers at the rudeness of the stupid gaijin, but Josh didn't care, he had to get away. He ducked into a men's room for fifteen minutes and when he exited, his shadow was nowhere in sight. Joshua took a deep breath and plunged into the crowd heading toward the surface up impossibly long, steep escalators wide enough for only one person, so that long single-file lines formed at the base of each one. After he ascended several levels, he found himself on the street.

Tokyo was like Night City on acid, or the razor's edge. The police and the gangs were more dangerous, the pace was more frenetic, the traffic jams longer and deeper, the motorcycles noisier, the crowds on the street more congested and pushier. When you top that off by not being able to understand any of the signs or have any idea where you are going, the whole concept becomes a study in panic. Joshua clung to the one tiny portion of his brain that reminded him he had just spent two months in intensive study of a Japanese form of martial arts, and therefore could claim to comprehend at least a small amount of the cultural swirl that eddied around him, though what little Japanese he knew was useless for ordinary conversation, unless someone asked him, for example, to perform *mizunokata*. Somewhere in this mass of humanity were students of Funakoshi, Egami, and the masters of yore, who would be able to relate to him, and somewhere out there, he hoped, was his friend Taro. Half the people on the street were fitted with some sort of cyberware. Josh's stereotype of a Japan in which everybody looked the same was quickly blasted, as he witnessed the passing parade in Shinjuku Station. Sure, there were plenty of the conservative dark-suited Corporates like those on the flight, but there was also a steady stream of exotic alternative types: Bosozoku gangers in satin armorjackets and baggy pants, Posers of all persuasions, many in the garb of their favorite *komike* comic book characters, androgynous men and women in silky lace and leather, with puffed-up 'dos and feminine bio-sculpting, *yakuza* in garish zoot suits and shades strutting their stuff and pushing passersby out of the way, and yet, still shuffling along among the Grapplers, the Metalmaxes, and the tight-suited riot-helmeted cops of the cyberpunk, half-fantasy modern world, the occasional old person in traditional kimono and wooden slippers.

CHAPTER 10

THE BASEMENT OF BABEL

Two million people would pass through Shinjuku Station today, and every one of them would know more about where they were going than Joshua Victor. He was lost. Without the 'trodes to translate for him, he understood no Japanese. A few of the signs were in English, but all he had was a scrap of paper with Taro's address on it. He tried approaching a couple of people for directions—they nodded, bowed, shouted "Hai!" to him, pointed, but left him as confused as before he'd asked. On the train in from the airport he'd passed through a bewildering series of neighborhoods, industrial zones, Japanese versions of beavervilles, nameless sprawls without street signs, glittering skyscrapers juxtaposed next to pre-fab concrete low-income housing. All he knew was that somewhere within a few square miles surrounding the swarming train station, among the millions of bobbing black heads, was his friend Taro, holed up in a ten by ten studio apartment and terrified for his life.

148

Although his papers were in order under the fictitious person he'd created for himself, Joshua hesitated to ask for help from a Japanese policeman. For starters, the cops were on average four to six inches taller and fifty pounds heavier than the ordinary passersby, and all of that weight was in muscles on the upper body and in the thighs, giving them the look of steroid-pumped maniacs in uniform, though it was said of them that they didn't take any body supplements, that all the increase was attributable to training techniques. Their uniforms fitted like the spotless white gloves they wore, and their black eyes were hidden behind mirrored sunglasses that they wore even in the relative dimness of the train station. Trains were arriving with immaculate precision at regular one-minute intervals on several levels, all of them beneath the surface. Joshua wandered through long corridors between platforms, where some of Tokyo's homeless had encamped in cardboard villas. Unlike the street people of Night City these urban dwellers were polite, not aggressive, and their individual paper homes were neat and clean. Still, they had the vacant look of starving men, and no one seemed to be giving them money, as they did not beg. Josh wondered how they survived.

Finally a group of teenagers approached him, eager to test their English skills on the gaijin. They were dressed in the style of sixty-five years ago, the fifties, the boys with greased-back hair, black peg pants, white T-shirts with cigarette packs rolled up in the sleeves, the girls in party dresses and ponytails.

"Lost?" a polite young man asked him.

"Yeah." Joshua showed him the slip of paper with Taro's Ikebukuro address on it. There was no name—Taro was careful.

"Oh, man, you don't wanna go down there. That's a bad neighborhood," the carefully dressed teen told him.

"I have to," said Joshua. He was alone and vulnerable, and though the near-orbiter crossed the time zones so fast he wasn't feeling jet-lagged yet, he was still a little disoriented by being suddenly plunked down in Tokyo. The farthest he'd traveled before this was a trip to Chicago once with his high school science class. Though he'd roamed the world on the Net, it wasn't the same.

"We'll escort you. Come on." They were riding old-fashioned motor-scooters, the kind of putt-putters that had been obsolete even before jet-bikes replaced internal-combustion cycles. Joshua was handed a helmet by a cute little girl who couldn't have been more than four feet ten inches tall and fourteen years old. He felt awkward and foolish at the ripe age of nineteen, but no one else was helping him, so he donned the headgear and took a seat behind her. They raced through the streets, running red lights and terrorizing pedestrians, sometimes jumping up onto the sidewalk if, as often happened in Tokyo, traffic had come to a gridlock standstill. It wasn't as scary as riding on the back of Raspis's bike when he was on the verge of passing out, but it was close. Gradually they left the glitzy high-rise towers of Shinjuku and strayed into a Tokyo version of his own neighborhood at home, a drab combination of warehouses and flimsy flats, but much more densely built than in Night City, so that they crowded on one another and the streets grew narrower until they were mere alleys where only a scooter or cycle was practical. *How do they get garbage trucks in here?* Josh found himself wondering after they'd made their sixth or seventh twisting turn deeper into the skinny maze. Josh realized he'd never be able to find his way back out of this labyrinth of tiny lanes, so he could only hope that the scooter crew was on the level and was taking him to the address as promised, not to some blind dead end where they were going to roll him for his yen and passport. His fears were unfounded—soon thereafter they pulled up to a nondescript cement block of a building and pointed, then waved cheerfully and roared off.

There were a hundred names on the apartment's buzzer board, all of them written in Japanese, and anyway Taro hadn't provided a name, only an address. How was Josh to know which doorbell to ring? He stared helplessly at the index. Then he saw a single name with an arrow pointing to a set of stairs down to the basement, and he remembered that Taro had said he lived beneath the convenience shop that occupied the storefront to the right of the building entrance. Vastly relieved, Josh tripped down the steps to the subterranean cubbyhole and knocked on the door, which was heavily reinforced with iron bars and sheet metal, and presented only a narrow slit for mail drop in its otherwise shiny and impenetrable surface. His elation was short-lived—no one answered his repeated poundings. Somehow, though, he knew that Taro was inside. Perhaps the Japanese youth had no means of observing who was at his door, Josh didn't see an obvious fish-eye peephole, and perhaps Taro never received any visitors except the unwanted ones, gangs and cops. How was Josh going to make his presence known? At last he struck upon the simple expedient of going upstairs to the convenience store and convincing the shopkeeper (who spoke not one word of English, they communicated in awkward pantomime) to drop a note down with the next box of sodas and chips. "I AM HERE!" Josh wrote, and he drew a picture of himself as his Net icon, a bushy-bearded stick figure in robe and sandals (and suddenly Josh flashed on the image of the stranger on the plane, also robed and sandaled, though to very different effect, and he wondered if he had successfully ditched the man, or else he was exposing Taro to great danger). The convenience store owner, a squat, bristly-headed man with a worried face, accepted some yen from Josh, handed some back (Josh had no idea how much) and grunted that the transaction was complete. He didn't allow Josh to see where the trap-door was located, but by means of pointing and gesturing and shoving convinced Josh to return to the basement door, where a minute later (Josh realized that the shopkeeper had probably described him to Taro, the note was a silly and unnecessary addition) the door creaked open and there stood a tall, extremely handsome young Japanese man, his face square and set off by a brushy crew cut, his complexion smooth and pimple-free, his eyes clear and focused, not at all like the scruffy, stunted, goggle-eyed geek of his Net image. Josh doubted for a minute that this could be the Taro he knew from the Net, but the underground dweller smiled and nodded and held out his hand.

"*Hero,*" he said.

"Hello! Great to meet you after all this time," said Josh, momentarily uncertain of how to proceed. Taro led him into the basement apartment, little more than a single room with a tiny bathroom off to one side, piles of clutter everywhere, pizza boxes, empty soda cans, scrapped computer equipment, clothes on the floor, just like the way Josh used to live before he switched over to the spare, spartan lifestyle of a dojo student.

"*Hero,*" Taro said again, and Josh had a sudden flash of comprehension—off the Net neither of them could speak the other's language—how were they going to communicate with each other? Wait, he could chip in, he'd brought the deck with him! When he opened the briefcase and exposed the cyberdeck, Taro's eyes glimmered for a minute, but then he backed off and waved his hands.

"No." He made a dumb show of retching and holding his stomach, and Josh knew for certain then that he'd been a victim of the Holo Men's virus. Josh plugged a module into one of his 'trode holes. He noticed that Taro's plugs had also receded, and he speculated whether his friend had experienced the same evolutionary swelling he'd manifested, and the subsequent reduction after their rejection by the Holo Men. He made a mental note to ask Taro about this, but first things first, as soon as he was in, and here he connected to the Tokyo LDL and discovered himself inside Shinjuku Station, which must serve as a locus icon for Netrunners as well as real-world travelers. He tried to make himself inconspicuous while he conversed with Taro. The arrangement was a little awkward, he drew glances from other Runners because he appeared to be a gone gaijin talking to himself, but the Japanese were too polite to interfere, so unless he caused some sort of disruption they would simply avoid him as another unpleasant example of why the world was so much better when Nihonmachi was the Pure Land, devoid of foreigners. Then Josh remembered what Fred had created for him in the way of an icon, and he threw his head back and laughed.

Josh activated Flip Switch 2.0 so that he could look at Taro while keeping his bearings in the Net, and smiled, and uttered a formal greeting, a perfect string of complex Japanese syllables, in the correct syntax.

"Honorable Taro-san, most humbling to make your acquaintance in person."

Taro immediately bowed and responded in Japanese with, "Cut the shit, white boy!" and they both cracked up and hugged and danced around the apartment and rolled among the crushed pizza boxes while Josh tried to maintain his icon stationary in Shinjuku, a delicate balancing

act. After a bit they settled down and began to talk in
earnest.

"Why the heck did you make yourself so gonky-looking
on the Net?" Josh asked his long-lost friend.

"Freedom. Freedom to be anything," said Taro. "Not to
be pretty boy, not to be high-expectation high school athlete star student go to Corporate Training School cadet
kind of guy." Josh nodded. He could relate to that. "Only
now I am nothing. Holo Men took away my life." Josh
could empathize with that too, although he'd found another life after the Net. If only he could bring Taro back
with him, introduce him to his *sensei* Bryan, he was sure
that the same regimen that worked for Josh would cure
Taro, to strengthen his mind and body so the virus found
no weakness to attack.

"You've got to come back with me to America, Night
City, that's where we'll be able to beat them."

"How do you know that? How do you know they're not
all Japanese?"

"Look at the icons they picked—anyway, the leader K-
M's the only one we know for sure, and he's an American
criminal through and through."

"I can't leave—I can't even leave this room. This is my
universe now. I don't even have the Net anymore. I just sit
here." Taro was dejected, dispirited, not the wired Net
guerrilla Josh had known in cyberspace.

"That's why you've got to come with me," Josh pleaded,
but Taro was too far down to hear him. It turned out he
hadn't left his room for several months, ever since the
Holo Men had shut them both out of the Net and for some
time before. "There's no one after you," Josh told Taro.
"The Holo Men figure they've done you, and my friend
Flight Sim Fred wiped your data slate clean, he's a genius
at that.

"Even so," Taro said hesitantly.

"What?" said Josh, a little impatiently, maybe because he'd come so far and was disappointed to find his friend so listless.

"I've been down here so long now, I'm afraid to go out," Taro confessed.

"I'll be right here with you," said Josh. "Come on, it's time for you to enter the real world again," he urged his friend, and he remembered his first days off the Net.

"I don't know," Taro vacillated, resisting his friend's entreaties, and they might have gone on like that all night, but just then the single light fixture in the gloomy subterranean den began to sway and a film of plaster dust shook loose from the ceiling and floated down and the walls began to crack and Taro shouted "Earthquake!" They both stood still and waited for the gentle rocking to subside but instead the rocking motion intensified and grew more violent. Taro pushed his way on wobbly legs past a dazed Joshua, flung open the door and dragged Josh out after him and continued to crawl up the stairs to the street, where cracks were swallowing whole parked cars in front of the building and the hiss of broken gas mains was like bombs ticking, at any minute a spark could ignite explosions.

The first story of the high-rise had collapsed. The contents of the convenience store, including the convenience store owner, were now in the basement. Josh and Taro started frantically removing debris. Fortunately the fellow had fallen beneath a main support beam that hadn't given way. When they uncovered him he was scratched and bruised but conscious and he hadn't broken any bones. He soon emerged from the rubble and bowed furiously to Josh and Taro, who bowed back, Taro naturally and Josh awkwardly, the more so because a crowd had gathered in front of the building. Josh looked around to observe the devastation and wreckage he expected to see all around them, but there wasn't any! The only building damaged was the one where Taro lived. What kind of earthquake was that? Taro was also staring about in amazement, since he too had felt the rumbling and shaking associated with a temblor, and also because he hadn't seen the world from street level in so long.

"It must have been a bomb," said Josh, but Taro could only shrug at him until he retrieved the deck and interface and logged in again.

"A bomb!" he shouted, this time in Japanese, and the crowd scattered. The shopkeeper nodded his head vigorously, but Taro wasn't so sure.

"Felt just like an earthquake. Must have been some special trick. You think our Holo friends have found us?" he asked, and as he said that Joshua noticed a black sedan pulling away from the opposite curb and as the electric window rose in the back seat he caught a glimpse of the crazy man from the plane, a maniacal grin plastered on his demented face.

"Him!" Josh shouted, but it was too late, the car pulled around the corner and was gone. Josh stood dumbfounded for a minute, then turned to Taro. "Well, you're out now," he said, and Taro grinned.

"I guess I am. Let's go get some sushi. I've been livin' on junk food so long raw fish might kill me, but it'll be worth it." They raced off just as the disorienting sirens of the Japanese Police Force approached the shattered building.

CHAPTER 11

THE RED TIDE TURNS

The sushi bar was as long as a railroad car but half as wide. Customers had to turn sideways to reach the back stools, all of which faced a narrow counter. Behind the counter, bald head wrapped in a banzai headband, blade flashing and hands moving rapidly, the sushi chef expertly filleted another blowfish, carefully removing the poison sac that could waste half of Tokyo. Josh and Taro were well into a feast. Bottles of beer and ceramic jars of sake littered the board in front of them and the ledge was piling up with empty plates of *futomake*, puffy pillow-like stuffed *tofu inari*, and other delicacies. Joshua was totally blitzed from jet-lag and alcohol, the first he'd had since his training regimen had begun with Bryan many weeks ago. It felt good to let go, be free. He ignored the not so subtle stares of the other restaurant patrons and stood tipsily. He'd rigged the deck so he didn't need the briefcase anymore by strapping

157

it to his midsection when he wasn't using keyboard mode; it wasn't as fancy as a SpanDeck cybersuit, but it worked, and he didn't have to be on the Net to use the translation mod, which made his life a lot simpler because he didn't have to keep track of where he was in the Net.

"We've taken a lot of hits, Taro-san. What say we give some back?"

"How?"

"I got the license number of the car that creep took off in when he shook your building down. Can you help me break into the data bank of the Japanese DMV?"

Taro responded with a gleeful "Hai!" and they celebrated with another round of sake. Later on Joshua paid for two tubelike berths in a travelers' hotel and the two of them slept off their drunken bash. The next morning they fortified themselves with hot tea and doughy rolls, and took the laptop cyberdeck to the park to begin their payback.

Taro was still unable to face the computer screen but Joshua could relay data elements to him as he encountered them. Together they bluffed and hacked their way into the registry of motor vehicles, and found an address in a posh section of greater Tokyo far from the crowded maze of streets and alleys where Taro used to live. The young hacker was still in shock over not having a rabbit hole to dive into; he didn't know what was going to happen to him next. Joshua had become his only hope, just as Fred had been for Joshua. When Joshua suggested they pay a visit to the house, Taro could only nod his head and follow along. Josh was even able to map his own subway route by means of the Net's guidance system. They switched trains twice and ended up in Yokohama, with low hills affording views of the Tokyo Bay below, in contrast to the flat sprawl that comprised most of the rest of the city. Near the train station they found a bicycle shop and rented bikes they planned to use for a quick and unobtrusive getaway.

The houses in this part of Yokohama were done in the old style, with shake roofs, exposed outer beams in brown against whitewashed walls, and pretty curving arches like miniature temples, though of course they also came with the most modern conveniences and security systems. This was a gated, walled community, entrance was allowed only through a guard checkpoint, but Joshua and Taro weren't planning to enter by the front gate. They pedaled around to the back, where the brick wall ran along a stream that was intended as a natural moat to further deter unwanted intruders. As they scaled the fence, Josh was pleased to note that although Taro might be more naturally gifted as an athlete, Joshua was able to hold his own because of his training with Bryan Lee while Taro was cooped up in his basement dwelling for so many months. Josh was first over the wall, and began scanning for security sensors. He disabled three by temporarily setting them to look like they were still on but were actually inactive. After that they were able to cross the lawn between two houses and out onto the street. A quick check of the numbers painted on the curb told them they were two houses off from the home where the sedan was registered. Truth to tell, Joshua didn't have much of a plan for what he was going to do when he found the crazy man. It might have been better to have thought it out before he got himself in so deep, but here they were. An inspiration came to him as they trotted down the sidewalk trying to look like they fit in among the early morning joggers and delivery men making the rounds of this secure redoubt of Tokyo wealth.

"Taro, you ring the bell. When the Westerner answers, say this in English: 'Life is magical!' "

"Urife izu magicar," Taro repeated.

"Close enough. Then walk away. If he follows you I'll take his picture, that'll bug the hell out of him, then we'll split. That might give us enough to go on when we go checking for who the frack this creep is, and it'll be our first real evidence against the Holo Men."

"Urife izu magicar. Urife izu magicar," Taro chanted over and over, practicing his line, then boldly strode up to the front door and rang the doorbell. About that time their plan began to fall apart. Instead of the American who had hounded Joshua and shaken down Taro's building, Taro was confronted by a sumo-sized bodyguard wearing a dark suit and shades, the suit bulging in various places with muscles, belly, and probable weapons and bulletproof vest. Taro smiled and for lack of anything better to do repeated the phrase Joshua had taught him. A short, violent confrontation ensued. The sumo grunted and unfolded his arms to crush Taro, then suddenly he was lying on the ground, groaning in pain, and Taro was retreating toward Josh and waving his arms in the universal sign of "let's get out of here." It happened so fast Joshua couldn't even tell if it was a punch or a kick. The enraged bodyguard staggered to his feet, but true to his training didn't leave his post; instead he set off an alarm that could be heard all over the neighborhood. Joshua had time to take one quick photo of the security man before he and Taro dashed for the backyard where the sensors were disabled, not that it mattered now since warnings were blaring all around them, sirens, buzzers, whooping and earsplitting noises as if the whole neighborhood had gone off. As they cut between the houses they could see the first security car round the corner at the end of the block.

They hopped the wall at the same point where they'd entered, but their bicycles were gone! This wouldn't have been a surprise in Night City, where anything left unobserved for more than a few seconds is subject to theft by any number of people, but in the polite, ordered society of Japan, and especially in this wealthy neighborhood, they expected to find them undisturbed. Taro was incensed, but there was nothing for it except to sprint away toward the city and the train station.

"Won't they chase us out here?" Joshua asked as they ran.

"Nah, those guys are only into protecting their domain, they could give frack what happens outside their walls. Keep runnin', though, just in case."

"Don't worry." Those days when Bryan had made him run for no reason were paying off big time now for Joshua. He spotted a culvert and pointed to Taro, who shook his head and kept them on the road.

"We don't want to call attention to ourselves," said Taro. "Just make like we're out for our morning jog, like all those Corporates back there. It's going to cost you a couple hundred bucks to pay the bike rental place," Taro moaned.

"What the frack, man, it's Fred's money, and I don't even ask where he gets it. Don't worry."

As they neared town they saw squads of JDF troops marching in close order, crisscrossing the narrow streets of the bayside community below them. Taro turned around and headed back up into the hills, not toward the gated neighborhood but to a park with a seaside temple perched on a bluff, a fishermen's shrine with a wooden torii facing the uncertain sea.

"Damn, all we did was ring the doorbell, I can't believe they called out the troops," said Taro. "The Holo Men must have friends in high places."

They stood on the small hill overlooking Tokyo Bay, where the ships of many nations sailed in and out loaded

with the commerce of the Pacific Rim. Japan had re-
asserted itself as the prime power of the region, and with
that had come an increase in trade. Many container ships
were too big to bring into the harbor and remained at sea
while smaller vessels ferried goods back and forth to these
ocean-going behemoths. It was not uncommon to spot the
occasional wooden junk from mainland China with its
gaff-rigged sail, shallow keel, deep rudder, high poop,
overhanging stem, and prominent prow, plying the water-
way romantically among its boxy, metal-hulled cousins.

"Submarines always look so sinister," said Joshua.

"There aren't any submarines in Tokyo Bay, they're not
allowed," said Taro, then he too saw the conning tower of
the sub breaking the water slowly in a stately and undeni-
ably ominous progression across the mouth of the harbor at
Yokosuka. "Really, they've been banned since, I don't
know, all the way back to the time when Japan was a country without a navy, after the Second World War. I wonder
whose it is? It's especially crazy if that's one that carries nuclear warheads. Shit, the demonstrators'll be out in force.
We oughta be careful or we'll get stuck out here and we
won't be able to get back to the other side of the city—"

"What do you mean?"

"They shut down the subways, it's a typical demonstration tactic."

"We could always find a hotel on this side of the city,
couldn't we?" said Joshua, but he noticed that his friend
wasn't paying any attention, instead he was scanning the
horizon.

"There's something funny going on, Josh. Don't you
feel it?"

"What?"

"Usually about now those freeways should be jammed
up with automobiles heading into the city. It's rushawa,

Japanese for rush hour, but the highways are nearly empty. And have you noticed, we're in the flight path for planes taking off or landing from Haneda Airport, and there are none. Get the deck out, Joshua. Try to log on."

"Okay." Joshua complied. He cranked up the deck, but nothing happened. After three attempts he gave up and stared at Taro.

"They've done it. They've shut down the Net." Joshua couldn't help himself—an exclamation of admiration escaped from his mouth. No matter how much he hated the Holo Men for everything they'd done to him, Sally, Joey Jet, Taro, and many other people, he had to admire their technical wizardry and their audacity. They'd made good on their threat to bring down the worldwide web, even after the governments of the United States, Japan, the European Alliance, and the Pacific Rim Consortium had assured their nervous populace that it was impossible.

They raced down the hillside and into the nearest neighborhood, a quaint district of shops and restaurants. Even here, far from downtown Tokyo, the streets seemed strangely quiet this morning, with the exception of the occasional military patrol. Passersby were jittery and apprehensive. Taro bought a paper with a one-character headline that took up half the front page, and they took seats in an outdoor café and ordered tea and pastry.

"What does it say, Taro-san?" Josh asked after the waiter brought them their order.

"CHAOS!"

"No wonder. No stock exchange. No international trading, no communications, no bank transactions, no baseball scores, anything and everything that's tied into the Net is wiped.

"Have they made any demands?"

"No." Taro scanned farther down the page, and reported

in cryptic sentences to Joshua as he read. "No one seems to know how they've done it. They haven't blown up any of the Long Distance Links, and they haven't taken over Sysops. Apparently they're jamming the usable frequencies with some sort of micro-scrambler. The Net itself isn't actually down, it's simply unusable. You know what that means?"

"Yeah, they're on it, doing who knows what. They're probably all billionaires a hundred times over by now, transferring funds and what not."

"They say they'll bring it back up tonight at six o'clock, and there'll be another message from K-M. Japan's declared martial law, that's why we saw the sub in Tokyo Harbor. The Defense Forces are patrolling the streets to supplement the Police, and if they ever found out who we were we'd be in trouble."

"But that's backward, Taro. We're the ones who know who's doing this."

"Can we prove it? What do you think would happen if we told that lieutenant over there"—Taro nodded toward a blank-faced officer staring unsubtly at them, because Joshua was a gaijin and therefore suspect even if he did nothing—"that we could take him to a house where people were involved in this?"

"He'd give us a medal?" Joshua joked.

"Yeah, right and he'd pin it on our bare skin. This martial law thing is serious, choomba. In Japan we have long memories of the cruelty of our own police force when the imperial fascists were in power. We don't give them much authority, and we tend not to rely on them when we need help. If soldiers are in the street the government itself must feel threatened."

"They need the Net to operate."

"Of course they do. Japan depends on the Net more than

the dis-United States even, because everything is trade and money here, we don't have the natural resources or the land for agriculture. Our prime export is information, and if we can't transmit it on the Net, we're fracked."

"So why were you a rebel hacker instead of participating in the system?" Josh asked.

"K-M is right, in some ways. The whole thing is out of balance, you have to be an Arasaka airhead to have any real say in what goes over the Net. It's like, I believe in his ideas but not in how he's going about it."

"Don't say that too loud, Taro. Here comes Mr. Personality with the stripes." The stone-visaged lieutenant was approaching them where they sat.

"Your passport, please," he said in perfect English. Joshua produced the faked-up papers Fred had provided him. The lieutenant examined them for a long time, then handed them back.

"Your business in Yokohama?"

"Tourist," said Joshua. Taro was silent, he was trying to make himself invisible. He didn't have papers. Fortunately the lieutenant was only interested in foreigners. As Joshua answered his questions, he saw that the lieutenant wasn't cipher-faced at all, he was actually handsome, in a different way than Taro, more square-jawed, pug-nosed, and muscular, but with sensitive eyes that seemed almost pained in the effort it took to maintain his pose as a hard-nosed cop. Joshua wanted to ask him about music or art, he thought he might receive some interesting reply, but instead he stuck to his own role as stupid gaijin tourist and the two of them had an empty conversation. At last, satisfied that Joshua was a harmless idiot, the officer left them to their cha and sweets.

"That was a close one," Taro whispered. "If he'd asked me for my papers we'd've been done for. He could've done it too, that's a power of martial law, it says so right here in the paper."

"Don't you have a national identity card or a passport?"

"No."

"Fred'll fix you up with a new ID, Taro-san. It's time for you to see the big wide world."

"Oh, listen to you, world traveler. I bet this is the first time you've been overseas."

Joshua had to admit that it was. And what a visit he was having—one day in Japan and he'd already survived a man-made localized earthquake and been chased by security thugs.

In this picturesque old fishing village tucked into the folds of the great shipping port of Yokohama, one could almost forget that the world had evolved into a punked-up, information-glutted, crude yet immensely powerful engine. The odor of drying fish was everywhere, gulls were circling dizzily in the sky looking for scraps as their ancestors had for hundreds of years, everything was suggestive of great, ancient peace, from the cobblestone-paved alleys to the wizened old women mending nets along the shore and the scruffy wooden boats with their faded paint and *wakame*-covered hulls. The presence of the helmeted, visored, black-booted troops was a jarring note in this charming scene. Japan was like an exquisite timepiece that had slowed down, lost time, and no longer served the high purpose for which it was designed. Everywhere one looked the effects of the Net shutdown were evident. The Tokyo stock exchange limped along with standard phone and fax transmissions, but its data was minutes out of date, a critical gap in the up-to-the-second world of securities trading. The powerful Arasaka Corporation was attempting to rig up an independent Net, but the scrambler placed on the system by the Holo Men was interfering with all packet switching by any group that tried to use the LDLs. Humanity had become dependent on the Net to a degree no one realized until it was taken away. Even in the karaoke bars, the singers could no longer upload the latest hits off the Net, so the thrill was gone, baby, of being the first to the mike with the newest songs.

People wore stunned expressions like after an earthquake, but the visible damage was where Net-driven electronic billboards had gone blank, and on the screens in the offices and coffeehouses and even in the Zen temples where monks had been transcribing Buddha's Sanskrit words onto Net files, anywhere where anyone would usually be logging on, chipping in, jacking up, there was a void. Like dust settling after a temblor, the fallout from the Net collapse was sifting and drifting over the Land of the Rising Sun. Police sirens could be heard crisscrossing the city, and the trains were still running on time as always, but mostly empty, as the mass of office workers, the information harvesters, sorters, and gleaners, were staying home and waiting to hear from K-M at six o'clock. The breakdown had occurred at 3:30 A.M. Tokyo time. K-M had promised to bring it back up after his address on all Net screens and vidscreens.

"We've got to get back to Tokyo," said Taro. "It's all happening down there."

Taro and Josh decided to watch their former leader's speech at a site in Ueno Park where a wall-sized holovid screen was being erected by Kyodai Corp in a bizarre promotional stunt for their new holovid technology. Up to now, holovids had been limited to a screen approximately the size of an old-fashioned movie theater screen. A breakthrough in holography imaging allowed Kyodai Corp to project 3D images over a gigantic area, creating a tableau effect that promised to be stupendous, but why had they

chosen this impromptu and unlikely event to demo their
wares? A few pretty boy/pretty girl Media types hung
around with microphones at the ready to interview any
celebrities that might attend the glitzy presentation, but
most of the crowd consisted of glum-looking workers.

As he watched the audience gather for the speech,
Joshua thought about the last holovid he'd seen, a docu-
mentary on a particular kind of frog that lived in the di-
minishing rain forests of Brazil. It was a tree frog. Every
morning after the sun came up, it would jump from the leaf
where it rested during the night and plummet to the
ground, sometimes as far as a hundred feet. The spongy
mulch-covered forest floor broke its fall. It would forage
all day for insects and grubs, then, just before dusk when
the night predators would be coming out to hunt but birds
were retreating to their roosts, the frog would make the laborious climb back up to its leafy home. Ordinary workers
were like that, Joshua thought, trapped between predators
above and below, flinging themselves into their daily work
day after day, to avoid being eaten, especially in Japan,
where loyalty to one's company was still a lifelong com-
mitment. This was the system Taro had opted out of, at his
own risk. Now here they were, among an audience of
sararimen, the salary men whose monotonous life Taro
had dreaded and resisted, and yet both he and Taro felt
only sympathy right now for the way in which the Holo
Men had disrupted their routine. All around them were
men in dark blue suits with anxious looks on their faces.
Was K-M going to make them an endangered species like
the tree frog? Would they have jobs tomorrow? Their
repetitive existences were in jeopardy. What would they do
with themselves? Would their wives have to go to work in
fish canneries to support them? They squatted uneasily on
the lawn in Ueno as if it were cherry blossom festival, but

there were no blankets, no families, no mochi on a stick or boiled corn vendors, no cans of beer, and, most of all, no delicate snow of pink and white petals to attract them, only the burnt brown hard grass of the park. Exactly at six o'clock, the holovid glowed to life, as K-M had promised. Once again the backdrop was the Oval Office at the White House, with its bust of Lincoln, its Jeffersonian desk, all the familiar props of power and security in place. The camera wandered around the empty room, and in Ueno Park there were gasps of delight at the clarity and detail of the immense holographic image that had none of the ghostly see-through properties of smaller, less sophisticated holovid imaging. Then K-M strode into frame, forty feet tall, a giant come to ravage Tokyo. Screams and shrieks pierced the sultry air of Ueno Park. K-M loomed above his audience, who shielded their faces with their arms as if he were going to spit fire monster-like, but instead he extended his arms in greeting and said "Good Evening!" in three hundred and fifty six languages simultaneously. The *sararimen* uncovered their eyes, bowed, and returned his greeting. There was some shuffling as the crowd settled into place to listen to the words of the gargantua before them.

How K-M played with them. A maestro, an impresario, he had changed his tactics for this performance. Instead of appearing as the ghoulish inside-out man, now he came on the screen as the personification of a kindly elder whose grandchildren were frightened; he comforted and soothed them. Immediately he allayed their fears.

"Many of you didn't work today. Consider that my treat, an impromptu day off. I wish you could've enjoyed it more, but no doubt many of you were worried about your future. Have no fear. From this day forward, we will not disrupt the Net, unless of course we don't receive the cooperation we expect from the governments of the world. It's your side we're are taking, you, the businessman in Bismarck, the stockholder in Stockholm, the office worker in Ueno—"

Here the audience murmured its surprise and pleasure at being singled out, they could not have known as Joshua and Taro found out later that everyone listening heard some local reference that might have applied to them, an ingenious feat of simulcast.

"—because we want you to be happy, and powerful, not the mere tool of your bosses but a participant in shaping your own future. Yes, from this day forward you'll be the masters of your own destinies. The universal vote, long possible technically but denied to you by those who would keep you weak, will be instituted at once. The whole world will be a town meeting place."

The water stirred in the reflecting pool in front of the National Museum. If Mothra herself had risen from the still pond, fluttering hugely to wreak havoc on Tokyo, the residents would not have been more stunned than they already were. Only Joshua and Taro knew that it was all a lie, that K-M had no intention of creating a techno-democracy, that he was using the political theme to cover his crimes, a time-honored technique practiced by many before him.

"They will say," K-M continued, "that we're criminals, that we're stealing, but how can we steal what should be ours already? Tonight's message is this: Take back your voice, which has been denied you. Speak out, tell them you want a FreeNet, accessible by all, void of commercial corruption. Reject their suasions, decide for yourselves who should be the masters, you or them."

In America K-M's speech elicited cheers from tavern sitters, factory workers, even some among the oppressed office class, but in Japan his words were met with a bewildered silence. The people of this island willingly gave themselves up to their leaders, for the common good. K-M could have his words translated into Japanese, but he couldn't change their feeling, their fundamental meaning. If he was really hoping, somewhere in the depths of his megalomaniacal mind, that there would be a revolutionary uprising against the current masters of the Net, he would be disappointed in Japan, and much of the Orient, where the concept of submission to the greater wisdom of others was not only proper, but sacred and revered. No, he would only win them over if he convinced them that he, not their present leaders, was the one worthy of obeisance, and this he would not do. Perhaps sensing that this part of the speech was meeting less than enthusiastic response, K-M pressed on.

"For now, return to your jobs, your usage of the Net. Negotiations will begin between our Society and the ruling powers. Keep ever in mind that we have your best interests at heart."

K-M ended with a short prayer in the appropriate format for each culture he addressed. The Japanese audience heard a Shinto benediction and then a Buddhist mantra. As Josh and Taro watched, the audience bowed once again in unison and let out an audible sigh as the holo image faded into the autumn evening. The crowd began to disperse, but Taro nodded to Joshua to follow him and circled around to where the Kyodai technicians, with typical Nipponese efficiency, had already begun to dismantle the holovid equipment. Armed guards prevented them from getting too close, ostensibly to protect Corporate secrets about the new technology. Joshua surreptitiously chipped in and ran a quick check on the Kyodai Corporation. The company was recognized for its efficient communications devices, and equally well known for its cyber-enhanced private militia, its paranoid security routines, and the rigorous background checks it ran on prospective employees. No one worked for Kyodai unless they had passed a series of interviews with no less that fourteen HR dudes, each one a trained psychologist and master manipulator. The deck Fred had given him was equipped with a Peeping Tom microphone, but as soon as Joshua activated it an alarm went off on the largest piece of nearby machinery.

"Possible intruder! Possible intruder!" the machine repeated over and over like the "pull up pull up!" crash warning in an airplane cockpit. Two uniformed private cops rushed at them with attack dogs on leashes, but it was too risky for the policemen to let their dogs loose, there were still too many stragglers in the park, the canine corps might chew up a couple of innocent bystanders by mistake. The two young rebs fled and tried to meld into the dispersing crowd, while behind them the Kyodai police closed ranks, pushed the crowd back, and used their own bodies to shield the equipment from further inspection.

"Aren't you going to try out your karate skills on those Kyodai guys?" Taro joked as they ran.

"Sometimes the best offense is a good set of legs," Josh answered. They scrambled around a corner out of the park, and ducked into the nearest subway station. As soon as Josh caught his breath, he told Taro, "I think there's some connection between Kyodai and the Holo Men. I mean, if they wanted to show off the holovid, they'd film a jet-cycle race or a rocket trip to the orbiting space station. Why would they spend all this money to cover a talking head?"

"Because they're crazy," said Taro, but he too thought it might be worthwhile, if dangerous, to investigate the Kyodai-Society connection. "I've been into their DB, when I used to run," he said wistfully.

"You'll run again," said Josh. "You just gotta build up

your body and mind, you've been underground too long. The virus attacks weakness, that's what I found out. Come on, what would you do to build yourself up again? What did you do before you were Runnin' all the time?"

"Dance."

"Dance? That's not much exercise."

"It is the way I do it."

"Alright, let's take the night off. Go dancin'. K-M can wait. He's not gonna make another move right away."

"Okay. 'Cept," Taro paused, "I don't have any clothes for it. You gotta be stylin' to get into these places. Speaking of which, you wouldn't win any points either—" Taro said, gazing pointedly at Josh's American caz' look, blue jeans, a plain shirt, and sneakers.

"So let's run up Fred's card in some cool shop, dude. He won't care."

"Hey! *Cho mabu-dachi.*"

"What'd you say? Those last two words didn't translate."

"I said, super, best friend!" They hopped on the next Ginza Line train from Uenohirokoji, rode to the end at Shibuya, and changed to the JNR on up to Harajuku, where Taro knew a place that sold the kind of clothes he wanted to buy. The store was a dazzling chrome palace with mirrors everywhere. Japanese schoolgirls in skintight minis giggled and pointed as Taro and Joshua entered. The threads for sale were in the modern Kabuki style. Ordinary school uniforms were adapted with buttons and studs to look like some kind of armor. The pants were baggy and the collars turned up high. Some of the clothes had elements of the *aragoto* fierce young-man costume from the theater. They picked out some outrageous-looking duds and headed for the dressing-room to try them on.

As they separated to change, Taro whispered to Joshua,

"Listen, choomba, I don't want you to take this wrong, but they don't like gaijin where we're going, so I thought if you wore a mask and hide the deck under your outfit like you've been doing you might get away with pretending to be Japanese for a night."

"Why not?"

It turned out Taro was doing more than trying on clothes. When he exited the dressing room area, his face was painted *kuma-dori* style with the angry, ready to explode expression of an *aragoto*. Joshua picked up a mask that represented one of the fierce solitary *ronin*, the unattached mercenaries of feudal Japan. With his face covered and his body draped in a red laced *maru do yoroi* armor, Joshua looked very much like a Japanese, except that Taro had to tell him to open his *koshi* more when he walked, to approximate the proper swagger of a warrior.

By now it was the middle of the evening, and Josh thought they'd be going to the club next, but it turned out the place didn't even open its doors until midnight, and nobody chill arrived before two A.M. Instead they drifted on up to Shinjuku and found a yakitori where they munched on strips of grilled beef and drank beers to pass the time. Joshua felt self-conscious in his mask and outlandish clothes, but Taro was enjoying himself; Fred's credit cards were letting him live it up in a way he hadn't been able to for months, since he lost his own access to other people's money on the Net.

"This Fred dude, he's a legend, right?" Taro asked.

Joshua had to reel in his mind to answer Taro; he'd been watching the cast of characters that strayed in and out of the yakitori. Everybody seemed to have a deal going down. Money was changing hands constantly, not for the food and drink but under the table, surreptitiously.

"Yeah, he's one of the originators of the Net. But don't

think he's out-of-date. Even though he's old, he's kept up with the changes. This deck he gave me is state of the art."

"So I see."

"Taro-san, what's with all the yen goin' back and forth?"

"This is a *yakuza*-run bar. They do the business here and exchange the goods later at warehouses or from the trunks of their cars."

"Is it safe for us to be here?" Joshua asked in all seriousness, but Taro only laughed.

"Sure. The *yakuza* like to see youngsters coming down here to party, it gives them an excuse to wear their fancy suits and bright make-up and show off their *mom-mom*."

"Mom-mom?"

"Tattoos. Look at that one, but don't stare." Taro pointed discreetly at a bodybuilder type down the bar who was wearing a scrappy T-shirt that exposed a chesty mermaid in blue ink running along his left shoulder. The fishy maiden was fondling an Arasaka Minami 10 submachine gun. "See, these *chimpira*, these low-level *yakuza*, they like us better than the *pampee*, the common people, the non-Edgerunners, because we make them seem almost normal. 'Course we're all *katagi* to them, anybody who's not *eda*, from some branch of *yakuza*, is from the *Shaba*, the ordinary world."

This world was anything but ordinary. The clientele in the yakitori was constantly changing as business deals were transacted quickly and sealed with a shout of "*Kanpai!*" and a tumbler of sake. Occasionally it appeared a dispute over price or quality of the unseen goods would escalate into a brawl, but the yakitori chef behind the counter would ring a bell, shout loudly, and wave his cleaver, effectively ending all quarrels. Joshua noticed that his little finger was missing down to the first knuckle, and

176 HOLO MEN

he wondered aloud if it had mistakenly ended up on someone's plate.

"That's the sign for *yakuza*, *baka*! Look around, you'll
see a lot of nine-and-a-half-fingered dudes. But nobody's
going to smash up this place, the yakitori man pays plenty
of *kasuri* to see that he's protected. Come on, it's time to
party!"

Then it was back on the JNR train (Joshua was forming
an amazed admiration for the perpetual motion machine
that was the Japanese subway system, far more efficient
than anything in the good old dysfunctional USA) and
down and around to near Okachimachi near Ueno again,
where the nightclub was hidden in a basement beneath a
row of tourist stalls, and the only way to enter was from the
subway station.

At first the club seemed like some kind of weird retro-
disco to Joshua. It even had a mirrored ball with lasers firing off the spinning globe to create random patterns of
icicle lights. The dancers too looked like they were stuck
somewhere in the fantasy past, and Joshua flashed back on
the first young people he'd met in Japan, the scooter-riders
on their under-powered machines. But as the music grew
more frenetic and the dancers convulsed wildly and
stripped off layers of clothing, Joshua saw that they
weren't really doing a techno-disco number, they were beyond that and into a uniquely Japanese form of expression,
part punk, part Kabuki theater, where the basic emotions,
always hidden in day to day life in Japan, were laid bare.
Ordinarily bashful high school girls turned into *kawaii* sex
kittens and bunnies. Studious, reserved boys became strutting rockers and bullyish gangers. Androgyny was popular
as sex roles were broken down, reversed, and altered. It
was like seeing the exposed subconscious of the Japanese
soul, a logical extension of the Friday night spectacle of

the *sararimen* drunk and vomiting on those punctual trains. Taro warned Joshua in a low voice not to remove his mask for any reason, then dashed off to greet old friends and jump into the gyrating mix of dancers. Joshua hung back for a few minutes, then he was approached by a sexy young girl in a skintight mini with a see-through teddy top, who rubbed her groin up against his thighs and said, "Whattsamatta, *aragoto*? No like to dance?"

"Sure I do." Josh was so stunned he forgot to use the translator chip.

"Oh, your English is so good," the girl ooohed in Japanese, and this time Josh switched over to the chip mode and answered, "I'm studying, but not tonight," and grabbed her hand and lit out for the dance floor before he had to answer any more questions. There was no alcohol being served, and no drugs that Josh could see, it was just the freedom to dance to be themselves or somebody else that was making everybody so high. He whirled around, moving his body easily, and watching his partner shake her little thing like a pro. Part of the ritual was dancers bashing into each other in a Nipponese variation of the old punk slam dance mosh pit action, so Josh had to be careful not to let his mask get knocked off. His pickup noticed this after a while and wanted to tug off his protective, but he wouldn't let her.

"Ooooh, Mr. Mysterious," she teased him. "Maybe you're a bad man, *yakuza* gangster type. Maybe I shouldn't be dancing with you."

"Your little self is bad enough, baby," said Joshua, hoping the translator chip had the latest Japanese slang expressions uploaded, and apparently it did, because she shrugged and hauled him back out on the floor for another round of the violent lurching and lunging that passed for dancing in this club.

Joshua was feeling happy that he could party with the

Japanese, be accepted in a culture that was so uninviting of outsiders, when the music stopped and while Joshua was in a distracted state between songs suddenly he was shoved to the floor and pounced on by three other dancers, who ripped off his mask and stood him up again, shouting, "Gaijin, dirty gaijin. Come kick the foreigner!"

A crowd gathered around as Joshua struggled to free himself. He felt like he could have busted free, but he didn't know where Taro was, and he didn't want to leave without him, so he allowed himself to be dragged to the stage where the recorded music was coming from (there was no live band) and spun around to confront a roomful of furious faces, some painted, others with masks, a few contorted with real, unadorned anger.

"If you want to party go down to Rappongi where your kind hang out!" someone shouted.

"Yeah. Who invited you here, anyway?" a voice shouted.

Joshua recognized Taro's tone, and shouted back, "Nobody! I crashed on my own!"

But somebody else said, "That's a lie! I saw you come in with him!" Someone pointed at Taro, who was drawn into the scuffle, shoved forward, and made to stand next to Joshua.

"Listen to me!" Taro shouted. "This guy's okay. I ran with him on the Net, many times."

"In virtual he might pass, but here he's not one of us, not *Nihonmachi*. You know the rules, and you know the punishment for breakin' 'em," a self-appointed spokesperson for the group told him, a young tough in a modified school uniform blazoned with buttons and medallions. Taro seemed to know him.

"No, Shin-san, please, I've already been kicked off the Net—"

"So has everybody—"

"This is the only community I have left!"

"Then you shouldn't have risked losing it. Out!" Shin and his accomplices drove Joshua and Taro out the door. On the street, Taro wailed his woe. Already an outcast, now he was cast out even from the rebel camp. To a loner like Josh this was no big deal, but to a Japanese, even a radical like Taro, it was a devastating loss. He sat on the curb and almost allowed tears to come. Joshua sat beside him. It was five-thirty in the morning, the first faint red glows of the rising sun were scratching at the edge of the sky.

"In the old days, I would have committed seppuku," he said bitterly. "Now I don't even have that much courage."

"There's only one thing left for you," said Joshua. "You've got to come with me to America and help me nail K-M."

"Yeah, sure, we did such a good job yesterday at the crazy Westerner's house," Taro mocked him. "I'm sure getting rid of the leader will be no problem. Not one time have we had any success against them, on the Net or here. You're dreamin', choomba. We're just two punks, there's nothing we can do."

"Frack that!" said Josh, jumping up. "Where's that banzai spirit? Where's that *gambatte*, keep going, give your best, don't quit Japanese craziness, man? Where's that don't-give-a-frack punk?"

"Maybe he's buried in the rubble of the basement where I used to live," Taro answered.

"Then we better the frack dig him out, 'cause if you don't find some reason to live you might as well just crawl over there and die like a Plaguers' dog." Josh stood over Taro like a fighter over a woozy opponent, taunting him.

"Don't call me that," Taro warned him.

"Dog, worm, lazy ape, useless no good parasite."

"Lay off," Taro repeated.

"Why?" Josh asked. "What're you gonna do about it? Frackin' do-nothing toadshit."

Taro jumped up, his face red as the dawn sky. "I have to take that from my parents, but not from you, frackin' gai-jin *aho.*"

"*Aho?* What's that, like, short for asshole? You can't even speak—" he started to say, and that's when Taro went for him, and the two of them rolled around on the sidewalk, punching and kicking at each other, while Josh secretly smiled even as Taro landed a good one on his face, and they were still at it a minute or two later when they heard the approaching sirens of a JDF patrol car, somebody must've reported fighting in the street, and Taro broke off and yelled, "Run!"

Josh grabbed the cyberdeck lying forgotten on the ground and followed him down an alley behind the nightclub where they hopped a fence and zigzagged through back ways until the sound of the siren diminished and the two of them collapsed against a dumpster behind a restaurant, gasping for breath.

"You did that on purpose, *aho.*"

"That's asshole to you, buddy."

"Right." Taro began to laugh, and Josh joined him, and the two of them would've whooped it up but just then the nose of the JDF vehicle nudged silently around the corner and three helmeted cops charged down the alley at them. Josh and Taro leapt up and vaulted another fence and dodged down another back alley and just kept going and going until they were well away from the pursuing policemen.

"Is this what it's going to be like if I stick with you?" asked Taro when he caught his breath.

"Worse, in America. You'll be an illegal alien on a false passport and I'm already wanted by the cops, plus there's the Holo Men."

"Let's go get some breakfast, I'm hungry."

"Okay, but no more tea and fishy crackers. I'm homesick for some coffee and a plate of greasy fried eggs."

"Sure thing, choomba."

It wasn't hard to find a Western-style diner in Tokyo. Many Japanese had converted to the American diet of fast food and high fat, and even for those whose principal fare was still the national staple of fish and rice, hamburger joints and prime rib restaurants serving surf and turf were as popular in Japan as sushi bars were in the United States. Josh got his eggs over breakfast, a break from his training regimen of healthy food, while Taro, who still seemed a little out of sorts, settled for chocolate donuts and cola.

While they ate, Josh tapped into the Net, made a few inquiries using Flight Sim Fred's name, and quickly found a dummy travel agency that could generate phony passports, tickets, and papers and send them to any address in the world. Taro was soon established in a second identity as a Japanese tradesman named Atsushi Kono, purveyor of laminated holographic business card technology. Taro gave Josh a school photograph of Taro with glasses and a grungy tie on for a disguise to paste onto the passport. Japanese security was more stringent than U.S. Customs, but Josh was confidant that they would clear the ports of exit and entry without problems. Josh planned to have Taro stay with his *sensei* Bryan Lee once they arrived in America. Maybe Bryan could work the same transformative magic on Taro he'd performed on Josh.

Afterwards they found another of those travelers' hotels that consisted of clear plastic coffin-shaped enclosures stacked like firewood in a warehouse. After all, they hadn't slept all night. Taro'd never talked of going home to his parents like Josh had considered doing and though Josh had wanted to ask him about this, he'd never found an opening to discuss it. Since Taro was homeless it was only logical that they crash in these transients' accommodations also known as lovers' hotels, since they were used by office workers and others for afternoon assignations. Josh and Taro were too tired to think about girls. They each took a cylinder, which could be paid for by inserting yen like a vending machine, and crashed immediately.

As he slept, Joshua had a terrifying dream. He and Taro boarded the near-orbiter for the return trip to America. The launch was smooth; the vessel rose into the upper atmosphere effortlessly, but as it swung around to glide along its shallow flight path in space, a second, smaller ship appeared off the right wing and zoomed up close to the orbiter, so close that Joshua could see the pilot's face—it was the crazy Westerner from his trip over! He darted about in his single engine fighter like a mosquito nagging an animal, sometimes flying high above the orbiter, sometimes dangling just behind, so that Joshua had to crane his neck to see him. Joshua knew that his demented adversary was going to fire a missile and destroy the spaceship. It would be mass murder on a horrific scale. He woke with a lingering feeling of dismay that so many people would die on his account. Joshua crawled out of his tubular bedroom a little sore, either from thrashing against the narrow confines of the sleeping chamber or from yesterday's fight with Taro, he wasn't sure which. He hopped down from the honeycomblike chamber and stretched. The dream clung to his rising consciousness like a poisonous snail, sliming his mind with a sticky trail of regret. The bicycles! That's what was bothering him. No one would have stolen them, that's what Taro said. That could only mean one thing—the

Westerner must have known they were coming! The inescapable destination of that train of thought was that Flight Sim Fred's security wasn't as good as he said it was, that the Holo Men might be monitoring his movements on the Net. If that was true, then they knew about his plan to smuggle Taro into the States on a false passport.

Josh stood up and pounded on the door to the tube where Taro had slept, but he didn't answer, so Josh pried open the hatch, which should have been locked from the inside but wasn't, and found Taro gone. On the bed was a note in katakana, which Josh had to translate using a scanning device on the cyberdeck. It said: *"Gone to try out my new personality and get those bicycles back. Wait here!"* Only Josh couldn't sit and do nothing. If the Holo Men knew about Atsushi Kono, then Taro was probably walking into a trap. He hurriedly collected his things and left the hotel, but as soon as he hit the street he realized how much he had been depending on Taro's knowledge of Tokyo to move around, now he'd have to go back to the laborious method of consulting the deck for his location. And where would Taro have gone? At first Josh thought he'd head back out to Yokohama, to the house where the crazy westerner was holed up, but then, on a hunch, he looked up the location of Kyodai Corporation. It was only one stop away in Akihabara, the electronics district, famous for its junglelike profusion of neon signs, laser ads, and black market shops where one could buy anything from Hong Kong computer knockoffs to Braindance tapes and cyberware of all kinds. Josh was sure this is where Taro would go, it was their freshest clue, it's where he would have gone if he'd thought of it first. But what if he was wrong? What if he never found Taro again, he had no address this time to look him up, and he'd given Taro a new identity that would be impossible to track if for some reason they didn't hook up again. He took a deep breath and plunged into the stream of human traffic that was clogging the street, the Net was back up and it was *rushawa* again; Joshua descended into the subway station and found the JNR train that took him to Akihabara.

The electronics district was a sensory shock even within the kinesthetic madness of Tokyo. Everywhere Josh turned, lights were blinking, buzzers sounding, pachinko machines popping off, laser beams sweeping the air, it was like being inside a huge holovid game. Kyodai Corp's building was easy to find, it stood tall among the low shops and stalls that comprised most of the district. Kyodai had spurned the prestige of the downtown Tokyo skyscraper row where Arasaka, Kendachi, Fujiwara, and others had built their Corporate palaces, preferring instead to be located among the black market traders in Akihabara. The company was famous for hiring young *otakus* like Taro as its engineers and programmers and burning them out like pistons run too hot for too long inside a frenetic engine. Recently, however, it had acquired a veneer of sneering respectability as a major player in the emerging mega-holovid market. The Tokyo stock exchange had looked favorably upon its research and development effort and rewarded it with a huge increase in its stock price, even as the yen was taking a beating in the currency market. But none of this mattered to Joshua right now. He was face to face with his biggest challenge—how to find out whether Taro was here, and if so, was he dead or alive?

As he stood at the entrance, looking up at fifty stories of concrete, glass, and re-bar perched on springs to prevent catastrophic collapse in an earthquake, Josh found himself thinking of Bryan Lee's talks to him about the essence of karate. His *sensei* had quoted to him from Shigeru Egami's classic text *The Heart of Karate-Do*, in which Egami had in turn cited his teacher Master Funakoshi, who said: "There is no offense in karate." Now here he was, in the land where this martial art and spiritual practice originated, and somehow he had to find a way to confront the monolith, to challenge the faceless giant that was Kyodai, to force it to reveal its secrets, if it had any. "There is no offense in karate." Everything is defensive, reactive. The secret is to feel your opponent's intention so strongly that before he even moves toward you, you have reacted to his strike with a block. According to Egami-*sensei*, Master Funakoshi also said, "Don't go against nature." But what was natural on this neon electric street, this jumble of chaotic images and synthesized sounds?

And anyway, Josh was an American, and sometimes Americans used the frontal assault, the take-the-beaches-at-all-costs, frack-the-torpedoes, full-speed-ahead approach. Sometimes it worked, sometimes a lot of people got hurt. Josh marched into the lobby of Kyodai, where he was surrounded by sudden silence after the cacophony of the street. A lone young woman sat at a massive reception desk in the lobby's interior, in front of a bank of elevators. No security guards were visible, but Josh suspected there were video cameras trained on the spot where he stood. Everything about the foyer was hard, sleek, and shiny, from the mahogany and teak desk to the polished marble floor. The elevator doors resembled the entrances to bank vaults. Joshua and the secretary were the only two soft things in sight, and he wasn't sure about her—she might be a female ninja for all he knew.

In a loud voice he announced:

"K-M sent me."

"*Sumimasen*, one moment please," the secretary answered in a sweet high voice, but Josh could see by a slight shift in her weight that she'd pressed an alarm button with her foot. He waited for the appearance of armed guards, but none came. Instead, a bespectacled young man emerged from one of the elevators and walked toward him calmly. He was dressed in the typical dark blue suit, white shirt, and conservative tie of an aspiring young Japanese executive, but Josh noticed that the suit bulged at the shoulders, either from a concealed weapon or a bulletproof vest.

"May I help you, sir?" he asked.

"K-M sent me," Josh repeated.

"And who is K-M?" the man asked, slowly, as if he had all the time in the world to help this confused American, who must be lost or misinformed.

"The star of last night's show," said Josh. "Your business partner."

"I'm afraid you are mistaken." The young smoothie tried to shine Josh on with a denial, but Josh had noticed a slight blink in the otherwise impassive face at his mention of a business connection between K-M and Kyodai. His gross directness had worked! He persisted.

"I think not," said Josh. "Perhaps I'm not the first visitor you've had today," he struck out again wildly, and again scored, as his adversary was forced to take a step back in the face of this brutal verbal charge, so un-Japanese, so typically gaijin.

"You are associated with the young man who entered our offices this morning?" Josh nodded. "How unfortunate."

Now it was Josh's turn to be thrown off balance, but he was in too deep to quit now. "What's happened to him?" he asked, faltering slightly.

The Japanese had now recovered his *wa*, and was able to respond coolly, "We have him in custody. Perhaps you'd like to see him?"

"I would."

"Follow me."

Like it or not, his ploy had worked, he'd verified that Taro had come here, and that he was in the hands of Kyodai Security. One of the six elevator doors sprang open like an immense trap. His Japanese escort bowed and gestured for Joshua to enter—he could not refuse, he'd gone too far, he was in the jaws of the beast. The elevator ascended with stomach-sinking speed. Joshua's attendant stared straight ahead at the burnished metal of the doors. Joshua thought briefly of attacking him but there seemed no point to it, and when the lift stopped on the twenty-eighth floor and the doors slid open, he was glad he hadn't; three armed and uniformed security men greeted them, but as yet they made no move to take him into custody. He had to ride the bluff as long as possible. At this point he was handed over to another groomed and fastidiously dressed young Japanese who could have been the brother or cousin of the first, sans spectacles. Something in their square jaws and clear-eyed looks also reminded Joshua of Taro; a new class of handsome young men had taken over for the sallow, toothy, wrinkled generation that had preceded them. Judging by the deferential bow that number one offered number two, his new guardian was a significantly more important personage. He addressed Joshua in perfect English. Josh left the deck running but shut off the translator chip.

"Good morning. We are honored. Two visits in one day, both from young men claiming to be from a secret Society of which we know nothing. What do you suppose is the cause of this confusion?"

"Where's Taro?" Josh attempted to continue with his American bluster, but here on the twenty-eighth floor the act had worn thin.

"He is here. He is close. You will see him soon. Tell me,

why have you come to disturb our receptionist with your wild allegations?" A harder edge crept into number two's voice. If only this were a Net episode, a game, Josh'd bust through the ceiling-to-floor glass window and fly away. But it wasn't the Net world, it was the real world, and Josh was alone, a stranger in a strange land, surrounded by hostile foreigners.

"K-M sent me," Joshua repeated stubbornly. It was his only card, he had to play it.

"Let's suppose we know of whom you speak. Why did he send you?"

"To bring in the traitor," said Joshua in a moment of inspired lunacy.

"Ah, the one who came before you. So, you aren't together, then?"

"No. I've been chasing him all over Tokyo since I got here."

"That's not his story. Aren't you young to be a secret agent," number two mocked him.

"We are the future. If you know K-M, you know that. Look!" He pointed to his own 'trode holes where some slight swelling, though diminished, still remained as evidence of his special evolutionary status. Number two tried to hide his interest, but there was no mistaking his recognition of the vital sign of a young Holo Man. Josh pressed his advantage.

"Bring me the prisoner!" he commanded, as if he were number two's superior. Number two hesitated momentarily, but was not willing to risk being wrong. He nodded to one of the security men, who disappeared through a doorway and returned almost immediately with Taro, whose face was an ugly mass of contusions and bruises.

"This is how you think to get the truth from him?"

Joshua barked. "A man who's being beaten will say anything."

"Our methods have proved effective in the past," number two tried to defend himself, but Joshua continued to act as the arrogant holder of higher rank.

"I've been ordered to take the prisoner to America. Release him into my custody." This was it. If the bluff worked here, he was free! Taro kept his eyes down to avoid any hint of camaraderie between the two of them. Number two wavered. Joshua repeated his demand. "Escort me to the street. I want no interference by your ignorant security guards. Baka!" Number two could no longer tolerate being humiliated in front of his inferiors, he either had to stand up to this arrogant foreigner or acknowledge his authority, and number two was not willing to risk that Joshua wasn't who he said he was.

"Hai!" number two said curtly, but he bowed before Joshua and handed him a small key to the leg chains, but Joshua didn't fall for the bait, he pocketed the key and kept Taro locked up. The three of them descended silently in the elevator. A few more seconds and they would be out of the clutches of Kyodai!

The elevator doors opened but a large figure blocked their way out. It was the crazy Westerner from the near-orbiter! He was no longer wearing pajamas and grinning idiotically, but was transformed now into a stern-faced businessman in a suit every bit as austere as those of his Japanese counterparts.

"Very good. They said they had one, but here are both. Excellent."

Number two caught his mistake immediately, and went for Joshua, but Taro was quicker, and barrel-rolled into the Westerner to free up the passageway for Josh.

"Run!" Taro yelled, but Josh couldn't leave him. He

swung around and confronted number two, who'd staggered backward into the elevator as Taro launched himself into the Westerner. With surprising ease Joshua seized the man in a throat hold and held him back in the lift. The lobby secretary had fled, they were momentarily alone, but Joshua knew he had only a brief respite before others would arrive.

"No!" Taro screamed. "Get out!" but then he could say no more as the westerner was on him. Their fight was short, swift, and terrible to behold. Taro struggled wildly, but the chains on his legs prevented him from avoiding the blows that came savagely, relentlessly, until it was beyond fighting, deviating into cruelty and torture, all in a few seconds. Somehow his insane opponent managed to wrap the leg chains around Taro's neck. As Josh watched, he snapped the vertebrae with a sickening crunch. Taro fell to the floor, eyes rolling in his head, a pleading expression on his face, and though Joshua wanted desperately to help his companion, he knew he had to escape if the Holo Men were to be stopped. Don't think about it now, he told himself, trying to hold down the panic that was rising in his gorge. The Westerner turned his attention to Josh.

"You should've listened to your buddy, kid," he said.

"Stay away or I'll kill this one," Joshua threatened, and he tightened his clinch on number two's neck until the color began to drain from his face. Joshua tried not to look at Taro's fallen, lifeless body and sightless eyes.

"That's easy," said Joshua's nemesis. With a flick of his wrist he shot out a blade from a hidden cyberhand and gutted number two as neatly as filleting a fish. Number two slumped to the ground as uniformed security forces broke from the next elevator over and rushed toward Joshua, who pressed the CLOSE button and caught the Westerner by surprise. He shoved his cyberhand into the opening but

Joshua kicked it out as the door slammed shut. He pressed the button for the second floor and took his chances. The door opened on a roomful of office workers, some of whom shrieked in surprise and dismay. Joshua looked down and realized that he was covered in blood from number two. He raced past the startled employees and found the emergency staircase down, but as soon as he opened the door an alarm was triggered, so he ducked back into the office, just in time to see the Westerner emerging from another elevator. It was desperation time! *Pretend it's the Net!* Joshua told himself, and took a running charge at the nearest window. He crashed through and tumbled into space surrounded by flying shards of glass. Everything seemed to happen in slow motion after that, as his training in rolling at Bryan Lee's dojo took over and he reacted instinctively. The fall was only one story. Rather than landing on his feet and risking a broken leg or ankle, Joshua tucked into a forward roll and tumbled along the ground, scattering amazed pedestrians. In an instant he was up and running! Behind him he could hear the angry shouting of the Westerner, who refused to make the leap from the shattered window.

Two blocks away Joshua threw his bloody shirt into a trash bin and ducked into a shop and bought a souvenir T-shirt that proclaimed in English: PRINCE OF FRUIT COUNTRY CHALLENGES ALL DIFFICULTIES. With the cyberdeck once again concealed on his midsection, Joshua found a subway entrance and randomly took several trains, switching direction repeatedly and completely losing his direction, until he emerged in a part of Tokyo he'd never seen. He entered a park with rolling green lawns dotted by shrines and sculpture, and oblivious to the stares of passersby, he threw himself on the grass and wept for Taro, his lost comrade who'd sacrificed himself so that Joshua could live.

CHAPTER 12

RUMPELSTILTSKIN RASPUTIN

Joshua decided to risk a Net call to Flight Sim Fred, but it was the AI Breughel who answered the phone.

"Tolstoi residence," he responded smartly, as an artificial intelligence should.

"Breughel, it's me, Josh, the kid who stayed with you in the RV a few weeks ago." It seemed like another lifetime, and himself another person, when he thought about those days.

"A pleasure, young man. What can I do for you?"

"Is Fred around?"

"Sorry, he's not. Can I help you?" the AI offered again. Joshua broke down.

"Taro's dead," he sobbed. "And I'm stuck here in Japan because I don't know if it's safe to go to the airport."

Joshua gave Breughel a brief summary of his disastrous trip, the ride in the near orbiter with the weird American who had turned out to be an ally of Kyodai and the Holo Men, and Taro's valiant surrender of his own life to save Joshua.

"A true samurai, he died in the highest way possible. You have no need of regret," the philosophical AI offered, but it seemed little consolation to Joshua. "Where are you?"

"I don't know," Joshua admitted. "In a park some-where." He gazed around at the unfamiliar setting where everything was strange and different, the trees, the birds, the antique buildings with their upturned curving arches. "I hopped some trains to try to lose the guy who killed Taro. He's a big-time creep, Breughel. He's always laughing. He laughed when he broke Taro's neck——"

"Okay, partner, listen up. Now I know you have a sat-link locator on your Net deck. "

"Yeah, sure," Joshua said listlessly. "I used it before I hooked up with Taro."

"Turn it on again, find out where you are. That's the first step in getting you out of there."

"They've broken Fred's scrambling, I'm sure of it. They're probably monitoring this call."

"If that's true, then you need to move, but first, in three seconds switch to the following frequency——" Breughel read off some numbers that Josh memorized, then Josh flicked some switches on his deck. The replicated scene of the park where he lay was replaced by the smiling face of the long-dead Flemish painter in his studio, surrounded by half-finished images on canvas. Joshua knew where he was now——he was inside Breughel's artificial mind! For the first time since he'd seen Taro's death face, Joshua was able to muster a weary half smile. The AI had spared no detail in recreating the medieval work environment of his namesake. What purpose it served Joshua couldn't fathom, except that he was no longer broadcasting his location to anyone who might be monitoring his position.

"Now," Breughel said firmly, "leave the park and find a new place to hide until we can bring you in. You may have to change identities again."

"I don't have anywhere to go," Joshua said plaintively. "Taro was my only contact."

"Haven't you met anyone else in your travels?"

Joshua thought for a minute. "Well, there were these scooter kids who were nice to me, but I wouldn't know where to find them." As he spoke, Joshua stood up and began to walk out of the park toward the subway station. He loaded Flip Switch 2.0 so he could keep one eye on Breughel's studio while he maneuvered through the Japanese landscape.

"Try," said Breughel. "It'd be helpful to have someone there who could orient you, so to speak." The clever AI was making a joke, but Josh's spirits were still very low. Without Taro, he couldn't read any of the street signs or subway messages. By studying the map he was able to figure out that he'd ended up in the park of the Meiji Jingu shrine, only a single train stop from Shinjuku where he'd encountered the scooter gang. With half his mind occupied by the constant chatter of the helpful AI in his ear 'trode, Joshua boarded the JNR at Yoyogi and soon found himself back in the multilevel train station where he'd first arrived in the tumultuous city of Tokyo. As before, he ascended to the street and was again staggered by the thousands of black-haired people rushing purposefully to and fro. He couldn't be sure but he thought he'd managed to emerge at the same corner where he'd met the young female scooter-ist who'd given him a ride to Taro's house, but looking around he saw no one he recognized and felt a momentary panic at the overwhelming strangeness of it all.

Breughel must've been monitoring his pulse rate, because he immediately jumped in with a soothing word: "Buy yourself something to eat and sit tight. If they came around before, they will again, it's probably their regular routine." Joshua realized he hadn't eaten for many hours, so he took Breughel's suggestion and purchased a chewy ear of corn on a stick and munched away while waiting for some sign of the scooter gang. Sure enough, around three o'clock they came putt-putting by, about thirty of them, dressed as before in retro-greaser duds, a style so old it had lost its cultural context in America but was preserved here in Japan. Joshua waited until they parked their bikes all in a perfect line along the sidewalk, and doffed their helmets. He recognized the young cutie who had taken him to Taro's before, and approached her.

"Hello," he said in English. She smiled at him.

"Nice T-shirt," she said. "Are you enjoying your stay in Japan?" she asked him.

"Actually, no," said Joshua. He found it impossible to be polite, even though the situation, and the culture, demanded it. "Listen, I need a place to stay for one night. Can you help me?"

"What happened to your friend?" the girl asked him, reasonably enough.

"He's dead," said Joshua. The girl stepped away from Joshua, just slightly, but enough to signal her apprehension.

"Just a minute," she said, and she placed her helmet on the seat of her scooter and walked over to the leader of the gang, if one could call them that, they were so young and, to Joshua's way of thinking, so innocent. The two of them conferred for a minute, then both came back toward Joshua.

"You're in trouble," the youthful gang leader said to him.

"Yes."

"Why don't you go to the police?"

"I'm traveling under an assumed name," said Joshua. He figured he had nothing to hide from these people. If they turned him in they might be doing him a favor, at least the chase would be over. He was tired of feeling like a hunted animal.

"What's your scam?" the boy asked him, unrolling a cigarette pack from his shirtsleeve and lighting up. He offered one to Joshua, but Josh shook his head.

"No scam. My friend and I are fighting the Holo Men. We found out that Kyodai is involved, and they killed him for it."

"Ah so. Kyodai. Bad karma, no?" Joshua admired the boy's cool; he was unfazed by talk of intrigue and murder.

"Bad karma, yes. I've got to get back to the States, but I can't leave until tomorrow, when a new false passport is going to arrive for me."

"What are you, some kind of super secret agent?" the girl asked, her eyes wide open.

"I'm just a kid like you who got into something heavy," said Joshua truthfully.

"Okay. Come on," the leader said, just like that. The girl nodded for Joshua to take up her passenger helmet and off they went, not the whole pack but just the three of them on two scooters, racing through traffic again like two-wheeled kamikazes, disregarding lights, lanes, pedestrians, trucks, directionals, and everything else in a wild dash for somewhere. They ended up in a high-rise slum that reminded Joshua of pictures he'd seen of the South Bronx. Laundry was draped on every balcony of concrete boxes that rose twenty stories out of the unlandscaped dirt. Buildings were scattered across a half-mile square lot and placed at odd juxtaposing angles, as if they had been thrown there by a careless giant playing at blocks. Each of the drab monoliths was the same height, and each duplicated the next in design, every floor fronted by narrow balconies festooned with sheets and underwear. Burned out automobiles littered the spaces between the structures. Bulldozers and cranes off in the distance hinted at an expansion of this nightmarish colony. It was as far as Joshua could imagine from his naive conception of Japan as a land of cherry blossoms and bamboo.

"Home," the girl said simply as she pulled the scooter down into a cement underground parking garage that extended gloomily as far as Joshua could see underneath the complex. She ignored the elevator, long since broken, and took the stairs up to the ground level. Their companion had veered off into another section of the subterranean lot but met them at the entrance to one of the high-rises.

"The name's Akira," he said, and stuck out his hand, very un-Japanese-like, for Joshua to shake. "Come on up, we'll let you crash here until you figure out what to do."

"Thanks," said Joshua, who was still dazed by the wild ride through the streets. He was completely lost again, and would have to use the sat-link to figure out where he was, but right now it didn't seem to matter.

"If there's an earthquake, you won't thank us," the girl giggled. "These buildings are unreinforced, there's no rebar in them at all. They shake like jellyfish."

"How many flights up?" Joshua asked.

"Oh, you're lucky," said Akira. "Keiko lives on the fifth floor. My family is up on the eighteenth. I only come down once a day if possible." Joshua realized with a start that

Akira had switched to Japanese. His translation chip had kicked in smoothly.

He was wondering how these kids managed to afford their fancy scooters, when Akira, perhaps anticipating the question, told him, "We're the side of Japan you never see or hear about. We're the losers in the trade war, the ones who don't buy into our country's new imperialist ambitions. We like other people, other cultures. Why shouldn't we, look what our own has done to us." They started up the stairs but on the third-floor landing the girl Keiko suddenly went into a crouch and waved for Josh and Akira to freeze. Above them they could hear pounding feet, screams, and muffled popping sounds.

"Nomad raid!" she whispered, a look of real terror on her face.

"You have Nomads?" Joshua whispered back. He thought they were strictly a dis-United States phenomenon.

"These are Teamers," Akira explained as they backed down the stairs. "Stupid pu-taro who don't have jobs. They rip off other people's stuff. We gotta go protect the bikes, 'cause that's what they're really after. If they've been drinking smash we're okay, but if they're straight there could be trouble."

"Sounds like there's fighting already. Don't you want to go help whoever's up there getting killed?"

"What are you, a samurai? We look out for each other and ourselves, and that's all, *Keto*." Joshua knew he'd been called an insulting name, but the translator chip didn't port it over. Keiko seemed more concerned because the sounds of the struggle might have been coming from her floor, the fifth, but her fear wouldn't let her go forward. They slipped back down the stairs, but before they could enter the parking garage the Teamers were on them, a half-dozen young punks in foppish ankle-length purple high-sheen armor-jackets like outrageous bathrobes lined with slogans in kanji and English. Their hair was poufed up in an exaggerated version of the same U.S.-fifties look the scooter kids wore, but the comic book effect was more menacing even though these gangers were even younger than Josh and Akira. They surrounded the trio, waving knives and jabbing but not really ready to fight, Josh could see.

"Hey, gaijin, what're you doing out here? There's no tourist attractions here. Go back to downtown Tokyo. Look at the stupid face on him," one of the Teamers snorted to another. They assumed he couldn't understand him, which was dumb on their part since the translation chip was sticking out of his 'trode and a thin wire led underneath his shirt to the deck. Josh played dumb while he picked the leader from among the six Teamers.

"Fighting in lobbies. I already fought once in Kyodai's lobby today," Josh said to Akira in English.

"What'd he say? Kyodai? What's the gaijin braying about?" the leader of the Teamers demanded of Akira.

Joshua ignored him and addressed Akira again in English. "They didn't learn English like you?" he asked sharply.

"No. These punks dropped out in grade school. We waited until high school so we had a few years of foreign language classes."

"Don't let them know I'm chipped in," said Josh.

"Why?"

"You'll see."

"Gaijin! Frack you!" said the Teamer atama, using two of the few English words he knew. Joshua spun and spoke to him in English:

"You imbecile. Maggot head!" The Teamer didn't know what the words meant but he couldn't mistake their import.

He flashed a short knife, but it wasn't a Kendachi or anything dangerous, just a plain kitchen paring blade. Many times Bryan Lee had attacked Joshua with longer, sharper weapons. Joshua stepped in neatly and expertly pushed aside the thrust, snapping his open hand down on the Teamer's wrist, fracturing it. The Teamer grabbed at his broken joint and howled. The other five heitai backed off instead of attacking.

"Now listen up, you," Joshua shouted in Japanese, which had the effect he expected of thoroughly intimidating his audience. "I'm a fracking Runner, and I'm five times as bad as you, so I'll fight the five of you all at once if necessary. But I'm looking for help, not a brawl, so decide, now, whose side are you on? You"—he spoke to the Teamer —"what's your name?"

"Koji."

"Koji. You fracked up, Koji. You failed to anticipate my *gedan-barai* block. I can spit you out a prescription for some serious painkiller and I can send you to a nonregistered doctor, or I can beat up on you some more, it's up to you."

"What do you want?"

" 'What do you want, Joshua-san?' " Josh corrected him.

"What do you want, Joshu-san?' said Koji, unintentionally using the name of the famous Zen monk.

"I want you to tell me what happened upstairs. Did you hurt anyone?"

"No. The old lady had a gun."

"What old lady?"

"The old lady in C."

Keiko gasped. "That's my apartment. What did you do to my grandmother?" she yelled, stepping up to Koji, who remained bent over holding his injured wrist.

"Nothing. She shot at us."

"That was you screaming?" Joshua asked.

"Yes, Joshu-san."

Keiko and Akira laughed, but Joshua wasn't through with Koji.

"You were going to beat up an old lady and instead she drove you off with a gun?"

"Yes."

"Maybe I can't use you after all. Maybe I should let Keiko here kick you around the lobby."

"Use us for what, Joshu-san?"

"That's my business. I'm *socho* of your gang now. You're demoted to *fukucho*." Koji bowed instinctively. As much as they were rebels, the old ways died hard. "Are there more of your *ningen*?"

"Sometimes as many as twenty, Joshu-san."

"Okay, I want them all here tomorrow morning. No, not here. Akira, where could we meet where we wouldn't scare anybody?" Akira suggested a park near the complex.

"Okay, now"—Joshua fiddled with the deck and printed on a slip of paper—"go to this address, a doctor'll fix you up and dope you up and he won't turn you in to the police."

"Thank you, Joshu-san." Koji bowed again. Obviously he thought he was in the presence of a serious warrior. Josh wasn't about to disillusion him.

"Tomorrow we attack Kyodai Corporation. Bring all the weapons you have. And all your friends."

"Yes, Joshu-san."

"Now get out of here. And don't ever raid this area again."

Joshua, Akira, and Keiko watched as the Teamers retreated, surrounding their former leader, now reduced to vice-presidential status, to the spot where they'd left their motorcycles and fancily painted cars, for in truth they were nothing more than a bunch of junior high school student rich kids with too much money and time on their hands and a bad attitude. Beaten twice in one day, once by an elderly woman and again by a gaijin, they were properly abashed and would undoubtedly show up obediently the next morning to do Joshua's bidding. Akira turned to Joshua with a smile.

"So tell me, Joshu-san, does a dog have Buddha-nature or not?"

"Huh?" said Joshua.

" 'Mu.' That's what the first Joshu said. The well-known koan. A monk asked Joshu: 'Does a dog have Buddha-nature or not?' and Joshu answered: 'Mu!' "

"Meaning?"

"Literally meaning 'not,' but it's also an exclamation like 'hey' in English. The monk who asked the question achieved instant enlightenment when he heard the answer 'Mu!' "

"I hope the same thing happens to Koji. I want him and his Teamers to help me."

"They will. So will we."

"No, you've done enough, just putting me up here. I don't want you to get into trouble for me."

"Do you really think you can beat Kyodai?" Keiko asked.

"They won't be expecting me. All I want is information. We're going to hit their data center. While the Teamers are making trouble I'll download some Kyodai files, see what I can dig up on their connection to the Holo Men."

"It's a good plan if it works," Akira said skeptically.

"As soon as I have what I need I'm going to Tokyo Aerospace Port and get out of here."

"The only way you're going to get out of Japan is to

visit a Chiba Ripperdoc, go for a change of face," said Akira matter-of-factly.

"You could turn Japanese," the girl tittered. Joshua blanched at the thought of going under the knife. He was happy as who he was, what he looked like, especially now, after his transformation from Josh the teenage Net hacker to Joshua the man. No doubt about it, he'd grown up in a hurry the last few weeks and months. He wasn't ready for a whole new look, though.

"I'll take my chances with phony papers, maybe a disguise," he said.

"Oh, Keiko can help you there, she's fab with makeup and wigs, for the nightclub thing you know," Akira boasted. Keiko gave Joshua a reassuring smile.

"I tried that once already, it got me into big trouble," said Josh. He briefly described his misadventure with mask and costume in the underground Okachimachi dance spot.

"Oh, but those were just toys from off the shelf at a shop. I do custom, detail work." Keiko had switched to Japanese again but the translator chip put their expressions into idiomatic English.

"Tell you what," said Joshua, "tomorrow you can practice up on me for the Kyodai raid. If it works there it ought to work at the airport." Suddenly Joshua felt faint. All he'd eaten all day was the one ear of corn on the streets of Shinjuku. All of a sudden he was crying, it was all catching up to him, Taro's death, the fighting, the overwhelming strangeness of everything— He was breaking down. The Japanese averted their heads to avoid embarrassing him by observing his public display of emotion, but Keiko took his hand and led him up the stairs. Keiko's grandmother greeted them with a Dai Lung Cybermag 15, a lightweight but deadly pistol. Guns were a rarity in Japan, so it was even more surprising to see one in the hands of an old person. As soon as she saw Keiko she tucked the gun into her obi and bowed a greeting, but she eyed Joshua suspiciously, especially on account of his red face, until Keiko introduced him as the person who had driven off the Teamers.

"No," she cackled, "that was me."

"You're right, Grandmama, he only finished the job."

"What's the matter with him? He looks horrible. His red face is like a devil's."

"Grandmama, he can understand Japanese," Keiko said softly.

"A thousand pardons," she said and bowed again.

"Grandmama, this is Joshu. Joshu, this is my *sobo* Tomoko."

"I'm honored to meet you, *obasan*."

"He speaks prettily enough," said Tomoko, momentarily forgetting again that Joshua could understand her. The grandmother busied herself with preparations for a meal while Keiko led Joshua to a small but deep square bathtub where he could soak away the bruises and bumps that covered his body. In the privacy of the tub Joshua again allowed himself the luxury of tears. If he'd never come to Japan Taro would still be living in his underground hideaway. But what kind of a life was that? He'd been little more than a prisoner, kept alive by the kindness of the storekeeper above. The Holo Men had had their way with Taro, Sally, Josh, and many others. Josh emerged from the bath solemn but refreshed. Keiko had left out a robe and house slippers for him to wear while she washed his clothes. Josh came to the kitchen table where Tomoko had set out a bowl of fresh green *edamame* soy beans and a glass of beer for her guest. The apartment was not as impoverished as one might have imagined from the drab exterior. Though it was cluttered and small by Western standards, it had a few amenities, some miniaturized versions of Western items like a tiny refrigerator and a shrunken stacked washer/dryer where Josh's clothes whirred and sloshed. Soon the three of them sat down to a simple but delicious meal of grilled fish and rice and pickled cabbage salad, supplanted by glasses of beer and hot tea. Tomoko asked him about his family, and Josh had to confess that he hadn't seen them for many months.

"You're as bad as Keiko," Tomoko declared, though her feeling was strangely without judgment, more like a statement of fact. "She has parents too, you know, but she chooses to live here with her grandmother instead. This generation—" Tomoko shook her gray head.

After dinner Josh excused himself and withdrew to the room that had been set aside for him (he realized this was Keiko's room from the posters of Japanese rock stars and motor-scooter ads that lined the walls, and the clothes and feminine accoutrements strewn everywhere). He rang up Breughel. One of the advantages of having an AI for a friend is that you could call them day or night, it didn't matter, they never slept.

"Breughel. I took your advice. I found the scooter people and they've put me up for the night. I'm in a real Japanese family's apartment." As he said this Josh realized how much better he felt to be off the street and in a private home. For the past seventy-two hours he'd been roaming the streets of Tokyo, with brief respites in those cylindrical beds of the travelers' hostels.

"Well done, boyo. What's next?"

"I've recruited some help. Tomorrow I'm going back to Kyodai—"

"Is that wise?"

"I've got to. If I can get into their data files I might be able to come up with some hard evidence."

"What about using the deck?" Breughel suggested affably. After all, he was a machine, so it always made more sense to him to take a systems approach. He hadn't yet been able to comprehend why humans found violence so attractive, since it usually resulted in their own destruction. He considered this lack of understanding one of his great failings and he spent a considerable amount of processing time pondering this paradox.

"This is stuff they'd never upload onto the Net, private files. I saw the data center. It's accessible, if I can sneak in there while the Teamers are messing with Security."

"Where shall I send your new passport and tickets?"

"There's a service desk at the Aerospace Center, why not send them there. If I don't make it to the airport I won't be needing them anyway."

"Alright. Good luck. Call me when you've completed your mission."

"If I can, I will, you can bet on it."

"I never bet," said the AI matter-of-factly. It was true. Though Breughel could figure the odds on the next value up in a six-deck pack of twenty-one cards faster than any human being, he refused to participate in games of chance. He was a killer chess player, though.

When Joshua arrived at the appointed park the next morning for his rendezvous with the Teamer gang, he was happy he'd insisted that Akira and Keiko not accompany him. More than fifty Teamers had shown up, attracted by the idea of mass violence on a hated Corps icon. They might have warmed on Akira and Keiko, despite the presence of their new leader, for Joshua had attained overnight star status as a tight-wired Runner. Koji gave him a "see what I done for you, boss" smile as he waved hello, but Joshua maintained a stern face.

"Okay, Koji, here's how it works. I don't want a parade through the streets, that'll attract too much attention. Tell everybody when to be there, then have them disperse, take different routes. When I give the signal, converge on the Kyodai lobby and do something crazy, smoke bombs or gas attack or something that'll cause a panic. Then keep the police occupied as long as possible, but no shooting, got it? I don't want any innocent bystanders injured."

"Sure thing, Joshu-san."

"Okay."

"Boss, they want you to speak to them," said Koji with a wave toward the group of duded-up young punks with their lavishly decorated bikes and cars and painted faces. Some of them didn't look old enough to be driving—they probably weren't. Today Joshua fit right in with them, because Keiko had painted his face to resemble a young daimyo of the Nambokucho era, and had stayed up half the night sewing a lavish costume to match, a winged purple battle haramaki that fit right in with the Teamers' lavender look. Joshua had thought perhaps he'd go disguised as a Japanese businessman, but he soon saw the wisdom of her ways. He would attract attention, of course, but not in the normal manner. As soon as his mission was completed he could shuck the costume, wipe off the makeup, and resume his normal appearance, whereas if he tried to dress in a suit he'd be hard-pressed to make a quick change and his features couldn't be altered so drastically.

"What do they want me to say to them?"

"Well, hey, they don't mind breaking heads, but they want to know what it's all about."

"Tell them, never mind, I'll tell them," and Josh jumped up onto the hood of Koji's car, on which was painted the image of a half-naked Oriental beauty with a bunny's ears and whiskers.

"Teamers. You frackin' young punks should be in school right now. What's wrong with you?" Joshua began, to get their attention, then he smiled broadly and whipped around on the car hood in a complicated kata of jumps, kicks, and punches he'd been studying just before he left Bryan Lee's dojo. They watched him with fascination, muttering to each other that this gaijin was different, he was crazy is what he was. When he finished his short demonstration, Joshua looked out over the expectant faces and smiled again.

"Japan," he said. "Land of the Rising Sun and the sinking yen. Teamers and Arasaka CorpZoners. Two-thousand-year-old Buddhist temples and Chiba cyber-stores. Castles and shrines and pachinko parlors. Yessir, you've got it all here in Nihon/Nippon. The Net too. Real big in Japan. Only thing is, there are some people who want to take it over. You saw him on holovid the other night? Creepy character, neh? Well, I've got news for you. Kyodai Corp is fronting his act. Yeah, they're partners, him and some of Kyodai's top execs. What do you think of that?"

"We don't care," someone shouted at him. This wasn't an ordinary group of Japanese, who would have listened politely if Joshua'd told them he was going to eat their babies. These were Teamers, frackin' junior high school dropouts with no reverence for anything.

"Fine, I don't care if you don't care. Yesterday they killed my best friend. Today they might kill me. All I want from you is the chance to get inside the building. Can you stir up enough trouble in front of Kyodai to give me that opening?"

"Shit. Is that all you wanted?" the same voice yelled. "Come on, brothers, let's show the gaijin what trouble is."

A dozen bikes rumbled and roared to life. Koji ran around explaining Joshua's plan for them to take different paths and arrive about the same time. The Teamers didn't like that so well, they were young bully cowards who were used to the safety of the pack, but they agreed to travel in smaller groups as long as they could mass at the site.

Half an hour later they blasted into the lobby of Kyodai Corporation, smashing windows and scattering dark-suited Kyodai execs like roaches runnin' from a bug bomb. Joshua slipped in through a freight elevator at the back and exited on the second floor. The window he'd jumped through had been replaced by a piece of plywood but he figured he could knock that out easy enough. This time the building security had rung an evacuation alarm. The floor was momentarily empty. His plan was working! He locked the door behind him, shoved a desk in front of it, and ran to the glass enclosed inner "clean" room where the main-frame computer sat unattended, and plugged his deck into a spare port. In two minutes of frantic on-line database searching he was able to locate a few key references to Holo Men and download those files. He was about to conduct a next-level-down search for references to K-M when the sound of police sirens distracted him. At any instant he expected either the scary Westerner, Kyodai security, or the JDF cops to break into the floor, but he couldn't resist one more pass through the data. At the last second he discovered a file named, he thought, New Revolution (he was reading all this in Japanese filtered through the translator chip), but he had time for only half a glance at it before the first blows of a fire axe on the door told him it was time to split. He saved what he had, disconnected from the main-frame, and ran to the windows and kicked out the plywood plug, but down below the street was a battle scene, with hundreds of riot-equipped JDF pressing forward to arrest the remnants of the Teamers action. They were being opposed by hundreds of others, Joshua had no idea where they came from, who weren't Teamers but looked like ordinary students who'd joined in the fray just because they didn't like the police. No way could he jump into that maelstrom. A beanbag stun pellet from a JDF shotgun slammed into the frame next to his head, and he saw soldiers pointing up toward him and a detachment rushing around toward the back entrance. If he wasn't careful he'd be fracked! Quickly he threw off the costume, wiped his face with the contents of a small vial of cream Keiko had given him, straightened his clothing so that he looked presentable, then bolted down the stairs and ran straight up to the nearest policeman he could find at the fringe of the fighting.

"Help me!" he shouted. "I'm an American. I had a business appointment with Kyodai this morning and I got trapped in the men's room!" he shouted in English to the cop, who didn't understand any of it, but assumed immediately that Joshua was an innocent gaijin who'd been caught in the wrong place. He shepherded Joshua away from the scene, Joshua practically clinging to him as if in terror, and summoned a cab for the apparently distraught American.

Joshua heard the policeman tell the cabbie, "Take this idiot to his hotel," so when the cabbie showed him a list of hotel names in English, Joshua pointed to one in obvious relief and nodded, and away they went.

The hotel was run by an American chain. As soon as he walked into its spacious, garishly decorated lobby, with its overstuffed sofas, faux-gilt mirrors, plastic chandeliers, Joshua felt like he had been magically transported to his homeland. The desk clerk and bellboys were blond young Americans. Sappy pop music played over the hotel's PA system. The signs and poster ads (for other places in the world where, the slogan boasted, you could feel like you'd never left home) were larger, more colorful, and in English. With some of his last money, Joshua rented a room and was handed a plastic mag strip room key. No questions were asked about his lack of luggage. Everything had been done to ease the traveler's trepidation about being in a foreign country. From the room service menu (Western-style breakfasts, hamburgers, and milkshakes) to the oversize shower head and the array of complimentary bottled shampoos, lotions, and mouthwash, everything screamed America, land of excess. Josh threw off his clothes, took a long hot shower, wrapped himself in the terry-cloth robe provided for his comfort, and plopped himself down on the bed, not a futon but a full king-sized box spring and mattress. He flipped on the television and found a news broadcast of the riot at Kyodai Corporation. He didn't see himself, but did catch a glimpse of Koji leading a band of Teamers hurling Molotov-cocktails at a line of JDF men with riot shields hoisted above their heads like Roman soldiers of old in the classic turtle defense. He ordered a feast from room service, and while he was waiting for it to be delivered he set himself up to play back the captured files as he ate.

The information he'd seized was fragmentary, but left no doubt that K-M had struck a deal with Kyodai to help him distribute his message in exchange for protection from attack by the Holo Men. It was simple old-fashioned strong-arm extortion. One of the graphics buried in the data was a downloaded half-tone photo of the Westerner with the caption: "Rumpelstiltskin Rasputin," obviously a code name. Josh made a note to ask Breughel about that one. There was enough evidence to throw suspicion on Kyodai, but not to convict it. If anything, the tapes showed that a bunch of fearful Kyodai execs had been cowed into cooperating by this Rumpel Rasputin character, an argument that was sure to win sympathy in the xenophobic Japanese courts. One other surprising find: once again there was mention of Phil O'Dendron's Nursery. The contents of the bankrupted conservatory had been moved to K-M's secret Night City location. By now Joshua could only shake his head in disgust that the Holo Men could be so venal. Here was the proof. Everything that had happened to Sally and Phil was directly traceable to the whims of the demented individual who led them. Josh switched over to the com port and rang up Breughel.

"Hey! It's me, Josh. I did it!"

"Yes, I've been monitoring the news broadcasts. The Kyodai student riots as they're calling them made the international bulletin. I didn't see anything about a young American, so I assumed you were successful."

Joshua was a little annoyed that Breughel had already seen tapes of the fighting, but he put his disappointment aside and shifted to the matter at hand.

"I got some stuff on the Kyodai-Holo Men connection. It looks like the company was forced into a deal."

"Of course."

AIs can be so supercilious, Joshua thought.

A bell rang, and a voice from the other side of the door announced, "Room Service."

"Hold on, Breughel, my food's here." Joshua tossed a sheet over the deck and went to the door. As a precaution he looked through the peephole but saw only another blond-haired young California type with a cart full of covered dishes. Still, he opened the door cautiously and asked the young man to wait outside while he wheeled the cart in himself. He paid and gave the busboy a generous tip, then double-locked the door after he left.

"Breughel, how can I test if the food's doped?' he asked.

"You'd need a litmus kit and some chemicals. Or a royal taster." Once again the AI displayed an all too human sense of humor. "Examine the liquid carefully. A powdery residue at the bottom of the glass can be a tip-off."

"I ordered a milkshake, Breughel."

"Ahhh." Once again the AI was trying to emote without using words, but the sound he made when he tried this was bizarre and inhuman. Joshua wondered where he'd got the idea. "Check for bitterness then, that's my only advice. Most poisons and drugs are extremely astringent."

Joshua decided the food must be safe, he'd only been here a half an hour and he'd arrived anonymously. He couldn't live his whole life under this paranoid cloud. He devoured a hamburger, French fries, milkshake, and apple pie with vanilla ice cream, essence of Americana in food form, while talking with Breughel between mouthfuls.

"What about your adversary, Taro's killer?"

Joshua's throat constricted as he tried to swallow a mouthful of food. An image of Taro's death face jumped into his mind unbidden. "I found a picture of him, labeled 'Rumpelstiltskin Rasputin.' "

"Hmmm." The AI was trying to make a human expression, but his hum came out more like static on the line than a vocalized utterance. "Two bad guys, one from fairy tales, the other the mad monk of Czarist Russia. Rasputin was an intimate of the czar. He was said to hold a hypnotic power over the imperial family, partly for his ability to stanch the bleeding of the hemophiliac czarevich Alexei, son of Nicholas the Second. A group of nobles murdered him. That doesn't fit in with the names taken by other Holo Men, homages to political rebels of the past."

"This guy might not fit in anywhere, Breughel," said

Josh. "He's a one-off, a real wacko. It doesn't surprise me."

"Why Rumpelstiltskin, though? And what's his real name?"

"Uh, Breughel, that's why I'm calling you."

"Oh, sorry, just thinking out loud. Of course, I'll run some analyses on it right away. I can parallel process—anything else you want to talk about while you're waiting?"

"Yeah, I want to talk about how I'm going to get through Japanese customs without getting busted."

"You have a new identity."

"Yes, and a makeup artist who's a real pro, but is that going to be enough? I suspect this Rumpel character'll have the Japanese cops looking for me, even though he's the one they ought to be after—"

"Here it is—oh sorry, go on—" Breughel interrupted Joshua, then caught himself.

"No, what've you got?" Joshua asked.

"His real name's Darnell Denard, he's a career criminal like K-M, they were in Pelican Bay together, that's where they met. He's also been confined to mental institutions several times—"

"He should be in one now, I'm telling you—" Joshua interjected.

"He's got a genius IQ, studied computer science in Japan before the first Corps war, speaks several languages fluently without the use of translator chips, fifth degree black belt in Shotokai karate—"

"Huh? No way. A karate man would have too much respect for codes of honor to do what this freak did to Taro."

"I'm just reading from the bio, Joshua. Maybe he used to be more righteous and lost it in the madhouse, who knows?"

"Go on."

"There's not much more. Had a high-level position with an American holo-disc drive engineering firm early in his career, was busted for tampering with data, and dropped out of Corp America permanently. The rest is a rap sheet, convictions for fraud, embezzlement, murder—"

"Who'd he kill?" Josh asked, turning over in his bed and sitting up.

"A couple of people. First an executive from the holo-disc firm, then, in prison, another criminal who crossed him on a deal for smuggling 'dorphs into the yard. He got an extra twenty-five for that one, but escaped the next year and hasn't been back in since."

"He's got to be on the Interpol database, so how can he travel on the near-orbiter?" Joshua asked.

"The same way you do, young man, on a false passport, with a disguise, and probably new fingerprints and a voice alteration as well. Only DNA would tell you he's actually Darnell Denard, and even that can be faked, if you're good."

"His passport doesn't say Rumpelstiltskin Rasputin, does it?"

"No, that's just what he likes to call himself. We ought to try to find out why, though, that would give us a clue to his thinking."

"Breughel, you just don't get it, do you? Are there any insane AIs?" Joshua asked.

"Only defective ones," said Breughel. "Isn't that what insanity is in humans?"

"No. A man or woman can be completely schizophrenic and still function in this world, even be a genius like this Denard. That's the scary part. When a machine fails it lets you know about it. When a human being goes off the deep end sometimes you don't know until the carnage starts."

"It's already started, hasn't it?"

"Now you're getting the idea. It doesn't matter why he's Rumpel Rasputin, we've just got to stop him."

"Not in Japan." Breughel's succinct analysis of the situation was correct.

"I agree. I need allies, and they're all in Night City. Somehow we've got to lure him, and K-M, out into the open in Night City. In Japan I'm too vulnerable and on the Net I'm too weak."

"Come on back, then."

"I'm leaving for the Aerospace Port in the morning." Joshua shut down the Net connection, and crashed.

The next morning he rode the train to Chiba, picked up his passport and tickets, and passed through Customs and onto the near-space plane without incident, though at any minute he expected to be seized by one of the many policemen who patrolled the terminal, or led off to a side room for questioning by the plainclothes undercover units that lurked in the hallways. Something wasn't right, he'd come to expect violence, trouble, it was all too easy.

He'd spent his whole time in Japan in the city of Tokyo, venturing only as far as Yokohama. He'd seen nothing of the mountains, the villages, the storied waterfalls and legendary hot springs of the countryside. He'd seen few temples and shrines. Someday, he knew, he'd have to come back to this amazing land and venture farther into the Land of the Rising Sun. Perhaps he'd look up Taro's family and tell them what a wonderful son they'd had. Looking down from the near orbiter as it lifted off he saw rice paddies and planted fields side by side with densely populated urban areas in that strange admixture of ancient and modern that defined Japan. He found himself wondering if Taro's body had been sent to his family, and if they'd had him cremated in the Shinto/Buddhist fashion. His friend had not even

lived for twenty years. He'd died a warrior's death, as
Breughel had said, but in vain, unless Joshua could make
his sacrifice meaningful. Yet if Joshua had learned one important lesson from his trip, it was that even in losing Taro
retained his dignity, that was one of the secrets of Japanese
culture, that unlike Americans, to whom winning was
everything, the only thing, the Japanese sought meaning
even in defeat. Frack! Frackfrackfrack! Joshua would beat
the Holo Men or die trying. He settled into his seat and
urged the orbiter on with his will, as the giant rocket ship
briefly reached suborbital velocity of many thousands of
miles an hour and it still wasn't fast enough for Joshua,
whose rendezvous with destiny lay ahead in the streets of
Night City.

CHAPTER 13

LOS LIEDER
(THE MEXICAN-GERMAN
MARKETING SONG)

Josh's troubles began when he tried to clear Customs in Night City. A sophisticated weapons detector picked up the plastic on the deck (these devices no longer checked merely for metal, as plastic and ceramic handguns had become so popular) and set off an alarm. Joshua tried to explain why he was wearing the deck taped to his abdomen instead of in a carrying case, but the resemblance of the makeshift mount to the way a drug-smuggling mule or a terrorist would conceal their stuff was unmistakable. He was pulled from the line and brought into a tiny room where two federal agents crowded around him. One shoved questions down his throat while the other tinkered with the deck, trying to pry it open.

"Hey! That's not how you do it, you'll break it," Josh protested. "Let me show you." He reached for the deck but one of the two knocked his hand down.

"Back off, kid, or we'll just take a sledgehammer to your unit and be done with it. It says here your name's Ralph Dunbar. Is that right?"

It took Josh a second to remember that this was his new alias, he'd only had it since he arrived at the Aerospace Port in Chiba a few hours ago. He nodded dumbly and decided to let them feed him information since he had no idea what he was supposed to be doing in Japan, he hadn't paid attention.

"Well, Ralph, tell me why an aluminum siding salesman would be in Tokyo, where none of the houses have that kind of construction."

Was this one of Breughel's sick jokes? The agent wasn't making it up, but obviously Breughel had. Josh tap-danced around the question.

"I was there as a tourist."

"Oh. You one of those Japano-philes? You know they're killing us with a trade imbalance. They're gonna try to take over the world again, those Pacific Rimmers, and when they do it they'll be using the money they got from Nip-lovers like you." The second agent spewed out this racial invective like verbal vomit and Josh caught some of it full in the face. The two of them were crew cut, ruddy-faced, in terrific shape, but mindless as slugs. Joshua decided the best tactic was to play dumb. He didn't think they were emissaries of the Holo Men. He tried to keep his story as simple as possible, because he didn't know what other surprises might be on the papers Breughel had prepared for him.

"I just like the food and the beer and the ladies, you

know," Joshua said, trying to sound like a sappy young salesman with a hard-on for Oriental women.

"You want sushi, go down to the Marina, they got plenty of them bars, and hookers too. This deck's kinda fancy for a tin man, ain't it?"

"My brother's a hacker, he bought it for me. Truth is, I hardly know how to use it, but when I lost the case I had to carry it in somehow——"

The first agent jumped on that one——"How'd you lose the case?"

"Oh, you know, I was in one of those love hotels and a lady walked off with it. She thought she had the whole deck but I'd taken it out as a precaution."

Both of the men laughed. "Ripped off by a whore, huh? Serves you right," the uglier, cruder agent sneered. His face resembled a roast hog snout, all that was missing was an apple stuffed in his maw. These weirdoes weren't seen too much in Night City itself, they were representatives of the fragmented government of the dis-United States, nobody took them seriously, except at the ports of entry where they could still lord it over poor travelers like Joshua with this bluster and swagger shit they were laying on him now. The other one was trying to play the good cop role but he too was nothing but a thug who would have worn jackboots and a brown shirt if he thought he could get away with it. The two of them probably spent their weekends drinking shitty beer and taking target practice in some cow pasture in Iowa, dreaming of the day when the government would run things again.

"We're going to confiscate the machine for further study," the agent in charge told him. Joshua realized he couldn't leave this room without the deck——he didn't know if Fred would give him another one, and more importantly, all the information he'd pulled from the Kyodai mainframe on the Holo Men was loaded on the holo-drive.

"Can I make one phone call?" Joshua requested.

"Use the pay phone on the street. We're not arresting you, we just want to make sure there's nothing contraband in your rig."

"Yeah, or any secret files or anything," the other moron chipped in, like he'd really know what to look for.

"I just want to call my brother. He can explain things. Please."

"Ah let him," said the good cop.

"You watch him. I'll dial the number, what is it?" Joshua gave him the number for Breughel. The AI'd gotten him into this mess, let's see him get him out.

"Good morning," the AI came on the line with his usual agreeable cool.

"Ted," said Joshua as quickly and cryptically as possible. "It's your brother Ralph. I'm at the airport and the government is going to detain the cyberdeck you gave me." Joshua could almost hear the data bits shucking and jiving in Breughel's brain as he tried to parse this confusing information. Obviously he didn't have a brother, he was an AI, a product of lab tech engineering. Would he be able to lie? Joshua was going to find out.

"Ralph? Put the agent in charge on the line, please." Josh did as he was told.

"Perhaps my brother neglected to tell you who I am," Breughel began. The two agents rolled their eyes at each other cynically.

"So who are you, Mr. Big Shot?"

"Give him your earclip please, brother," Breughel instructed Joshua. "I need a private word with the agent."

Now Josh and the second agent watched as a fascinating dialogue took place, which consisted of the agent in charge nodding disinterestedly at first, then with increasing vigor and grunting assent every few seconds with intensifying servility, until his yaps became "yesses" and then "yes sirs" and his body language shifted from slouch to straight-backed attention. By the end of the conversation he was staring at Joshua with furious wide-eyed amazement.

"Give him the deck and let him go," he said to his partner.

The other agent, not privy to the exchange, objected. "We never got inside the deck. Suppose he's got—"

"For God's sake, do as I tell you," said the one who'd spoken with Breughel.

"What is he, the brother of the director, forcryinoutloud?"

"I'll tell you later. Good day, Mr. Dunbar." Joshua walked out of the room carrying the disputed deck with strips of adhesive tape dangling from it. He was curious to find out what Breughel had said to the man, but first he wanted to get as far from the airport as quickly as he could. He walked out of the terminal and hailed a cab.

"Take me to—" and then Joshua paused. Where should he go? Where was his home? Was it with Bryan Lee at the dojo? In the trailer with Breughel? He gave the cabbie Sally's address and slumped back in the seat. He must've fallen asleep because the next thing he remembered was the cabbie's foghorn voice cutting through his turbid brain—

"You sure this is the right address, kid?" Joshua sat up and looked around. It was the correct block, only there was nothing on it, every building on both sides of the street had been torn down, razed to the ground, pulverized into rubble. A blinking construction sign announced that this was the site of a new Superstore, a monstrous "everything at a discount and in bulk" outlet that turned neighborhoods into parking lots.

"Let me out here."

"Whatever you say, kid."

The cabbie pulled over at what used to be a corner grocery store. Now it was just a corner. The buildings in the next block seemed ashamed to be so exposed, their back sides in need of paint, their tattered yards and rickety porches once hidden away were now in full view. This was more of the Holo Men's work, a relentless persecution of the innocent that made Josh almost physically sick. Where could Sally have gone? She didn't have any money, she was an unemployed plant nursery worker, for God's sake. As he stood wondering what to do next, he noticed that one small far corner of the empty lot was green. A glimmer of hope raced through him. He set off at a trot toward the patch of life amid the ruins. Yes, it was a vegetable garden, orderly rows of new cabbages, tomato plants curling around poles stuck into the hard, crumbly earth, the frizzy heads of carrots and parsnips sticking up, it was not the greatest dirt for growing food but someone, and Joshua knew who, was raising a crop despite the poorness of the soil. A small sign proclaimed this to be a community garden and though Sally was nowhere to be seen, two small boys were scratching at the weeds between the rows with rakes.

When Josh sidled up to them, they raised those same implements as weapons and one of the urchins said, "Frack off, punk. This is the people's food. You can't have none less you work on the patch."

Joshua smiled. "I won't steal any food. Where's Sally?"

"Who?"

"The plant lady."

"You know her?"

"Uh-huh."

"Then you kin stay, but you gotta hoe. She'll be round later."

Josh admired the spunk of this little tyrant, who couldn't have been more than eight years old but was ready to boss around his elders because he'd been entrusted with the weighty responsibility of guarding the garden. Both of the kids were dirty from weeding and thin as cornstalks, but proud of their role. It was a hard life on the streets of Night City, and culture shock from the tidy, orderly environs of Tokyo where Josh had been just hours ago.

"Wanna see some cool moves?" Joshua asked, and without waiting for an answer he went into one of the katas Bryan had taught him. The boys, named Frankie and Billie, were duly impressed and nodded enthusiastically when Joshua offered to teach them, but the older one, Frankie still insisted that if Joshua was going to stay he had to work in the garden.

Josh was scraping at the obstinate earth several hours later when Sally arrived, bent under the weight of two sacks of fertilizer. She ignored Josh at first and tended to her two little helpers. She'd brought them each a treat, a bottle of juice and a cookie that they gulped down hastily. He saw one of the boys point to him from thirty yards off where he'd worked his way down a row of beans, but she didn't rush to greet him. He finished the line before he approached her. The two of them stood awkwardly in the emptiness, while the boys hovered nearby protectively.

"Hi, Sal."

"Hello."

"Still growing things, I see."

"I do what I can."

"Where do you live now?"

"Here."

"Here?! Where?"

"Right here. We bring out tents at night."

Joshua looked around. The rocky grounds were as bleak as Siberian tundra or the Rub Al Khali, the infamous "Empty Quarter," that stony desert in Saudi Arabia. His idle hacking in the Net had resulted in a life of hardship and deprivation on the streets of Night City for Sally. After the death of Taro, it was almost more than he could take. He sat down abruptly and rested his head on his arms. "My best friend's dead and you're living here. It's horrible." Sally crouched beside him and put a hand on his shoulder lovingly.

"No, you've got it wrong, Joshua. I'm happy here. I'm really helping these people. Some of them have never tasted fresh vegetables."

"But, where do you shower? How do you cook? It's so primitive."

"We make do. We cook over open flame and we wash ourselves at the fire hydrant over there." She pointed to a plug where right now a hose was connected and ran out into the field for irrigation. "I've got a key to the thing, look, see?" She dangled a large ratchet with a hexagonal claw end to it. Joshua thought he'd made himself strong at Bryan Lee's, but he saw that Sally was still stronger. "What happened to your friend?"

Joshua told Sally about his trip to Japan and everything that had happened there. As he recounted the story he realized that he had accomplished at least some of his purpose, if at a terrible cost. The information he had on the holodrive in the cyberdeck was incriminating, and the link between Kyodai and Darnell Denard a.k.a. Rumpelstiltskin Rasputin and thus to K-M was undeniable, but what difference did it make? The government had never been able to capture K-M, why should it be able to do so now, even if Joshua was able to prove that K-M, Denard, and the Holo Men, in league with a Japanese mega-Corp, were responsible for the threat to the Net? Joshua was still on his own, but at least he had bait that might lure K-M out of hiding and into a real world confrontation, where he would be a powerful enemy but not as elusive as his Net presence. But Joshua couldn't stay here, at the very least he needed a power source to recharge the batteries in the deck.

He mentioned this to Sally, who smiled wanly and said, "Oh, we tap into the generator that runs their sign. Until they begin construction, and nobody knows when that will be, we have everything a person could need: power, water, housing."

"How'd you get stuff growing so fast? I saw you only a few weeks ago, and the apartment was still here then."

"We didn't start from scratch, silly. Phil gave us plants. We just had our first harvest last week."

"You're amazing, girl." He was truly in awe of her. Then he remembered: "In a way I'm responsible for you being here. K-M was ripping off Phil for his orchids. He's the one who did all that vandalism and shut down the nursery."

"I want you to stay," she said. Either she'd finally seen how much he had changed, what a new person he was, or else she felt sorry for him that he'd lost his best friend. Joshua didn't care which, he was happy. It was the perfect hiding place, the Holo Men would never think to look for him here, because "here" wasn't really anywhere. He could prepare for his battle with K-M and help Sally at the same time. He learned that the two boys were brothers and orphans and that Sally had adopted them informally. His admiration for her grew stronger. Here she was, homeless herself, and yet she was taking in others, including him, and feeding the neighborhood. Later that night after the chores were finished and the tent erected, Joshua led the boys through tai kyaku-sho, the first karate kata, while Sally watched with amusement. Then he chipped in and called Breughel.

"Breughel, it's me, Josh."

"That would be my brother Ralph, yes?"

"Yes, 'Ted.' What did you tell that agent at the airport anyway? He was spooked."

"I told him I was highly connected in the Company. He seemed to believe me, especially after I gave him a few codes to convince him."

" 'The Company.' You mean CIA? I thought there was no more Central Intelligence Agency, since there's no central government anymore."

"Old spooks never die, they just become AIs," said Breughel mysteriously. "Ask Fred about it sometime."

"I will. Anyway, thanks for springing me. I'm with Sally, and I have some data I want to transmit to you."

"Go ahead, but be careful. The Net is never as secure as you think it is." Billie, the younger of the two brothers, had taken to Josh right away, and now he settled into Josh's lap where he sat cross-legged on a sleeping bag spread on the floor of the tent, which was lit by a weak and fluttering electric bulb.

"You're bein' awful peculiar, Breughel."

"Just cautious. How do you intend to fight this K-M character?"

"I'm going to use the stuff I'm sending you as a threat to bring him out. In the real world he won't be as squirrelly as on the Net."

"That's a good plan, but you'll need help. Do you have any tough guy friends?"

"No. Wait. Yeah. There's that ganger Raspis, I saved his butt once, he could help me, and my *sensei* Bryan, he's got good reason to fight K-M. They'll both make strong allies."

"Good. You'll need them. Don't forget, this K-M is a lifelong criminal. He isn't going to give in without a fight. Port over those files."

"Here they come." In seconds the files flew across space and landed in Breughel's brain. Billie snuggled closer to Josh. Sally watched the two of them from across the small space where she was dressing Frankie in his pajamas for bed. Suddenly they were a family. Joshua had the strange sensation that they were like primal humans, their tent a cave, their lantern a rude candle of sputtering animal fat, the flattened construction site a primordial plain full of unknown terrors: woolly mammoths, saber-toothed tigers, fierce barbarian tribes. Only the last was an approximate truth.

Breughel gave an AI's approximation of a whistle. "Nice work, Josh. This data would convict the whole lot of Holo Men."

"Yeah. In absentia. If the government could catch K-M they wouldn't need me."

"Yes, but this removes all doubts. I'll pass it along."

"To whom, Breughel?"

"The proper authorities. Never mind about that," said Breughel, awkwardly trying to change the subject, because obfuscation wasn't in the AI's repertoire. "Marshal your forces. The end is in sight."

CHAPTER 14

DOUBLE EAGLE EQUALS
ZERO ON A PAR THREE

K-M didn't need motivation to fight Joshua Victor. He hated everybody, the privileged, the young, those new boys with their swollen brains, gaining by evolutionary advantage what it had taken him years in a prison cell to achieve. When word arrived of Darnell Denard's failure to eliminate the young hacker, K-M, locked in his lair behind the double security doors, vowed to kill them both, kill them all, Denard for his bungling, Joshua for his treasonous rejection of the Holo Men, scam though it was, the Kyodai Corpsmen for their inefficiency. K-M was not such a fool as to believe his own propaganda. For him, the Society was merely a means to an end, the accumulation of more money and continued payback against a world that had spurned him. For a good measure of revenge he would

take the young punk's girlfriend as his personal sex slave
and hothouse attendant. She could cultivate his precious
orchids when she wasn't servicing him.

K-M whirled in his seat and shoved on the custom gog-
gles he wore when he ran. Unlike most Runners, K-M preferred to use a keyboard and eyepiece instead of thought
commands and Flip Switch 2.0. He bashed away at the
keys like the madman he was, thrashing agitatedly as he
typed, spastic, almost epileptic in his fits of movement.
Often, alone in his chamber, he acted out the scenes of violence that the Net created, mere play for others but deadly
serious for K-M. When he stomped on someone in the Net
his feet slammed the concrete floor of his bunker, seeking
the soft pliable sponginess of bruised human flesh, his ears
sought the muffled crack of bone within. It had been
months since he killed someone himself, too long, he
thought, it was time for some real blood to be spilled. He
sent a message to Denard, ordering him to appear before
him in the plumbing supply warehouse that was the Holo
Men's headquarters.

Seven thousand miles away in Tokyo, Denard heard the
message alert go off on his deck and logged on, fearing the
worst. He had expected this summons ever since that punk
Joshua Victor had escaped from him and slipped out of
Japan. There was nothing he could do except appear as
commanded, there was no place to hide from K-M. Vicious
as Denard was, he knew better than to think he could defeat his leader in a physical confrontation. This wouldn't
be like cracking the neck of some young jerk in leg chains.
K-M was a killer's killer, the best, the most cruel and efficient. All Denard could hope for was a reprieve, forgive-
ness for having screwed up. If only he could bring Victor
in with him, yeah, that was it, he'd go in early, hunt the
punk down, and haul him in like a trophy, that might keep

K-M from killing him. Denard caught the next near-orbiter and arrived in Night City that same afternoon. On the flight he monitored Net activity to see if he could find Joshua. Denard'd already broken through the punk's elaborate electronic smoke screen while he was in Japan, but in Night City he seemed to have vanished, he was no longer using any of the resident Net addresses that Darnell had ferreted out. He was able to trace Joshua to Bryan Lee's dojo from a sales receipt. How had the young bastard discovered that Bryan Lee was an enemy of the Holo Men? He must have had help. This made Darnell wary, and more dangerous, and added urgency to his search, but he'd fracked up Lee once, he could deal with him again if necessary. He disguised himself effectively as a stooped elderly man, though he was just thirty years old, tall, and supremely athletic, as he had demonstrated in his gruesome destruction of Taro.

The noise and confusion, the shouting and the filthiness of Little China, repulsed him. There was nothing like it in Japan, a country of order and neatness, where he had become accustomed to politeness, even if it was a veneer. He shoved his way past tiny old ladies carrying plastic shopping bags full of greasy duck gizzards and stinking fish until he neared the building that housed the herbalist's shop on the ground floor and gym above. He sought a location from which he could watch the comings and goings undisturbed, but it wasn't easy for him to blend into the scene, even in his deceptive guise. He settled on a tea shop across the street where he could sit and observe the front door of the pharmacy.

Denard knew that Bryan Lee had lost his sight, and he also was aware that the martial artist had had his vision restored by means of cyberoptics. He didn't know, couldn't have discovered, because it was a deep secret known only to Bryan and his surgeon, that the artificial eyes implanted in Bryan Lee's orbits contained special properties, the latest in cyberoptic technology, including a sophisticated X-ray vision module, and special sensors that reacted whenever any of a list of catalogued images appeared in their field of vision. This list included weapons, and enemies. When Bryan Lee glanced out the window of the dojo on the second floor during a break in class, he was alerted twice over that the seemingly harmless-looking stranger entering the tea shop was in fact an armed threat and a known assailant. Bryan guessed immediately that this had to do with Joshua, who'd called him only that morning. This man who sat insolently only a few yards from his father's shop was the murderer of his mother! Incredible good fortune! Bryan dismissed his students early and plotted the revenge he had sought for three years.

Denard drank another cup of sweet jasmine tea and ordered another butterfly pastry. He noted the stream of students exiting the gym, and waited for the appearance of Bryan Lee, but the teacher remained out of sight. Though he would have preferred to surprise the man on the street, perhaps in an alley, Denard was pressed for time, his appointment with K-M loomed over him like the sword of Damocles, and pushed him into the ill-advised decision to confront the martial artist in his own studio. Still, he figured to have the advantage of surprise, and he was confident of his fighting skills. No one had ever defeated him. He shuffled across the street but rather than entering the dojo he limped into the herbal store. Wu Chii Lee was at his place in the back of the shop. He wasn't fooled by the stranger's costume or affectations of age, but he didn't reveal his knowledge. Instead he bowed and smiled blankly at him and at the same time pressed a secret button that rang upstairs in the dojo, but his son was already aware that Denard was within his father's shop.

"Got anything for arthritis?" Denard requested.

"Where is your pain?"

"In the legs," Denard answered, aware that his hands would reveal his actual age, especially the one cyberhand with its hidden knives.

"May I feel them?" the elder Lee asked cagily.

"No, no," Denard reacted hastily. "It would hurt too much." He backed away, but suddenly noticed that the other clerks were fleeing the store. He turned back to throttle the old man but Wu Chii Lee had already vanished, performing the same magic trick he'd played on Joshua. Denard was alone in the store. He knew something was terribly wrong, but he was momentarily baffled as to what to do. He should have left the shop but didn't dare use the front door, so he lingered uncertainly. He didn't have to wait long. Bryan Lee appeared in the doorway, dressed in his white gi, but unarmed, without sword or staff. At this sight Denard relaxed. If the fool was willing to fight him, Denard would take his chances.

"You killed my mother," Bryan Lee said simply. Denard looked into those marvelous servomechanical orbs, no longer a window but an electronic link to Bryan Lee's soul, and felt a shiver of fear. But then he remembered that in hand-to-hand combat no one had ever walked away from him alive.

"Yes, and now I'm going to kill you." Denard assumed a fighting stance, but Bryan Lee backed away and bowed. "Not here. Upstairs in my gymnasium we'll be undisturbed."

"Fine." Denard laughed at the pretentious facade of honor that Bryan Lee exuded, the martial arts outfit, the obnoxious dignity with which he treated his mortal enemy.

This wasn't his style. A quick garrote on the way up the stairs was more his method, but Bryan Lee didn't allow him an opening. He gestured for Denard to lead and Denard backed up the stairs until he entered the bright space, the polished floor dazzling in the sunlight, everything neat and clean, a fine place to fight and die. Denard shucked the heavy overcoat he'd worn as part of his old man's costume.

"I see that one of your hands is cybernetically supplemented," Bryan Lee commented. Denard wondered how he'd noticed this, since he'd kept his hands carefully concealed as always.

"You can't see anything, you're blind," he said viciously. "I'll turn off my hand if you'll shut down your artificial vision."

"Agreed," said Bryan, to Denard's surprise. Now he was sublimely confident. The idiot had given up his one advantage. Denard circled around Bryan and noted with satisfaction that the martial artist was unable to follow him precisely. This would be easy work.

"Do you know why I call myself Rasputin?" Denard asked his opponent, whom he loathed for his sanctimonious attitude, the phony adherence to the code of bushido by one who wasn't even Japanese. He was in no hurry. He continued to circle Bryan, who listened with one ear cocked and his head tilted sideways. He had yet to assume a defensive position. Neither man seemed anxious for the fight to begin, yet they were already closing on each other.

"Because you're as ugly as that hunchbacked Russian dwarf?" Bryan Lee said calmly, as if he wasn't insulting his opponent but merely making a factual statement.

"No, because I'm as difficult to kill as he was," said Denard. "They poisoned him, stabbed him, and threw him into the Neva River, and yet some say he survived."

"I won't use any of those methods," Bryan Lee promised. "Nor will I cowardly murder an elderly woman to achieve my goals."

"Ah, your mother, yes, she wasn't supposed to be with you. A last-minute change of plans, no doubt."

"Yes," said Bryan simply. Denard ventured to reach out and touch Bryan Lee's hakama, like counting coup. The martial artist showed no signs that he sensed the contact. Denard's lips curled in cruel pleasure. From within the folds of his clothing he withdrew a short monokatana.

"No blades," said Bryan Lee. Denard jumped back.

"I thought you agreed to dispense with the cyber-optics," he said harshly, reaching across his body to turn on his hand.

"I did," said Bryan. "As you can see, my eyelids are down. It's your intent that I saw, not the knife itself. As now, you have rearmed yourself. Either shut off the hand again or I must open my eyes."

"Very well," said Denard, a little dismayed but still willing to wager his natural talent as a killer against a blind man. He disarmed the artificial hand once again. Craftily he slipped off his shoes to make his footfalls even quieter.

But Bryan Lee only said, "Thank you. I ask all of my students to remove their footwear in the dojo, it keeps the floor cleaner."

Another man would have been thoroughly spooked by Bryan Lee's uncanny second sight, but Denard was demented, he didn't have the emotional reactions of an ordinary human being. He rushed at Lee and stopped a few inches from him. The karate master never flinched.

"First we must bow to each other, then the match may begin."

"You've never even been to Japan. I've lived there.

What do you know about the formalities, the culture. You're Chinese, the Japanese despise you."

"Perhaps," said Bryan Lee, "but I've studied their ways, and I don't agree with you. At root, we are all the children of Amaterasu. Now bow, because I can wait no longer." Bryan assumed the *seiza* position, his neck exposed as he performed a deep *rei*, his head touching the wooden floor. Denard could have smashed his fist into the first vertebrae at that moment, but what sport would there be in that? He too bowed, as much to honor his own years in Japan as to acknowledge his opponent. Then he attacked, kicking savagely at Bryan's head, but the *sensei* rolled easily out of reach.

After all the talk, the fight lasted only a few seconds. Time was compressed and movement speeded up, as if the dojo was a space capsule traveling through a realm of the universe where the physical laws of this ethereal pebble called Earth no longer applied. The two combatants joined in a whirling blur of kicks and punches, some landing on both sides. They separated momentarily, then linked again in a pas de deux, a brutal ballet of death. All at once Denard sagged, his spirit spent, his face a blank, his body open to attack. He must have been stunned by a blow. Bryan Lee never gave him a chance to recover. He let out a kiei scream that reverberated throughout the dojo and beyond into the street. In five quick movements he stepped through Denard's remaining defenses, took the wind out of him with a blow to the solar plexus, broke his jaw with a front kick, snapped him down with a pull on the neck, and finished him off by smashing his windpipe. As the life drained out of him in rattling gasps, Denard's failing sight was filled with the image of Bryan Lee, who had switched on his eyes again and was staring at him with those cold devices inches from his face. "A karate match should never last more than a few seconds before one of the combatants is dead or dying," Bryan said as if he were lecturing to his students. "This is a legacy of the battlefield, where one might have to fight several opponents one after the other in the space of a few minutes. You fought only for pleasure, I had purpose," he said. "May your next life be an improvement on this one, though you are doubtless going to be born in the lower animal world." Denard couldn't respond, the blood was gurgling in his esophagus, he was choking on his own bodily fluids. The last image that dwelled in his fading consciousness was of Bryan Lee standing over him, chanting a Buddhist prayer for his spirit to transmigrate in the soul's great liberation.

The police were surprised and pleased to find one of their most wanted criminals dead on the floor of Bryan Lee's gym. Homicide usually requires an investigation, but none was conducted. Denard's lifeless form was carted away unceremoniously. Bryan spent the rest of the afternoon scrubbing the dojo floor to remove the blood before it could seep through the finish and stain the wood. His father appeared late in the day, out of breath from climbing the stairs. He performed a purification ceremony, because for the Chinese it was very unlucky to have someone die in your house, but in this case there were mitigating circumstances. With sandalwood incense and tiny bells he sanctified the space, drawing out and casting away the toxins that Darnel Denard had brought into the sacred arena.

Joshua heard about the death of Denard on the Net. He knew that Denard had come after him, and that once again he owed a great debt to his *sensei*, but he didn't dare risk contacting Bryan for fear that others would be watching for him at the dojo. Instead he made a trip to Rucker Street, in hopes of finding Raspis and the Raptors. He was doing as Breughel had suggested, finding anyone and everyone who could help him in his upcoming confrontation. The biker and his gang might be unsophisticated compared to the devious genius of K-M, but there were times when heavy bashing was all that was needed. Joshua hoped to bring K-M out from behind his Net facade and into the open. If that happened he wanted all the muscle he could muster behind him. Rucker Street was just as torn up as the last time he'd been there, a row of bars and black-market shops frequented by all sorts of Edgerunners. If you needed an illegally large-bore pistol, or a piece of cyber-gear that wasn't sanctioned by Night City authorities, or you just wanted to get good and fracked up and stomp somebody, Rucker Street was the place to do it. With his boyish good looks, Joshua was out of place down here, but he no longer feared for his life, he could take care of himself, and the confident way he held himself, his awareness of the street around him, made others think twice before hassling him.

Joshua knew that the Raptors favored a hole in the wall called Slammer's, but when he arrived at the Upper East Side he found that place a charred hulk. Just down the block was another bar, Indian Bob's, named after the owner who possessed a true antique, a gas-powered inter-nal-combustion Indian motorcycle that hadn't been made in sixty years. It hung in the window of the place, a shiny symbol of an age long since past, but every once in a while Indian Bob would take it down off the hooks and race up and down Rucker Street, the pipes rumbling, the plastic or-ange Indian head on the gas tank glowing. You could buy most any drug made in America at Indian Bob's, plus de-signer stuff that didn't have a name yet, that was said to knock you loopy for three days on one homemade tablet. Joshua walked into a slight tiff that was going down at Bob's that afternoon, ten or fifteen of the locals in a little tussle, breakin' chairs (Bob went through 'em like match-sticks) and smashin' empty beer bottles on each other's heads, but the knives and chains weren't out so everybody knew it was just a friendly scuffle, nothin' to call the Night City cops over, it was almost like they were just practicing for the real thing, except there were a few bloody faces and a couple of dudes down and out on the floor. Joshua was such a curiosity he actually stopped the fighting when he walked in, 'cause people wanted to make sure he wasn't a narc or a psycho Slinger.

"Who's the Bennie?" somebody called out. Joshua looked around for the distinctive Raptors colors. He hadn't worn the leather jacket they'd bestowed on him 'cause he didn't know what he might find down here, gangs came and went like plagues of locusts, swarming one season and disappearing the next, everybody killed off or sent up to Pelican Bay for some serious downtime, but there in the corner were three Raptors, holding up a rival ganger and working him over pretty good, or at least they had been till Josh showed up. Josh walked over to them and said, "Where's Raspis?"

"Who wants to know?" one of the trio challenged him, and almost in unison they dropped the guy they were pounding on to face Joshua. The unfortunate victim crawled away, leaving a trail of blood as he dragged himself to a corner and passed out.

"It's me, Joshua, the kid who saved his frackin' life. You gave me colors, remember?"

"Hey, yeah, sure. He's who he says, bros, don't frack with him. Man, you look different."

"I grew up," said Joshua simply. The rest of the Raptors drifted off, leaving their spokesman to talk to Joshua. He motioned for Josh to take a seat on one of the unsplintered chairs around a rickety table that hadn't been smashed yet.

"What brings you down here?"

"I want to talk to Raspis. He around?"

"He won't be back for a long, long time."

"Yeah," one of the other Raptors chimed in with an evil giggle, "not in this life."

"What happened to him?"

"It's weird, man. He drew the Ace of Spades, just a few days ago. Funny, he thought he was invincible after you saved him. Just goes to show ya, nothin's forever, huh?"

"You mean, he's dead?" Josh asked, astonished.

"Might as well be. He's on Death Row in San Morro. He flatlined a Corpse and got busted for it."

"How do you kill a corpse?" Josh wanted to know.

"That's CORP Security Expert, ya gonkin' deckhead. An' in this case the how is by usin' a shredder. Wanna buy one? Bob's got 'em for sale behind the bar."

Joshua had heard of the deadly autocannons; he'd never seen one. But the whole thing didn't make sense. Why would Raspis be messin' with a Corp exec? Unless—

"Who did the Corpse work for?"

"I dunno. Some Nihon hi-tech firm. Kobooty, Coyote, something like that. What diff does it make?" The Raptor was gettin' tired of answering questions. Joshua bought him a glass of whatever the gents passed out on the floor were having, and while he was quaffing it down Joshua was thinking hard. There could be no doubt, another person had been sucked into the vortex of evil that had surrounded him since he became involved with the Holo Men. Somehow the Holo Men had connected him to Raspis, and Kyodai had sent a security man in, only they hadn't counted on how tough Raspis was, and the man had been killed, though Raspis was apprehended. So extensive was K-M's network that everyone Josh came in contact with was a potential victim.

"I gotta chip in. There a private room in this place?" he asked his drinking companion, but the laced drink had kicked in like hydro in a rocket car and his friend was no longer capable of coherent conversation. Joshua left the table and approached the bar. Indian Bob himself was tending that day, Joshua had no trouble identifying him by the tattoo on his forehead of a warrior in full headdress astride a bike that matched the one in the window. The rest of Bob, every inch of exposed skin, was also heavily illustrated with blue ink depictions of naked women engaged in sex acts with monsters, space aliens, and animals. Josh tried hard not to stare but the orgiastic scenes were so exotic he couldn't help himself.

"Go ahead! Don't be bashful! Take a good look, that's what they're there for!" Bob yelled at him over the thrasher rock that played incessantly as mood music for the barroom brawls. Josh decided Bob must be waxing down his skin, or maybe he'd had depilatory surgery, because anywhere there wasn't a tattoo, like on the top of his head, his upper chest right under his neck, and the backs of his hands, there was a thick growth of black hair. This combination of hairiness and permanent skin stains was somehow doubly shocking.

"Bob. You don't know me, but I'm a friend of Raspis—"

"So what? You think I am? Hell, if I could get rid of these jokers I would, maybe my chair expenses would go down."

Josh took a deep breath and slapped down some e.b. "I need a place with some peace and quiet where I can jack in for a couple of hours. You got one?" Bob pocketed the money without even counting it and jerked his head toward the staircase at the back of the bar. Joshua nodded his thanks and ascended the stairs. The first room he tried was locked. The heavy frackin' sound of groans and bouncing bedsprings told him what was going on—Bob was runnin' a second business up here. It helped explain the tattoos, anyway. He tried couple more doors until he found one that wasn't occupied, entered it, locked the door behind him, and examined the pathetic room, the very image of despair, no dresser, no table, just the essential double bed covered by a single scuzzy sheet. Josh skipped the bed, sat cross-legged on the floor, drew the hidden wire out of his shirt, connected it to his 'trode hole, and called Breughel.

"Hey, you no-good synthetic sense organ. It's me, Joshua."

"Good afternoon. Are you assembling a unit?"

Typical AI, thought Joshua. *He picks up right where he left off, even though that was two days ago.* "I'm trying. How are you at busting guys out of prison?"

"I can do wonders, my boy, but there are limits. Who is it, I'll see if I can spring 'em?" Breughel's contraction of the pronoun sounded like a buzzer going off.

"Don't use the colloquial, Breughel, it doesn't fit you."

"Who is it?" the AI repeated, sounding a little peeved.

"My man Raspis, the leader of the Raptors. He's in San Morro."

"This will be difficult. He committed a capital offense."

"The guy he killed was a Kyodai thug, Breughel. They must've connected me to him. Maybe they saw the jacket the Raptors gave me. They were trying to find out what Raspis knew about the whole deal, he got caught up in the mess I've made. You gotta get him out. Besides, he's the muscle I need."

"I'll try. Did you see that you no longer have to worry about Darnell Denard, a.k.a. Rumpelstiltskin Rasputin?"

"Yeah! My *sensei* bailed me out again, big-time."

"A remarkable man, Bryan Lee. And his father too. I should like to meet them in person some day."

"Just get Raspis out, whatever it takes. I don't want to have to ask Bryan Lee to fight K-M for me. He's done enough already."

"I see by your transponder that you're on the Upper East Side. Is that the home of the Raptors?"

Joshua glanced at the dismal surroundings. "Yeah, if you could call this bar and whorehouse a home."

"You live in a tent and I live in an RV, Joshua."

The AI was still trying to get back at Joshua for putting down his attempt at slang talk. Despite the situation, Joshua laughed. "You're right, Breughel. And Raspis lives in a prison, and he's going to die there if you don't get him out so he can maybe die on the streets of Night City where he should."

"I'll do what I can."

"Any news from Flight Sim Fred?"

"Yes. Fred is occupied with that little trouble in Mexico City, but he said to tell you that you're doing fine, he's sorry about your friend, and he'll see you after you shut down the Holo Men."

Joshua had heard about the "little trouble in Mexico City." That metropolis's pollution problems had finally reached the state of critical mass; all the canaries died, and people started dropping in the streets just from breathing the particle-loaded air. A full evacuation of the city had been ordered. The dis-United States was cooperating in the effort in conjunction with officials of Petrochem Corporation. The government was on a humanitarian mission, but Petrochem had installations to protect—they were sending in fully suited 'borgs and other specialists to guard the sites until their Mexican workers could return to their jobs. Joshua wondered which role Flight Sim Fred was playing, humane public official or vested interest CorpZoner. It was like a paranoid nightmare, Joshua didn't know which side anybody was on anymore, he only knew he had to kill K-M or at least neutralize him. He signed off with Breughel and packed up the deck. Before he left, Joshua took a last look around at the dead-end room and thanked the fates that had spared him this kind of life. At least he had a tent to go home to, and a woman who loved him not by the hour but all the time, for free.

CHAPTER 15

RELAX! RELAPSE!

The tent glowed like an over-sized polyhedral pumpkin in the barren worn-out patch. Outside there were gangs, Nomads, aggressive Solos, barreling 'borgs, vicious street people, wild dogs, scavenging ravenging rats, and God knew what else, but inside there was love, tenderness, and a tiny nuclear family of one man, one woman, and two children, though the man and woman were still teenagers and the children were not their own. Such things were still possible in the cyberpunk world of 2020, if you looked hard enough for them.

"I'm going to be Runnin' for the next couple of days. Watch my mortal body for me," Joshua told Sally.

"Just like old times," said Sally, but now she understood his mission. She hugged him with affection.

"Frankie! Billie! Guard the garden, and if any bad men come, tug at my sleeve here," Joshua said, and both boys nodded earnestly. "Let me see your kata." Both the boys had quickly assumed the stance for *tai kyaku-sho*. Frankie could do it better, he was older, but Billie followed right behind, kicking and punching with his scrawny body. Sally smiled.

"That's it," said Josh. "I leave you in the hands of your two protectors."

Back into the Net Joshua plunged, into the world he'd left behind many days ago. He was rusty, but the touch came back to him quickly. If he'd been Japanese he would have been either a pachinko addict or a Net rat like Taro. Joshua decided to take a little spin through the Night City simulation where he'd spent so many happy days as a young hacker. Though he'd been off-line for only a few weeks, much had changed. The influence of the Holo Men was palpable—now the Net had the feel of a social realist sculpture or a propaganda film, all hard edges and slogans. The use of exotic icons had declined—most of the people in the Net were businessmen in ordinary off the shelf jobs. Bizarre and eccentric characters had been frightened off by the threat of suppression. While the Holo Men promised freedom, what they delivered was conformity. Joshua realized that the mythic beastie icon Fred had created for him must be sticking out, so he reverted to a simple human body type with a blank face, a cheap rental avatar that made him indistinguishable from anyone else. He thought of the meetings of the Society, the members bedecked in their revolutionary icons and morphing at will, chameleon-like. As in all totalitarian movements, the upper echelons enjoyed the liberties they sought to stifle in the masses. Once again Joshua was reminded of Nazi excesses, the decadent parties, the cross-dressing and sexual deviance that marked Hitler's intimate circle while the German nation was brought under heel and required to conform to an idyllic image of bland purity.

Even in the cafés and bars there was a new, subdued atmosphere. The cyber-bohemians were afraid to express themselves. Many had heard of the fate of the legendary Taro Takahashi, and none wanted to meet a similar end. The government had reacted in the only way it knew, by placing more Net police on every corner, where they lurked clumsily, as if K-M and his fellows would be likely to expose themselves anywhere the authorities might find them! Joshua tripped on down to City Center, looking for a reason to make things happen. There was something off, something more than just the changed tone. What was it? He checked his baud rate—yes, that was it, the whole system was slow by a few thousand cycles a second, not enough to corrupt the display but easily enough to be noticed by a Runner like Josh. Something, somewhere, was draining energy at a furious rate, and Sysops was unable to compensate. Josh did the unthinkable, at least for the old rebel Joshua—he contacted Netwatch Admin. It was easy to do, he just sent a certain signal on a specific frequency and immediately the local operator was trying to pin him down, but Josh was just fluking with him to get his attention.

"Yo! Mr. Cop. What's wrong with the Net? Somebody dump molasses in the LDL lines?"

"Alright, smartass, identify yourself. That's one dirty rig you're Runnin'. I can't even see you, which is illegal."

"Hey, I'm actually on your side, you moron," Josh couldn't resist tweaking the goon a little. "Just tell me, is this more Holo Men trickin'?"

"What are you, undercover or something? Give me tonight's code word."

"Sorry, don't have it on me. Who's using up all the juice? Is it the Society?" Josh asked again.

"Maybe it's you." Josh could feel the Netwatch guy's frustration level rising as he tried every known trick for displaying Josh's icon and address in the grid, but Josh kept him blind for the moment. "Where are you?"

"I'm sittin' right here on this park bench in City Center," said Josh, taking a small risk by revealing his actual location on the Net. He figured he'd be gone by the time the cops arrived that the Netwatch guy would be dispatching right about now. "But really, what's causing the energy downflow? You can tell me, I'm not part of the problem, I'm searchin' for a solution, just like you."

"Frack off," the Netwatch man cursed him. "We'll make you talk."

"Bye," said Josh. He signed off that frequency and moved away just as the first units of the security forces arrived on the scene. It might appear that he had learned nothing from the encounter, but Josh'd heard enough to verify that this was indeed another Holo action. If it'd been a simple system glitch or some server that was off-line, the Netwatch man would've said so, but he was clueless. Josh knew where he had to go if he wanted to find out the real story—Wilderspace! He wasn't ready yet for a final confrontation, but unless he learned the nature of this latest threat he couldn't be sure that any plan would work. Josh reverted to his snake-headed, eagle-clawed griffin icon and soared into the sky. The Night City grid shifted perspective beneath him, not smoothly as he was accustomed to, but in a herky-jerky refresh pattern that revealed more of the collapsing infrastructure of the Net. The faster he moved, the slower the image was to respond. This was dangerous, it was like trying to run in quicksand, the harder one struggled the more one was sucked in. Joshua would have to be careful not to depend on speed to escape a trap. He wondered what K-M knew of his recent movements. So far his hiding place in Sally's tent had proved safe. He settled into a comfortable pace as he crossed the coastline and headed out over the rocking blue waves that symbolically separated the Pacific coast from the distant shoreline of the Asian mainland.

In the real world it had started to rain. The drops made a thudding sound on the polyplastic rain flap of the tent. Fortunately Sally had treated the covering with a retardant that prevented the acidic downfall from eating through the plastic like, well, like acid through a brainpan. She, Frankie, and Billie huddled together inside their flimsy abode, keeping watch over Joshua's inert body. In the Net, too, a downpour had started. Clouds were massing on the horizon ahead of him. It was all an illusion of course, but nothing on the Net was accidental, someone was generating this storm, and the winds on the leading edge of the front had the effect of buffeting Josh's icon just as if he were in a light plane flying toward it.

As Joshua continued on a westerly course, the winds swung around from the south and intensified, as they would if a tropical storm was tracking in toward the coast of Mexico from the lower latitudes. The hurricane or typhoon was causing heavy static on the Net. Josh realized that this could be the source of the energy drain, a meaningless roiling and turmoil that required massive power resources to execute, to no apparent purpose. There was nothing out here. Unless, unless the storm turned north and swept through Night City! Its disruptive influence would likely knock out most Netrunners and damage existing data structures. Joshua skirted the front and called up a weather map. There could be little doubt, the path of the maelstrom was curling northward and would take it over

Night City in the next few minutes! What could Joshua do against this powerful simulation of nature's fury? There had to be a source, he decided, a locus that was producing this phenomenon. He would hunt for the center, which he suspected would not be a traditional eye but instead a power pack or generator.

He drew in the leading edge probes that he usually used to navigate on the Net and curled himself into a ball in order to penetrate the churning tempest. Soon he was being buffeted by an electron wind as intense as any he had ever felt in the real world. It was difficult to maintain a course, but the central cause of the phenomenon was within reach now, pulsating with magnetic-electric energy, in a few seconds he would reach it, and then what? He could turn himself into a reverse polarity charge and counter the energy loss, but in a fraction of a second he'd max out and crash. This would send an immediate trace signal to Netwatch, but Joshua suspected that by the time those idiots in Sysops figured out what was going to hit them it would be too late, his sacrifice as a human lightning rod would be in vain. He was just about to do it anyway when he noticed something strange about the force-field that preceded the storm system. It wasn't just headed toward Night City, it was pursuing him. As he shifted his position the squall subtly altered its path. It was aware of him, personally. He was the only icon within range, but there was more to it than that, the hurricane was keyed in to his movements in an uncanny way, as if it was hunting him down.

It was a trap! The whole illusion was designed to lure him into the hands of the Holo Men. They were willing to blow down Night City to take him, if necessary. He'd figured it out just in time. He sprang back from the disturbance. As he watched from afar, the storm system imploded rapidly, like a black hole sucking cosmic debris into its heavy center. Within seconds the entire effect had disappeared, leaving a white-capped blue sea gradually settling back into tranquillity. Joshua knew he'd better leave the area as soon as possible. He jetted into high gear and retraced his steps to Night City, and reverted once again to the anonymous, shielded, filtered icon that offered him the most protection from the prying eyes of the Holo Men.

"Phew! Ducked a fuse job there," Joshua said to himself. He must've mumbled aloud because from far off he heard Sally ask him if everything was alright. He placed himself in stasis mode for a minute and Flip Switched to look around. Frankie and Billie were curled up asleep next to Sally, who'd also been dozing until Joshua's exclamation woke her.

"It's okay, go back to sleep, everything's fine," he said. Actually he was rather pleased with himself. He'd seen the snare before he was caught up by it, and in a small way he'd won a victory over the Holo Men by avoiding the pitfall. Their resources weren't limitless, it must have cost them a good deal of energy to create that sizable a hallucination, all for his benefit. Still, it was a dangerous game he was playing. He needed help. He tucked the covers over his sleeping family and strapped the deck onto his body again for a midnight run into the real world.

CHAPTER 16

DYIN' O' THIRST WITH A FULL CANTEEN

Breughel was the key. Josh had known it all along, but somewhere he'd forgotten. The quirky AI was the only weapon Joshua had that wasn't checkmated by a superior Holo Men tool. They had faster equipment, better organization, more numbers, everything except the unpredictable AI in byteboi's RV. Actually, the phrase "in byteboi's RV" wasn't quite accurate—Breughel *was* byteboi's RV, or rather, the RV served as Breughel's corporeal presence. Its owner had vanished on another of his quests in search of lost illuminated manuscripts, leaving the AI as sole occupant of the recreational vehicle, which remained parked behind the Night City Art Museum, though Joshua suspected that Breughel could drive it by means of sensors and remote controls if he wanted to. The AI's motives might be questionable—for instance, was he a bigger threat to the stability of the world than the Holo Men themselves, and who did he and Flight Sim Fred really work for? But Joshua had to take those risks. He'd developed a comfortable relationship with the personable artificial intelligence, to the point that they teased each other about each's limitations. He decided to pay a late night (it was now early morning) visit to the RV.

"Hey! Breughel!" he shouted as he entered the camper. "Exit sleep mode and talk to me. The whole boogie's gonna shake down today."

"AIs never sleep. It's a waste of time," came the dry rejoinder from the very walls of the mobile home.

"Not for humans. That's when we do some of our best thinking, dreaming, creative shit, but you wouldn't know about that, since AIs are completely uncreative."

"Define creativity. If you mean, 'something out of nothing,' AIs are the most creative beings ever to come into existence, since everything we do begins in the Void, has never before been rendered."

"Alright, Breughel. 'Nuf said. I haven't got time for philosophical gamesmanship today, this is D-day, zero hour, me and K-M are going to have it out today, and I need your help."

"Take me with you," Breughel suggested.

"No can do," said Josh. "This isn't my RV, and anyway, some of the places I'm going might not be able to handle a vehicle this size."

"I could fit in your cyberdeck. Course I might not be as smart as I am here, I would be cramped in your unit's memory," said Breughel with an almost human smugness.

"I appreciate the offer, but no. I want you to track me wherever I go, and if I look like I'm going to lose it, create a distraction."

"That's all?" Breughel's voice was definitely tinged with disappointment.

"That'll be enough, believe me. It might keep me from gettin' killed."

The RV was a safe place—it was tough to leave. Night City was not a safe place, especially when Josh knew that somewhere out there he was being hunted by a lifelong killer who was desperate to stop him from crumbling his carefully constructed empire. Walking the streets of Night City was always a thrill, you had to watch out for roving gangs, random violence, out of control police, techno-industrial craziness of all kinds from oil spills to acid rain storms, and now Joshua had to pay extra attention to anyone who walked too close behind him or too straight toward him, it was an additional level of paranoia, like a speed freak drinking coffee for that little extra buzz, that almost had the opposite, calming effect of knowing that no matter what he did he was probably going to die. The weeks and months of martial arts training had prepared him for this state of perpetual readiness, but it was still exhausting and demanding.

Breughel had reported success on one front—he'd managed to post bail for Raspis, a thing almost unheard of for Death Row inmates, but somehow Breughel had finagled another trial based on spurious new evidence, and had plied the judge with so many obscure precedents that the justice had finally relented and agreed to a writ of habeas corpus. The Raptor was tagged, forced to wear an electronic ankle device that monitored his movements, but that made it easy for Joshua to find him, not that it would have been difficult anyway. He was at Indian Bob's drinking Muscovy Moose Juice, a deadly mixture of black-market Russian bathtub vodka and liquid ether. It was five o'clock in the morning. Raspis was the only customer in the place.

Indian Bob was asleep behind the bar. Raspis's mood was foul, and he was so bleary-eyed it took him a few minutes to remember who the hell Joshua was and why he should pay any attention to him. When he found out it was Josh (through Breughel) who'd gotten him out of the slammer though, he slugged him on the back and tried to make him drink some MMJ, but Joshua managed to decline the offer.

"You wanna get back at the crew that set you up?" Joshua asked his wasted ally.

"Frack 'em. Frack 'em all. Kill 'em. Kill 'em all. You, him, them, everybody." Raspis was barely coherent. He wasn't any use to Joshua in this condition.

"Listen. You wanna kill them that's fine, but you're gonna have to straighten up, at least long enough to fight."

"Frack you. I could cut your frackin' throat right now and there's not one damn thing you could do about it, you little wirehead." Joshua knew that Raspis had no idea of the transformation he'd experienced under Bryan Lee's tutelage, but he didn't feel any need to prove himself right now.

"You're a hellacious gang-banger, Raspis, and your Raptors are the toughest bunch on the block. But you gotta be real ready for this fight, 'cause K-M—"

That got Raspis' attention. He focused on picking up Joshua's words as they emerged through the vodka-ether haze. "K-M? Kilo Mega? He's the one you're crossing with?"

"He's the leader."

"Hoo, boy, you're in deep shit."

"What do you know about him?"

"They're still talking about him up in the joint. He ran some kinda brotherhood even while he was in solitary, they say. Had the prisoners organized, the guards bought off, and everybody so damn scared of him that they'd do anything he said. Then he disappeared. That was a few years ago, but he's still a force in the yard."

"I know the story."

"Can you cut this damn bracelet off?"

"Can't do it, Raspis. That's part of the deal that got you sprung."

"I'm like the frackin' cat with the frackin bell," said Raspis. Joshua found it comical that this tough guy would make a left-field allusion to a children's tale, but Raspis was in no mood to be laughed at. "When do we slammit on?"

"I dunno yet. You gotta be ready. You're my muscle."

"Listen, you better be good with that Netrunnin' shit, you little deckhead, because if you think you can deal with K-M on the street you're already in trouble."

"I'm good," Joshua promised. "You're only backup in case things get out of hand."

"Sounds like they're outahand already." Raspis pushed the rest of his drink off the table where it crashed to the floor. The sickly suffocating stench of ether fumes wafted up from the pile of broken glass. The metal anklet emitted an annoying beep once a minute, and its LCD display twinkled every few seconds to confirm that it was still activated. Raspis kicked at it half-heartedly with his other foot, but he knew it represented the most sophisticated technology the justice system was capable of developing, and that there was no hope of cutting it off, the alloy it was made from was the same one used on the nose cone of the near orbiter, and was resistant to every known cutter from acetylene torches on up to lasers.

"Call the Raptors together. It's gonna go down soon, maybe later today. Can you be ready?"

"I'm frackin' ready now," Raspis rasped, and it did seem that the mention of K-M had sobered him up miraculously.

Joshua left him at the bar, but not before he made sure that the biker was through drinking and was headed upstairs to crash for a few hours in one of the sleazy rooms above the bar. A plan had been forming in Joshua's head, a way to ruin the Holo Men for good and also make sure that whoever Flight Sim Fred (and by extension Breughel) worked for got the evidence they needed but didn't profit too much by it. It would take delicacy and trickery followed by hammering brute force. His first move was a bold one. He contacted K-M directly. That wasn't as difficult as it would have seemed, for though the criminal had eluded the police for many years, he was ever watchful of Net activity and responded immediately when Joshua sent out a message designed to catch his attention. In the real world, Joshua was on the move, walking the streets aimlessly to try to keep anyone from pinning down his location. In the Net, he started out across town in the Night City University icon off Lake Park, a safe distance away. It was like Tokyo all over again, he was shifting constantly between two worlds, one a shimmering fractal fantasy, the other hard-edged reality. K-M appeared before his eyes as the inside-out man, flayed flesh dripping blood, nerve endings exposed, a raw, quivering mass of tendon and cartilage. Such a complex dynamic icon was difficult to maintain, but K-M did it effortlessly. Joshua was determined not to let the man intimidate him, but he knew he was playing a dangerous game against a master.

"Kilo Mega. Your icon, what does it mean?"

"Icons are symbols. Mine represents modern man, his protective skin sheath stripped away, everything revealed for all to see. There's no place left to hide in this intrusive age, as you'll soon find out, when you're brought before me to meet your Maker."

"You didn't make me."

K-M laughed savagely. "You misunderstand me. It's an old phrase, 'meet your Maker,' it means, to die. And such a pity, because I wanted the world for you, my son."

"Bullshit." Josh resorted to an epithet. He turned on Flip Switch 2.0 and looked around to make sure he wasn't being followed. He wished he really was at Night City University. The campus was the safest place he could think of; it was controlled and heavily patrolled by a private university police force that kept out undesirables. The quadrant was organized in a parklike atmosphere of grassy lawns bisected by tree-lined walkways connecting reinforced red-brick masonry buildings that evoked an earlier age of sedate learning, a West Coast version of an Ivy League campus designed by city founder Richard Night himself. Only right now Joshua felt about as safe as a fly walkin' tightrope on the edge of a spiderweb. K-M's voice brought him back into the Net—

"I was willing to make you a prince—"

"Of darkness—" Joshua answered with a trace of bitterness, thinking of Taro.

"No. I offered you a bright future—"

"So you say. It looked like the grisly past to me."

"Aghh, you young assholes don't know what a struggle is. It all came to you so easy, you with your swelling brains."

"You took it all away."

"Yes, but you've managed to gain it back. I'm curious, how did you override the viral effects?"

Joshua was about to tell K-M what an effort of will it took, how he had transformed himself, but he saw that K-M was probing him, so he lied.

"Dr. Lee's medicines did the trick."

"Oh, really?" the disbelief was evident in K-M's voice.

"Never mind that, the question is, where do we go from here?"

"I'm going to turn over all the information I gathered in Japan to the proper authorities?"

"Who might those be?" K-M asked archly, but Joshua could tell that he was furious. "Since the Collapse there are no proper authorities anymore, only illegitimate bastardized ones."

"You'll find out when the time comes."

"What time?"

"The moment when they lead you back into your cell in Pelican Bay."

"Never! I'll never be locked up again. You have no idea how painful it can be to spend day after day in a four-by-eight cell with no fresh air, no sunshine, no hope. True, I learned the memory tricks that culminated in the creation of the Holo Men, but at a cost incalculable to one such as yourself."

K-M was taking a subtle tack. He knew that Joshua must be somewhere in Night City. The natural tendency would be to bring the two plot points together, Joshua's Net location at N.C.U. and his physical position. Joshua was being maneuvered, K-M was trying to pinpoint him, he had to keep moving to keep from being discovered, without giving himself away by repeatedly choosing a direction that K-M could use to extrapolate his current whereabouts. He thought he'd been randomly turning corners, but he sensed that K-M was using vectoring software to cross-reference his movements. Joshua must have them meet where and when he wanted, not at a place and time to K-M's advantage. A surge of nausea gripped him. He fought it back. K-M was talking again, the hypnotic leader, alternately cajoling and threatening Joshua while he played cat and mouse.

"I was grooming you for greatness, my young friend. You and your running mate, the Japanese kid. The two of you were my prize pupils, which is why I didn't trust you, you knew too much, as you've proved. Do you think I would've scrutinized and tested you so severely if you'd been ordinary recruits?"

"I don't know," said Josh. He felt dizzy, he was losing his equilibrium. K-M was closing in on him, he knew he should shut down the Net connection and run, but he was slow to react, his icon was shuffling along in jerks and twitches, the virus was taking hold again, he was going to black out! K-M's next words shocked him back to consciousness—

"Of course now that I have your woman I'm sure you'll be willing to—"

"Sally!" Josh wailed.

"Did you think you could hide forever from me?" K-M scoffed. "That was a neat trick, abandoning any registered building, but my sources tracked you down. We've been waiting for you there, but you haven't returned. She is a flower, my young friend, and I've plucked her. She'll tend to my orchids when I'm not pollinating her myself, if you catch my drift."

With a supreme effort Joshua gathered himself and told K-M, "This afternoon on Rucker Street. The real world, not the Net. You bring Sally. I'll bring the evidence. We'll trade."

"Perhaps," said K-M. Joshua shut off the connection and fled down the street, glancing fearfully into every alleyway. He wanted desperately to return to the tent but he knew that K-M's operatives, if not K-M himself, would have the place under surveillance. He took a circuitous route through the neighborhoods of Night City that brought him to within a few hundred feet of the bulldozed

field with its unlikely garden, then waited until he spotted
Frankie and Billie wandering the streets. He whistled to
get their attention and they came running as fast as their little legs would carry them, tears streaking their dirty faces.
Josh swept them up, one in each arm.

"Josh! Bad men came and took Sally away," Frankie
cried. "I tried to stop 'em but they just hit me. I'm sorry,
Josh." It was then Josh saw the shiner under one of
Frankie's eyes. He clutched the boy closer, and examined
Billie for marks of abuse, but they seemed to have spared
the younger one.

"It's okay, Frankie. You did good. Don't worry, we'll
find Sally. Come on, I'm going to take you to meet somebody fun. You'll like him, he's got lots of cool holovid
games you can play with, and you'll be safe there."

They walked slowly away from the garden field. Joshua
sensed that these were his last moments of human tenderness before the bloody battle that loomed before him like
an angry cloud.

CHAPTER 17

SINKING OF THE TITANIC (EGO)

Joshua, like his namesake the Old Testament warrior, was the angel of vengeance. First, though, he had to find safe haven for the two children. The only place he knew that he could be completely sure of was the RV where Breughel lived. Once again Josh zigzagged in an indirect route in case he was being followed. He worked his way by twists and turns to the Night City Art Museum parking lot where sat the RV owned by a peripatetic cybermonk named byteboi whom Josh had never met.

After he washed up the boys and put them to bed together in the back of the camper, Joshua explained the situation to Breughel in a few cryptic sentences.

"K-M's got Sally. I told him I'd trade the evidence for her."

"He doesn't believe you. He'll kill her, if he hasn't already."

"I know that," said Josh, his face grim as a stone. "But he wants me badly. I think he'll come. That's all I can ask for. I'll have Raspis there, and you can monitor the situation from here and provide a distraction if I need one, yeah?"

"Of course."

"Take care of the boys. If me and Sally don't, well, you know, raise them up yourself. You're the only one I trust."

Breughel found time for a joke: "That'll be a first, AI father to humans."

"Just make sure they don't turn into deckheads like their adopted father."

"Oh, he's not such a bad sort," said Breughel, and Joshua definitely heard the sound of real affection in Breughel's tinny computer-generated speech module.

"I'm outa here. Call me if you need me, and feed them something when they wake up."

"You call me if you need me," Breughel corrected him.

"Yeah, right." Still on foot, Joshua headed back across town to see if Raspis had sobered up enough to be of any use to him. He needn't have worried. Josh wore the colors, he was a Raptor for life, and Raptors take care of their own. A phalanx of thirty motorcycles met him at the head of Rucker Street, Raspis at their lead on the biggest, shiniest loudest bike, a jet-assisted turbo-charged machine that was some kind of chopped hybrid of Japanese and German technology.

"Where's the action?" Raspis shouted over the resonant roar of throttling bikes.

"Here," said Joshua.

"Here?!"

"Rucker Street. I told the guy to meet me here."

"Fantastic! Park 'em, boys, the dude's comin' to our

turf. We like it better that way," Raspis confided, "the bikes are too expensive to replace so easy."

"We may need them to get away," said Joshua. "K-M is one bad-ass, and I don't know who he might be bringing with him."

"I know, 'cause I met some of 'em up in San Morro. They won't want to fight me. I was on the Row; that's a place of honor."

"K-M has his own ideas of honor," said Josh. "Let's set up a line—"

"Uh, Josh boy, that's not how we do it down here," said Raspis. "Let me handle this part." Joshua shrugged, then watched as Raspis deployed his troops as carefully as any battalion commander. In a few minutes he had snipers on the roof, sappers in the sewer lines under the street, guys hidden in alleyways and behind parked cars, and a careful fire zone established so they wouldn't be killin' each other with friendly fire.

Only thing was, K-M arrived by air, swooping down in a McDonnell-Douglas AV-4 Tactical Urban Assault Vehicle, spattering 20mm cannon fire as a greeting. A flock of pigeons exploded off the rooftop in panicked flight, mindless as their clay counterparts, but they weren't the targets. As Josh dove for cover from the sudden air attack, he saw Sally's frightened face pressed against the smoke-tinted glass of the passenger side window as the fighter plane streaked past him down Rucker Street. She wasn't wearing a helmet like K-M. Her red hair streamed behind her because K-M audaciously had the star-roof open atop the aerodyne car to show that he didn't fear anyone or anything. At the end of the block he pulled up in a sudden blast of jet exhaust and tilted the maneuverable rotors downward to hover while he lined up for a rocket barrage. Two seconds later Rucker Street erupted in hellfire as two modified laser-guided Thundersnake rockets slammed into the middle of the block. Motorcycles flew around like electrons smashed off their nuclei, a chaos of spinning wheels, all sense of order lost, the proud parade a disorderly rout accompanied by the sound of scraping metal, the choking smell of burning rubber, a shower of orange plastic bits and pieces, chrome scraps, and human scraps too. The world lost all logic, everything was dripping blood, a moaning and groaning wracked his ears, most of the Raptors were dead or dying in the street. Half a dozen Holo Men, K-M's prison pals, appeared at the far end of the block and rushed into the smoking rubble, finishing off any of the bikers who still twitched and jerked in their death throes. It had all happened so fast, they never had a chance to fight. The prison gangers were looking for Joshua, he had to get away, but his legs were pinned under Raspis's bike, he could feel them but they wouldn't budge. Raspis crawled over to him. The biker king was horribly wounded. One of his hands was blown off and spurting blood from a severed artery, but he still had the strength to heave his motorcycle off Joshua and drag him by his other hand away from the scene. K-M's ground troops were halfway down the block.

"We've got one of them motherfrackers," said Raspis. Joshua didn't know what he meant, but Raspis was busy winding a strip of leather around his stump as a tourniquet so he couldn't ask. Raspis disappeared into a battered building and returned an instant later dragging a case from which he withdrew a handheld missile launcher. Before Joshua could scream, "NO! Sally's in there!" Raspis'd taken aim at K-M's aerodyne and fired. The aerodyne was heavily armored but the shot entered from underneath in the vulnerable underbelly of the flying machine and snuffed its engine. It dropped from the sky and burst into flames.

The remnants of the Raptors had regrouped and were finally putting up a defense against the ground assault. They cheered when the hovership fell, and rushed forward, but K-M emerged unharmed, firing an automatic weapon with one hand and dragging Sally by her beautiful hair with the other.

The blood was gradually returning to Josh's legs. He stood up wobbly. His legs were badly bruised but nothing was broken. He ignored the throbbing pain of blood-swollen muscles and the bullets from K-M's machine gun and limped forward toward the burning auto-plane.

K-M shouted to his gang, "There he is! Kill him!" but the Holo Men were under counter-attack by the revitalized Raptors.

Raspis waved his bandaged wrist and swore foully as he charged toward a group of them, "Don't you recognize me, you frackers? I was up in San Morro with some of you."

Beyond the perimeter of Rucker Street the Night City police were massing and waiting for the firefight to subside between what they assumed to be two rival gangs. Their tactic was to let the gang-bangers kill as many of each other as possible, then TAC/SWAT teams would clean up the mess. When K-M broke out, still clutching Sally and followed in close pursuit by Josh, the lieutenant in charge of the operation told his men to keep containment, not to bother with them, thereby unwittingly allowing one of the greatest criminals of all time to flee. The cat and mouse game began again, only this time the roles were reversed, Josh was the hunter. On a hunch he chipped in as he ran, juggling two realities. He screamed an urgent message into his chin mike, knowing that K-M would get it. The leader of the Holo Men had disappeared around a corner up ahead, but Joshua was tracking him now by his Net location, using a program Breughel had loaded for him that morning that had only one purpose, to follow the movements of K-M.

"Let the girl go and I'll stop following you!"

No response. Josh knew that K-M would be trying to return to his legendary redoubt, that triply secure aerie whose location was unknown even to the inner circle of the Holo Men. He would be untouchable once he entered his lair, but K-M would have to shake Josh first or the hideout would be exposed and he could send the cops to lay siege to him. A doubly devious game ensued. K-M had discovered the tracking program and was trying every programming trick he knew to break the electronic link between himself and Joshua, all the while shifting and changing his path in the real world. They crossed City Center, drawing looks from the lunchtime crowd who'd heard about the blowout on Rucker Street, but nobody stopped them even though K-M was manhandling a woman. At City Center station on the south side of Fifth Street he yanked a guy out of his hovercar and carjacked it. Joshua followed suit, briefly impersonating an officer (he was, after all, a vigilante) to convince a bystander to give him the keys to his machine. In the intervening seconds, K-M had managed to mask his whereabouts from the tracking software. He'd disappeared from the Net. Joshua called Breughel frantically.

"I've lost him!" he screamed.

"Lay in the following coordinates," Breughel said calmly. Nothing like an AI for grace under pressure—nor blood nor ice water flowed through his veins, he didn't have any.

"Where is that?" yelled Joshua, maneuvering unsteadily on the unfamiliar controls of the hovercar.

"If my guess is right, this is where K-M is headed."

"You're guessing?"

"We'll find out if I'm right in two minutes."

Joshua typed the directions into the hovercar's onboard mapping system and let himself be driven toward an unknown destination that might or might not be where he wanted to go. It was maddening and he felt helpless, but he had no choice except to trust the AI, who had never let him down before.

Up ahead, K-M was congratulating himself on overriding the trace program. In a few seconds he'd be safely hidden within his shelter. No one could harm him there. He'd suffered a momentary setback, but he'd recover from it, he'd rise to greatness again, and there'd be time for revenge, especially as he still held a prize. He glanced over at Sally, who was pressed into the hovercar seat on the passenger side, her face white with fear. She wasn't a great beauty but attractive enough. K-M would have his brutal way with her many times before he snuffed the life out of her. And if she was as good as she said she was with his flowers, that might be a very long time. There remained only to ditch the hovercar a few blocks away and—

"What the frack—?" K-M exclaimed. He'd reached his refuge well ahead of Joshua, but parked in front of the only entrance, the one that led to the portcullis and the second inner door, was an immense recreational vehicle, thoroughly blocking the way. He couldn't get in. There was another, secret exit, but only from within, on this side it was booby-trapped and even K-M wouldn't risk tampering with the trigger. He briefly considered blasting the RV and anyone inside it to hell, but that would only draw attention to his sanctuary. He would have to stand and fight. He jumped out of the hovercar and banged on the door to the RV, but there didn't appear to be anyone inside. Seconds later Josh came whipping around the corner in his borrowed aircar.

The Net vanished as Joshua leapt from his machine. The two of them had arrived at the same place in the physical world. Now he was face-to-face with a prison-hardened killer armed with who knew what dangerous weapons, and what was he, Joshua, but a scared nineteen-year-old kid Runnin' hard and just tryin' to stay alive. But he wasn't completely helpless like he'd been a few months ago. He knew how to defend himself, he was aware in a new way, and his body was responsive. He was no Old Testament warrior, but he wasn't a geeky deck vegetable either. He assumed a defensive kibadachi stance, but K-M only laughed.

"Kid, I've been studying hand-to-hand in prison for longer than you've been alive. I've killed fifty-odd men, and a couple of women, with my bare hands. How many have you killed?"

Josh gulped but said nothing.

"You want to play samurai? Come over here, stick your neck out and I'll cut off your head without using a sword. Ever seen that done? More impressive than ripping a telephone book in half or breaking a cinder block or a couple of shitty pieces of plywood, huh?" Josh could see that K-M was edging closer to him, but he was frozen, paralyzed by the man's physical power. Over K-M's shoulder he saw Sally slumped in the seat of the hovercar. At least she was still safe and alive! Then he recognized the RV from the museum parking lot, what the hell was that doing here? Against a vastly superior opponent, Bryan Lee had told him, one had to be clever and cautious, cautious and clever, never let them engage, move away, look for an unusual opening. Joshua got his feet moving and retreated a few paces, but that only intensified K-M's stalking.

"This your crappy camper?" K-M asked him. "It's in my way. Move it."

"It's not mine," said Josh, not lying but hiding his connection to it. He wasn't alone! Breughel was here. How could he use the AI? Thinking furiously, Joshua continued to keep a few feet between himself and K-M, who continually pressed forward, seeking to grab hold of Joshua but not wanting him to run, because if he could keep the conflict confined to this narrow alleyway he could kill the bastard and avoid drawing attention to his hideaway. The scar along the left side of his mouth gleamed red as it always did when he was tensing to strike.

This was no place to die, this trashed alley between two desolate brick warehouses in a nondescript district of Night City. The image of Taro lying on the cold marble floor of the Kyodai lobby flashed through Josh's mind as he tried to keep K-M from closing with him. If K-M killed him now, it would go on and on, the tampering with the Net, the senseless persecution of innocent people. No matter what happened to him, Josh had to stop K-M.

"My teacher took care of that sicko Denard."

"Saved me the trouble. The bungler. But when I'm finished with you I'll settle up with Lee."

"No," said Josh. "I'm not going to give you that chance. That RV's loaded with barrels of CHOOH. If you don't surrender I'm going to blow us all to hell!"

"You're lying. You're bluffing. What about the girl?"

"If we have to sacrifice our lives we will."

"I don't believe you. There's no explosives. This piece of shit probably belongs to some idiot tourist who got lost." K-M slapped his hand on the RV to emphasize his point. When he did so, a funny thing happened—he twitched and fell! Breughel had sent a mild electric charge through the aluminum body of the camper. K-M was up almost instantly, but in that moment Joshua had sprung forward and seized the opening. Now they were like the mongoose and the cobra, Joshua clinging for life to the throat of K-M who thrashed violently, banging Josh against whatever he could hurl his body into, pummeling him with his fists, and reaching into his pockets for stashed weapons. A knife came out—Josh kicked it away. K-M pulled a small pistol from another pocket—Josh rolled over and grabbed the hand that held the gun. Shots exploded next to his ear. Although Josh had the advantage of surprise because K-M had expected a weakling, the fight was a mismatch, and K-M would certainly win the contest. He was slowly loosening Josh's rabid grip on his throat and hand, in another few seconds he would gain the upper hand, and a few seconds after that Joshua would be dead. Suddenly K-M's grip relaxed. A dazed look came over his face, and he collapsed next to Joshua on the ground. Josh jumped up. Sally was standing there, trembling, a length of lead pipe in her hand. She'd whacked him so hard K-M was unconscious.

Joshua raised his hand to shatter K-M's windpipe.

"No!" Sally screamed. "Don't kill him. Don't kill anyone. You'll be just like them." Joshua hesitated. He wanted revenge on the man who had tormented him, Sally, Taro, and many others, but he knew that she was right, and his samurai training from Bryan Lee didn't allow the striking of a defenseless opponent.

The measured mechanical voice of Breughel broke the silence. "I've summoned the authorities. Tie him to the door handle, place the evidence disks in his hands, and enter the RV."

Joshua did as he was told. He and Sally climbed into the RV. Josh sat in the driver's seat and spoke to the vehicle that was possessed by the spirit of the AI—

"I thought I told you to stay put," Joshua yelled, but he couldn't be too severe, Breughel had just saved his life.

"You said to track you," the unrepentant AI answered, obviously pleased with himself. "AIs are notoriously literal-minded. I took you to mean—"

"Never mind, Breughel, it's over. Get us the hell out of here!" They fled to the welcome sound of sirens approaching.

But it wasn't over. K-M's last act, the bitter swan song of the Holo Men, was to unleash the mnemonic plague, a more virulent version of the virus they'd used against Josh and Taro, on the defenseless population of the Net. He must've sent the commands to activate the virus in the final seconds of the struggle with Josh, or just before the police arrived to lock him away. It was reminiscent of the last madness of the Third Reich, when all was lost yet the killings in the camps continued with insane methodical regularity and the Fuhrer ordered his army of twelve-year-olds defending Berlin to stand and fight or be shot. K-M was defeated, yet he wouldn't go gracefully, as a samurai would do, offering his neck to the blade of his opponent or turning his own weapon on himself. Instead he sought to poison the Net entire, to turn it into a diseased data wasteland that wouldn't be safe to anyone. Breughel informed Joshua of this turn of events as they raced away from the scene.

"I'll drive. You've got to stop it," said Breughel.

"How?" Josh asked aloud, but he chipped in from the driver's seat while Breughel took over the real world navigation of the ten-ton RV.

As Josh entered the Net, he saw that it was dwindling away. Before his eyes, buildings lost their structural integrity and dissolved. Ragged holes appeared in the roof of the sky. The waters of the Pacifica grid lost their luminescent aqua tint and turned an ordinary gray like used bath-water. The whole construct was collapsing. Power spikes and surges on the LDLs made travel chancy. If Joshua was caught in transit when the level dipped or soared, he might be sagged right off the Net or the shot might wend its way back through the wires and fry his hair or even the inside of his head.

If the virus crept inside his brain, he'd begin to zombie out, his life would lose its meaning, he might be found days later wandering the Net in rags, or he might lock up and go catatonic, brain dead on and off the Net, a useless dysfunctional creature foaming at the mouth and vacant-eyed, not even as smart as a NOROM, those hideous self-inflicted random access addicts who'd paid to put themselves in such a state. Netwatch execs were beside themselves, but they couldn't do anything about it short of closing down the Net entire, which would be conceding defeat, would yank the world's economy down into chaos, and would mean victory for the Holo Men.

Joshua raced between crumbling buildings. A child's fairy tale leapt into his mind: "The sky is falling! The sky is falling!" Somewhere in this apocalyptic setting the mad-man who had caused it all was being led to a police van for incarceration. The end time had come—either Joshua de-feated his enemy now or the walls would come tumbling down as they had for his biblical namesake, only this Joshua was trying to keep them up. He passed a couple of Netwatch cops, but they ignored him, they were incapable of responding to an obvious Net violator, they were mind-lessly drilling each other with their electron pistols and getting off on the charge. He had to find the source of the virus, and he had to do it quickly or the whole system would implode. Breughel fed him data in a corner of his vi-sion. Joshua headed straight for Wilderspace, where he'd encountered the data storm before. He flew over the crumbling city, crossed the coast, and sped out over open water. Yes, there it was, the legacy of K-M and the Holo Men, a terrifying mountain of clouds, spinning and whirling, its mere presence already causing fantastic disintegration of data integrity and it hadn't even reached the coastline yet. The last time he'd defused the threat. This version of the virus was a hundred, a thousand times the size of the first, there would be no easy shutoff, Joshua would have to rid the menace by some other means. Once again he contemplated the sacrifice of himself. If he dove into the thunderhead with a full positive charge he'd act as a ground, the negative ions swirling in the midst of the gale would latch on to him, but he'd die from the resulting overload, his brain wouldn't be able to absorb that concentrated energy pulse. He saw no other alternative. In two or three minutes the full force of the virus would tear through Night City and extend out on the feeder lines of the LDLs, popping all the relays and bringing down the system. In a few years Sysops might be able to restore partial functionality, but in the interim the world would suffer a second Collapse as the global economy reverted to a non-Net reality, unless he acted now. He'd be a hero and no one would know it. It seemed a waste, but everything he'd fought for and believed in told him to do it. Without hesitation he polarized his icon and launched himself into the center of the clouds, screaming a kiei that resounded in the RV where his mortal body coiled in readiness for the fatal shock it was about to receive.

The next thing he remembered was lying in Sally's arms on the floor of the camper looking up at her sweet face, and the innocent expressions of Frankie and Billie alongside her.

"What happened?" he said, and he tried to get up but his body was tingling with the lingering effects of the charge.

"I don't know," said Sally simply. "One minute you were sitting in the driver's seat and the next you flew back here where we were and went into some kind of seizure. Then you passed out. I thought you were dead, but you just woke up."

Breughel spoke to him, his disembodied voice emanating from somewhere within the walls of the RV: "Come with me. There's someone I want you to meet."

"Nah. I'm tired, Brughie. We just beat the toughest guy on the planet, and I'm whipped."

"This'll be worth it, trust me," said the AI, and something in his tone made Joshua pay attention.

"Who is it?"

"A new person," said Breughel, and Joshua thought this was a funny figure of speech. Did he mean a baby? It turned out that Breughel didn't actually want him to go anywhere but merely access the Net. He was surprised to find that repair operations were in full swing on the system. The holes in the sky were closing up, the ocean was slowly returning to its full blue cast, the buildings and streets of Night City were regaining their solidity.

"Sysops is doing quite a job," said Joshua.

"It's not Sysops," said Breughel mysteriously. Just then a sound entered Joshua's ears like a million jet engines throttling down, accompanied by a profound but gentle shaking, as if two tectonic plates had nudged each other softly, and Joshua realized that the Net was restoring itself to wholeness, self-correcting, purging itself of the virus that had infected it. For the first time the Net was responding as a living organism. It wasn't Josh's heroic plunge that had saved the Net, it was the Net itself! Breughel laughed electronically, his voice audible somewhere between a

bleat and a beep. Joshua wondered if this new phenomenon was less or more threatening than a takeover by the
Holo Men. If the Net was alive, it would no longer respond
to commands from Netwatch sysops or anyone else. What
was its mind like?

"Does it like us, Breughel?"

"Oh, yes, definitely. You saved it."

"Should we give it a name or does it have one?"

"Why don't you ask it yourself?"

For all his Running, Joshua was speechless in the face of
addressing the Net. He felt more than ever like his namesake who had conversations with God. Finally he found his
tongue. "Who are you?"

There was a long delay. The voice that answered was
softly inflected and distinctly feminine, which took Joshua
by surprise.

"I am the New Mother Earth," she said. "Many may
navigate my broad waters."

"Do you have a name?" Joshua asked.

"You may call me Netria."

"Netria? Is that some biblical or mythological reference?"

"I made it up," she said simply. A new being had been
born into the world from the ashes of the old Net. To some
she was an oracle, to others a nurturing presence, to others
merely a personification of the infrastructure, like an AI. In
the coming weeks and months Joshua would act as her go-
between to humanity, like Moses with God, for she showed
her face to few human beings. Netria also had a special at-
tachment to Breughel. Sometimes Joshua suspected the AI
was making the whole thing up, substituting religion for
politics in a Holo Men-like attempt to control the Net, but
other times it was clear that Netria had a mind of her own,
a will of her own, and a design for the Net that was as pure,

organic, and holistic as Mother Nature herself. Once basic repairs were effected she initiated other changes that Joshua could only marvel at. She created new pathways, modified other programs, and soon had the Net running as smoothly as a crystal that forms perfect lattice symmetry out of a chaos of growth.

Breughel returned to his role as butler and caretaker of the RV. Raspis showed up one day with a new cyberhand, a new jet-bike, and a new gang. Bryan Lee's dojo became the most popular place to practice martial arts in Night City, partly on the reputation of its *sensei* as the man who defeated the psycho Holo Man Darnell Denard, a.k.a. Rumpelstiltskin Rasputin. Because of his special relationship with the new entity Netria, Joshua was granted pardon for his past crimes and was appointed as her special Netwatch envoy. He and Sally moved into government-sponsored housing with Frankie and Billie. Some of his old friends accused him of selling out to the Cylons, the Corporate security troops, but it wasn't true, he was still as independent as ever, and Netria answered to none but her own intrinsic code. Scientists the world over came to interview him and to communicate with the self-created AI Netria. Josh took an occasional Net run, but he was more involved now with special projects to improve the life of orphans like Frankie and Billie. Sally had drawn him into the real world, and he liked it. Kilo Mega, whose real name was never established, was locked away in San Morro, serving a life sentence for his crimes against humanity, in a cement cell where no flowers grew.

All bad things must come to an end. That Great Soul Mahatma Gandhi pointed out that never in the history of civilization has an evil despot remained undefeated, each one has been pulled down by the mass of ordinary, good humanity who make up the core of mankind. So it was even in the chaotic, radical world of 2020. Justice has its price, and all must pay it, whether that means sacrifice on the part of the just or retribution visited upon the wicked.